FAMILY OF FIRE

Dragon's Mate 1

Hope Bennett

CONTENTS

Title Page	1
Copyright	2
Chapter 1: Lew	7
Chapter 2: Lew	17
Chapter 3: Lew	25
Chapter 4: Morgan	33
Chapter 5: Morgan	46
Chapter 6: Morgan	55
Chapter 7: Lew	64
Chapter 8: Lew	70
Chapter 9: Morgan	83
Chapter 10: Lew	97
Chapter 11: Morgan	106
Chapter 12: Lew	114
Chapter 13: Morgan	127
Chapter 14: Lew	140

Chapter 15: Lew   149

Chapter 16: Morgan   160

Chapter 17: Lew   174

Chapter 18: Lew   183

Chapter 19: Lew   191

Chapter 20: Lew   203

Chapter 21: Morgan   210

Chapter 22: Morgan   224

Chapter 23: Lew   234

Chapter 24: Morgan   246

Chapter 25: Lew   256

Chapter 26: Morgan   266

Chapter 27: Lew   275

Chapter 28: Lew   283

Chapter 29: Morgan   290

Chapter 30: Morgan   300

Chapter 31: Lew   310

Chapter 32: Morgan   318

Chapter 33: Morgan   327

Chapter 34: Lew   335

Chapter 35: Morgan   342

Chapter 36: Lew   352

Chapter 37: Morgan   358

Chapter 38: Lew   365

Chapter 39: Morgan   373

Chapter 40: Morgan   387

Chapter 41: Lew   395

Chapter 42: Morgan   402

Chapter 43: Lew   410

Chapter 44: Morgan   421

Chapter 45: Lew   428

Chapter 46: Morgan   438

Leave a Review   445

Other books in this series   446

Other books by Hope   448

Stay in touch   451

About Hope   452

CHAPTER 1: LEW

We'd been preparing for this for weeks, so it's not like I didn't know it was coming. It was just that I didn't like it. To be fair, none of us liked it much. That's just the way with dragons.

We didn't like other people coming into our territory, *especially* other dragons. It was our nature to protect our family, which meant it was our nature to be territorial and possessive and unwelcoming. Yeah, I know, dragons are great, huh? But we're not that bad really. We just didn't like douche-bag *uasal* coming to our homes with their noses in the air and acting like they stepped in something nasty on our doorstep. And that's exactly what every *uasal* I'd ever met had been like. Charming bunch.

It meant I was a little cranky that morning and I'd been up early cleaning the house so the Somervilles wouldn't have any excuse to stick their noses up at us. We had a lot of house to clean, since we lived in a castle. Most dragons did.

Our castle was the best, though. It was thick stone, with four turrets stretching high into the sky and looking down over the cliff to the churning sea below. We had the best view of any of the families, not that I was biased in any way.

Around me, the rest of the family started to gather and we started giving each other those looks, the ones that said *I hear ya* and let me know that nobody was looking forward to that morning. But Nana was the elder and she was adamant. I wasn't about to go against her – and not just because she could burn my balls off, it was because she was also right but, like I said, I didn't like it.

I heard the car turn into the driveway. In fact, I heard two cars pulling up, which was not what I'd been expecting.

"What the hell?" said Dane. He sounded angry already, which wasn't great. Dane hated *uasal* more than I did.

"It's alright, Dane," I said, trying to sound calm. It came to something when *I* was the one being calm and reasonable. "One car, two cars, what difference does it make?"

He turned to face me. I had to look up at him since he towered over me by a good five inches, the only dragon in the whole castle who was bigger than me. If I didn't know he would never harm me, I'd be frightened by the look on his face. He looked murderous.

"They're bringing more. That wasn't what we agreed."

Making sure I kept the same level tone, I said, "We're only keeping one."

"One too many."

"They won't stay long, they just want to say goodbye to Morgan. He won't see his family again for weeks, we can't begrudge him a good-bye."

I knew I'd hate to be parted from my family for that long and it made me think perhaps I'd misjudged the *uasal* before even meeting him. Perhaps he wasn't as bad as all that. Not that we'd be friends – *uasal* and *curaidh* didn't mix – but maybe we wouldn't hate each other as much as I'd thought we would.

The cars pulled up outside the front entrance and I stepped closer to the window, wanting to see their reaction when they got out of the car. Our castle was beautiful and imposing and ancient and I loved to see the awed look on people's faces when they first stood in front of it.

I was disappointed.

Before the car door even opened, I heard a voice from inside it say, "Seriously? What a dump."

I clenched my fists. That was not a great

start.

Another voice added, "I can't believe you've got to stay here, Morgan. It's too bad." They also did not sound impressed and my dragon began to stir irritably inside.

"Now boys," said a voice I recognised. It was Barrington Somerville, the head of the Somerville family.

I was prepared to hate them all on sight. I was not prepared for the bolt of lust that lanced through my whole body at the sight of the slim young man who emerged from the car behind Lord Somerville. He was the most beautiful creature I'd ever seen. If he ever managed to get the proud look of distaste off his smug face, he'd be almost too beautiful to look at.

I couldn't take my eyes off him as he walked from the car, up the steps to the front doors and through them. I heard the faint hum of voices as the guests were greeted by my family and then I couldn't see him at all. And that's when I realised I was practically hanging out the window, trying to track the hottie. I stood upright, clearing my throat, and glanced at Dane beside me. His face was pinched with anger still and I wasn't sure whether he was more or less angry than before.

"What's the matter?" I asked carefully.

"Nothing."

"Did you think he'd come?"

"No."

I kept my mouth closed after that. Because I liked breathing and Dane was not in the mood for me to dig into his aversion to *uasal*, particularly Somerville *uasal*. Or, to be more precise, one specific *uasal* who was too stupid to know a good thing when it was in front of him.

"Tell Nana I'm going to check the border."

He pulled his t-shirt over his head and slipped his jeans down his legs and stepped out of them, and then, naked, walked over to the open window and jumped up onto the stone sill. He was silhouetted there for a second, so big he almost filled the frame, and then he bent his legs and pushed off and leapt out into the air.

Just as he began to fall, his skin grew darker and became grey, scaly wings burst from his shoulders and he shifted fully into dragon form. His tail whipped out, his huge wings beat against the air and he was out of sight in under a minute, and I was faced with the prospect of telling Nana that he'd gone. Great. We both knew he wouldn't be back that night.

I turned to face some of the others in the room behind me. A couple of my cousins had been hanging out of the windows like I was, a few others were standing around, looking bored, and my cousin Nadia was lounging in an armchair looking like she couldn't care less. I was never sure whether she really couldn't care less or whether she was just really, really good at faking it.

I always got the impression that Nadia was small but that was probably just in comparison to me. She was average height and curvy. She looked very feminine. I was not fooled. She had the same simmering strength that all dragons had, and the advantage of being fast, too. And she was totally ruthless when it came to letting me know who was boss. Spoiler: it was her.

She saw me eyeing her and raised an eyebrow. "What?"

"Don't suppose you want to tell Nana?"

"Nope."

"You sure?" I asked. "It'll be good practice for you."

The other eyebrow rose up to join the first. How she could control them separately was beyond me. If I tried it, I ended up squinting with my head to one side, looking, and I quote, *even more moronic than usual.*

"Practice for what?" Nadia asked with a surprised, curious air, exuding innocence. I was not fooled.

"For when you're head of the family."

She stood then, languid and uncaring.

"You keep saying that, but I'll never be head of the family, Lew darling. Tell Nana yourself."

She sauntered to the door and opened it.

Without even turning round to look at me, she added, "And stop frowning. If the wind changes, your face will stick that way and then you'll look like Dane for the rest of your life."

"Low blow," I muttered as she left.

It wasn't Dane's fault he frowned all the time. At least, *I* wouldn't blame him for it.

A little hand reached out to tug at the hem of my t-shirt.

"Are we allowed downstairs now?"

I looked down to see Hannah, my cousin. Or was she my niece? Maybe my great-niece? Anyway, she was small and female and definitely related to me.

"Not yet," I said.

Hannah was sweet but she was also doggedly determined to get to the bottom of things if she didn't understand. Usually I admired it. I may even have encouraged it, a little too much if her mother was to be believed. But at that particular time, it was awkward, because she gave me a quizzical look and said, "But Auntie Nadia did."

Her logic was irrefutable.

"Yes, but Nadia is older than you."

"But you're older than Nadia."

Again, she was right. I wasn't good with kids. I knew I was supposed to say something like 'because I say so' and leave it at that but it seemed unfair. She asked a question, the least I could do was answer it.

"Yes, but Nana is even older than me and she told us to wait up here."

I was pleased with that. It was true.

"Ok."

"Why don't you play a game while you wait?"

"Will you play with us?"

I sighed heavily. "Isn't there someone else you can bother?"

Her wide, innocent eyes told me that, no, there wasn't, even though there were at least eight other people in the room she could be bothering instead of me right then. "Nobody else lets me ride their dragon."

And that's why I was in my dragon form, clattering round the large open lounge on the second floor with three kids on my back squealing and giggling when the door opened and Jill came in. She was older than me, stern and prim, and she was already talking when the door opened.

"You know we can hear you all the way downstairs."

I stopped, the three children on my back quietened but didn't move, which meant I was stuck in that position since I didn't want to shift with them on my back and I didn't want to just tip them off, either.

Jill continued. "Nana told you to be quiet. I'm surprised at you, Hannah, you're normally such a good girl."

That was a bit much. I shuddered, trying to hint to them to get off my back. They slid off and tumbled to the floor and I shifted, standing up and cupping my hands in front of my groin. Modesty was a thing of the past in my family but it was respectful not to flash your junk at your aunties. Although maybe Jill was my second cousin?

"It's not her fault. I'm in charge up here."

"Then you should have known better, Lew." She said my name like I was the most exasperating person on the planet. "We're trying to make a good impression and we can hear the children squealing."

"They were enjoying themselves. Doesn't that make a good impression?"

"Not to that lot." She jerked her head behind her at the door. "They're too stuck up to play with their children."

That sounded awful.

"Never?"

"It's not in their nature. It was bred out of them centuries ago."

Unfortunately, it didn't surprise me. *Uasal* would never do anything so undignified.

Hannah stepped tentatively forward. "But you're not like them, are you Jill?"

"No, I'm not," she said, sounding offended at the idea.

Hannah tilted her head. "Do you want to play with us, then?"

I nearly laughed at that. Jill was cornered. And it had been a beautiful move by Hannah. I actually had to turn my back to them and go and fetch my clothes where I'd left them in a pile in the corner of the room so she wouldn't see my smile.

Jill said, "Of course I'll play with you. But we'll need to play something quieter. We don't want to be heard downstairs. And Lew?"

I slipped my t-shirt over my head and faced Jill. "Yes?"

"Nana wants you downstairs. Barrington Somerville wants to meet the trainers."

"Right," I said. I'd been dreading that. It was bad enough that I had to spend time with one *uasal*, I didn't want to have to spend time with a whole group of them.

As I walked towards the door, Jill asked, "Where's Dane? He should go as well."

"He went to check the borders," I said. There was no point sugaring that pill.

Jill pursed her lips. "Good luck telling Nana."

"Thanks," I grouched as I went out the door. "Don't suppose you want to tell her?"

She snorted and I took that as a no.

CHAPTER 2: LEW

The west room was one of the best in the whole castle. It had large windows that had been expanded years before to let in more natural light and they overlooked the rolling clifftop and the jagged edge. In the evening, it was lit with the glorious red sunsets over the water. The room itself wasn't shabby, either, especially as it was where we entertained guests. Upstairs rooms were more homely, but the west room was large and open, with rich red-patterned rugs and mahogany furniture. The Somervilles didn't look like they appreciated it, though.

Lord Somerville was sitting upright in a large chair, looking like a petulant king on his throne. Beside him sat three younger men, each as upright and expressionless as the next.

Nana, who was always a gracious host, introduced me. Her eyes flicked behind me, looking for Dane, and I gave just the smallest shake of my head, trying to tell her that he wasn't coming. I saw her lips pinch ever so slightly and knew that, even if I got a reprieve, I was going to be questioned about that later.

"Lord Somerville, may I present my grandson, Lewis Hoskins. He's one of the finest dragon warriors in the country. He'll be training your son."

Somerville looked me over with cold, cold eyes. They were silver, like all *uasal*'s eyes, but they were light silver, so light they almost vanished in the white of the eye. They reminded me of ice and I repressed a shiver as they raked over me. I was sure I was colder than I had been a few seconds before.

"What are your qualifications?" he asked bluntly. I tried not to prickle at his rudeness.

"A hundred years in the Fife Army," I said, trying to keep the growl from my throat. My dragon didn't like the man and it was speculating whether we could fry him. We couldn't.

His face was practically a mask, carved into indifference, but I thought I saw just the faintest flicker in his eyes at my answer. I wanted to smirk and say, "That's right, suck it up, I was in the fucking Fife Army," but I didn't. Nana didn't allow bad language and I could only imagine the bonfire she'd start with me in the middle if I said anything so rude to a guest.

Either I'd imagined the glimpse of respect or he was over it already, because he turned his gaze back to Nana and asked, "Who else will be training my son?"

It seemed I wasn't good enough on my own.

And Nana was going to have to think fast, since the other person doing most of the training would be Dane, who was famously... not there.

Nana rallied. She sat calmly and said with dignified grace, "Morgan will be trained as per our agreement, Lord Somerville. I hope you don't doubt the quality of our training."

Barrington huffed and asked pointless questions, probably trying to give the impression that he was deigning to let his precious son stay with us rather than what had actually happened, which was the Somervilles practically begging us to train him. We were *curaidh*. We were warriors. Had been for generations. Fighting was what we were good at. And *uasal* like the Somervilles were nobles and had spent centuries being protected by my kind. Now we were no longer personal guards, they had to either pay us for our services or protect themselves. It wasn't exactly like dragons were weak – even *uasal* could shift and fight and breathe fire – but there were people out there who hunted us and all dragons needed to be prepared.

While Barrington blustered and picked

holes in the training programme we'd *generously* offered his son, I let my gaze wander. I'd kept it firmly on Barrington because he was the one talking and he was the one who gave me chills from his creepy eyes, but, once his attention was back on Nana, I looked at the other three Somervilles.

They sat quietly and looked like dolls lined up. They were all handsome, I had to admit. The *uasal* were smaller and leaner than us, and their dragons were silver instead of grey. But two of them, no matter how pretty, were completely eclipsed by the third.

The beautiful man sat closest to Barrington and stared straight ahead. He was pale and fragile-looking, with a slim frame and delicate features. His high cheekbones and slim, straight nose made him look a touch hawk-like, lending him a regal air. It was unfortunate that his whole expression was cut into bored and haughty lines. It couldn't make him ugly but it showed he had an ugly personality. It was a shame because, seriously, that amount of physical perfection was wasted on someone like that.

His eyes slid to mine and he held my gaze. I was almost embarrassed to be caught staring but I couldn't seem to stop. His irises were darker silver than Barrington's, with a hint of blue in their depths. I was convinced, as I stared into them, that they were deep pools of cool, clear water.

And then he shifted his gaze back onto

Nana. I felt thoroughly dismissed and had to resist the urge to draw his attention back to me. I watched him carefully but he never looked at me again. I was completely gone from his thoughts.

My dragon stirred inside me and I felt the uneasiness that was rousing it. We didn't like being looked at like that, and we liked being dismissed even less. The only thing I could hope for was that the beautiful man wasn't the son Barrington was leaving with us. I'd much rather have one of the others, who were silent and still and didn't rile my dragon.

But, of course, my life wasn't like that, and if there was something the Somervilles could do to make my life more difficult, that's what would happen. Hence it was the cold, beautiful young man who turned out to be Morgan and would be staying with us for a long six months.

When Barrington was preparing to leave, Nana stood and said tactfully, "We'll leave you to say your goodbyes." I turned to go, not wanting to see anyone cry. Turns out, I needn't have bothered.

Barrington's cold, flat voice stopped me in my tracks. "That will not be necessary."

He turned to Morgan and gave a curt nod to the other two men. I still didn't know who they were. On cue, they each offered Morgan a hand to shake and said, "Goodbye, Morgan."

Seriously, that was it. I knew I was staring

in complete bemusement and I did not look my most intelligent when I did that – it had been actually pointed out to me by no fewer than three of my cousins – but I couldn't help it. Goodbye Morgan? That was it? They weren't going to see him for six months. And, sure, we had technology, they could call him, or video chat, but a handshake would in no way sustain me for six months without my family. When I'd been a soldier, I'd flown home every chance I could and I'd been hugged to within an inch of my life every time. In fact, I'd been more at risk of suffocation on my visits home than I ever was of death during my service.

Barrington's goodbye was even less effusive. He looked gravely into the younger man's face and said, "Do the Somerville name proud, son." And with that, he left. Morgan didn't seem bothered either way. He looked like he was already cataloguing all the things he would need to do to make our castle habitable for his refined tastes.

Nana saved the day. She said goodbye to them in grand fashion and sent them out the door before turning to little Morgan standing there alone. If it had been anyone else, my heart would have gone out to them, being left with strangers, alone and unfamiliar, but his expressionless face made it hard to pity him.

"Morgan, why don't you go up to your

room and settle in? Your bags have been taken up. We'll dine at eight, so you have time to freshen up and change."

That's what I liked about Nana – she was kind, but she made it clear exactly what she wanted from you. Of course, that didn't necessarily apply when she was angry, and I was about to get roasted for letting Dane fly off so I said, "I'll show him."

Nana gave me a look that said she knew exactly what I was doing and it was only going to delay the inevitable. I didn't care, I'd take it.

"This way," I said, and led Morgan out of the room.

We'd put him on the south side where the sunlight shone into his room all day and he could look out over the rolling hills. The castle was on high ground and we could see for miles over the surrounding countryside.

When I got to the stairs, I gestured in front of me, thinking it was polite to let him go first. I realised that was a mistake when he walked up the stairs and I followed, and his pert little butt was wiggling in front of me all the way. I'd never hated the fact that we had so many stairs before – dragons needed a lot of space and the castle was wide and high – but that climb seemed to go on forever and I followed the two perfectly-formed globes encased in sleek black trousers like I was being led on a lead.

By the time we reached the top of the stairs, I was hard. I wasn't proud of it – far from it – but I was only flesh and blood and it had been a long time since I'd got any action but my own hand, and so watching an attractive man was bound to make the blood flow south. It just meant that I had to position myself slightly behind him the rest of the way and give him directions so he wouldn't catch a glimpse of my erection. He probably thought I was an idiot. And, to be fair, I was. I have no idea how I got into the situation in the first place but I showed him his room, told him to ask for anything he needed and then practically fled back to the safety of my own room where I climbed into a chilling shower to chase my erection away. There was no way I was going to touch myself. I did *not* want to give my body any reason to believe that Morgan Somerville was associated with sex.

CHAPTER 3: LEW

I was incredibly glad I'd taken that cold shower. It had been freezing but it had still taken more than five minutes for my dick to stand down. I'd nearly had to climb back into it when I was dressing because I accidentally let myself think about Morgan's tight arse in those slacks when I wondered whether he always wore such fancy suits.

Still, I was glad I didn't have to face Nana with an erection. Modesty may be something we didn't grow up with but walking around with a hard-on was a bit much. The whole family shifted when we wanted and flew around and my cousin Daniel, for example, spent most of his time as a dragon and only shifted into human form when he absolutely had to. We were used to nakedness. But it was an innocent nakedness, just being there without clothes on until you could find something to cover yourself. That was the way I wanted it to stay.

On the other hand, walking into Nana's room and knowing she was going to chew me out for letting Dane fly off would have killed my hard-on anyway, so I needn't have bothered with the shower.

I knocked on the door to Nana's room and waited.

"Come in."

I stepped inside and shut the door behind me. Not that it would stop anyone from hearing what she was about to say if they wanted to stand outside and listen to it, but it felt more private. Privacy was also pretty much a thing of the past for my family.

Nana was sitting on a sofa, looking small and bird-like. She had sharp dark eyes and her hair was still black, despite her age. Only the wrinkles around her eyes and mouth gave away her age at all, as she was as slim and sharp as ever.

Her suite of rooms was surprisingly pretty, with a charming little living room with a few rose-pink sofas and treats stashed around the place for the kids to find when they came in. It was obvious that I was there for a talking-to since she'd thrown the kids out. There was always one or two in there otherwise.

The kids – I remembered from my own childhood – weren't really there to see Nana, they were there to see Gramps.

My eyes flicked around the room to find him and there he was, sitting by the large window in his high-backed armchair and smiling at me like I was his favourite. Everyone always thought they were Gramps' favourite, but I knew I really was.

"Hello Gramps. I missed you this morning."

"I thought I'd stay up here and read my book while Edith dealt with those *uasal*."

I nodded. It was for the best, seeing as Gramps was human and the Somervilles were incredible snobs. Some dragons didn't like other dragons mating humans and, since the Somervilles didn't even like mating outside of other *uasal*, I could only assume they would have a problem with Gramps.

Nana's voice became rough as she snapped, "You didn't need to. If they've got a problem with my mate, then they're not welcome in my house."

Gramps smiled. For some reason, he always seemed to like it when Nana got angry. I tended to hide, if I could.

"If I'd wanted to sit there and be bored to tears by some *uasal* snob, darling, I would have gone downstairs and done that. As it was, you had to sit through his awful company and I got to enjoy a couple of chapters of my book and have a little snooze."

He looked at me and I couldn't help but smile at him. He was the best Gramps in the world. He looked like he was just passing middle-age, maybe around sixty or so, but I knew he was nearing a thousand years old. He was still several hundred years younger than Nana, though. She'd been considered a young dragon when she'd mated him, and they'd bonded. He had the life-span of the dragons now. I was hoping he'd make it to two thousand.

Nana huffed but didn't carry on, so I suppose he won. He was the only one who ever did, where Nana was concerned.

He gave me a wink and said, "There might be a little treat in the box behind you."

That's what I liked about Gramps. No matter how old you got, he always treated you like you were a child. Or maybe that was only me, since I was his favourite.

Nana interrupted before I could turn around and search out whatever chocolate he'd hidden for me.

"He's not here to see you, John, he's here to let me flay him alive."

"I didn't—" I began, thinking I should probably explain myself quickly if I intended to make it through the meeting, but Nana cut me off.

"If he wasn't the only one qualified to train Morgan, I'd throw him in the dungeons."

That wasn't a threat. The castle did have dungeons, from centuries before, but they were used for storage and there were a few very pleasant games rooms down there, too, now.

"I didn't know he'd—"

"And if he interrupts me again, I shall hang him upside-down and crack every bone in his body, one at a time."

Legend had it that she'd done something very similar, once – years before I was born – to a dragon who'd tried to kill Gramps.

Gramps yawned. "Sounds exhausting."

I tried not to let my smile show in case that caught Nana's attention.

She sighed.

Good old Gramps, totally deflating her anger. I had no idea how he did it. If *I*'d yawned and said, "Sounds exhausting," she'd have added some scalds to the flaying she'd had in mind. As it was, she just said, "Lew, sit down. You're towering over me and it's giving me a crick in my neck."

I obediently sat.

"So," she began. "Tell me how you managed to let Dane escape."

"I didn't realise he was a prisoner."

She raised one eyebrow. That must be where Nadia got it from. Shame I hadn't inherited it, too. Of course, when Nadia did it, I didn't feel the same tremor of unease as I did with Nana.

"You know it's not a good idea for him to be out, especially alone."

"He was—" I began, but couldn't think of a word to describe exactly what Dane was. "Upset," I settled on, in the end.

"Yes, he would be. I hoped Lord Somerville would mellow a bit towards us if we agreed to train his son, but it doesn't look like that will happen."

"Why did you want him to like us? We don't need him."

That eyebrow twitched but didn't go up again. "I have my reasons."

It sounded like Nana wanted the Somervilles to like us so they'd let Dane court the little *uasal* he'd fallen for a few years ago. I said nothing, since I didn't think that was ever going to happen.

"Do you want me to see if I can find Dane?"

I tried to give the impression that I didn't know exactly where he would be, since I didn't want anyone else to know.

I should have realised that Nana already knew. She knew everything.

"I know where he is. I don't think he'll cause trouble."

Guaranteed, Dane had flown to the Somerville estate to see if he could catch a glimpse of his man. Well, not *his* man, since Dane had been well and truly dumped before they'd even kissed.

I knew that because I'd got Dane outrageously drunk three years before and made him spill his secrets. I'd never done it again, since I hadn't liked the hangover, and since Dane had shifted into dragon form and threatened to slaughter the entire Somerville family. In the state he'd been in, and with the size of him and the raw strength he had, I'd had to call for back-up just to keep him grounded. My personal opinion was that, if the man didn't want him, Dane was well rid of him.

Nana said, calmly, like it wasn't a risk that one of her grandsons was about to start a bloody war with a *uasal* family, "He'll be back tomorrow."

"Yeah."

She leaned forward and slapped my arm. "Yes."

"Sorry, Nana. Yes."

She eyed me keenly. "You'll need to speak properly if you're going to train Morgan."

"Yes, Nana."

"He's smaller than I expected."

"Yes," I said, trying not to remember his delicate limbs and his pretty face.

"You'll need to get him in good condition. I'll trust you to do that, just report to me what you've done and how well he's learning. Lord Somerville wants regular updates. Unless you'd like to update him?"

"No, you do it."

I shuddered at the idea of trying to explain to Barrington Somerville what I'd been doing with his son. And, when I thought that, I really shouldn't have made it sound naughty. It wasn't helping.

"I'll keep Dane away from you for the first couple of weeks. Let me know if you want any of the others to come and train with you, for practice or demonstration."

"Yes, Nana."

"Go and put a shirt on so you don't look like a complete slob at dinner."

I grinned and stood up, and then swooped down to plant a kiss on Nana's cheek. She clucked at me and shooed me off with a quick, "Don't think you'll get around me like that," and I grinned harder.

On my way out, I stopped to sniff out the little trinket box with chocolate in and opened it to find a tiny wrapped square of dark chocolate orange. Yum.

I swiped it, looked over my shoulder and said, "Thanks, Gramps," and bolted out the door before Nana could realise she'd just let me away scot-free. As I unwrapped my chocolate and popped it into my mouth, I heard Gramps' laughter from inside the room.

CHAPTER 4:
MORGAN

It was disconcerting to sit in the curaidh's castle with the elder flicking her black eyes at me every few minutes and talking to Lord Somerville about my training like I wasn't there. But I was used to having decisions made for me, especially where my duty to my family was concerned. What was more disconcerting was the curaidh dragon who stood behind the elder like a bodyguard and watched me with his predator's eyes. I felt... vulnerable. And that was absolutely not normal for me.

I may not be as big as him – the elder called him Lewis – but there was more to a dragon than brute strength. It was just that, sitting under the watchful eye of a warrior, and one who'd been in the Fife Army no less, I began to wonder whether his sheer size and strength would be enough to kill me if he wanted.

What made the whole situation worse was that he was incredibly handsome, which was unfair. The man looked like every sexual fantasy I'd ever had, all rolled into one deliciously muscled package. I hadn't realised that being watched like prey could be a turn-on, but apparently it was. I was uneasy with it, but my body had decided that, if I was going to be hunted, it wanted the killing blow to come from Lewis.

When I'd first seen him, I'd felt a faint flush of arousal when I'd met his gaze. He hadn't given me any sign that he was pleased to have me there or that he was looking forward to training me – which was exactly what I'd expected so I didn't know why I was so put out by it – and I knew better than to talk when Lord Somerville was, so I just took in his perfect face for a minute and then turned away, hoping he would look somewhere else but feeling his eyes burning into my skin right up until my father left.

The only consolation I had was that dragons muted their scent habitually and so nobody would be able to smell my arousal. I would probably die of embarrassment if I got turned on right in front of Lord Somerville, and by a *curaidh* no less. Not that I'd be given much time to die of embarrassment, since, if my father knew I'd been eyeing up the trainer, he'd either drag me home and keep me there like my poor cousin Seren or he'd outright kill me before the humiliation could finish me off. Lord Somerville was old-school about that sort of thing.

It might have sounded harsh but dragons were like that, and Lord Somerville took the nobility of our family blood very seriously. Hence I'd been sent to be trained by warriors in the first place. The Somervilles were one of the oldest noble families in existence. We had treasure. We needed it guarded. Since the *curaidh* had relinquished their duty to protect us, we had to do it ourselves. I was young, I was fit, I was strong, and I was Lord Somerville's son, which meant I was the one who would spend six months learning to fight.

When my father left, I was pretty glad to be left alone in what was to be my room for the next six months. It wasn't exactly what I was used to but that was only to be expected. The Somervilles had a particularly fine castle and anything else was bound to pale in comparison.

I'd just been left there by Lewis, the warrior who was going to be my trainer for six whole months, and I stood in the middle of the room for several minutes, just listening to the sound of his footsteps walking away from my door and the sounds of the castle around me.

I locked the door.

What I expected that to achieve, I don't

know, since any dragon in the place could have kicked it down, but I still had that vulnerable, exposed feeling and I didn't like it. I wanted to crawl under the bed and hide. I hadn't felt like that in a long time.

Eventually, I decided there was nothing better to do than unpack. I hung my suits in the wardrobe and folded the rest of my clothes into the chest of drawers and put my toiletries in the absolutely tiny attached bathroom, and then I took the large bottle of lube I'd brought with me and tried to decide where to put it.

I hadn't been sure whether to bring it or not. In the end, I'd decided that I wasn't going to spend six months completely sexless, so I'd brought it but I was definitely going to hide it. After all, I didn't want any of the *curaidh* to find it. I had no idea whether they were ok with homosexuality but, on the basis I didn't intend to actually sleep with anyone on their property, I figured they didn't need to know. I was just a bit worried that one of them would find my lube. They shouldn't go through my things, of course, but I had no idea what kind of people they were.

In the end, I put it in my sock drawer and tried to bury it under a mound of socks. It looked safe enough.

I began to sweat at the thought of anyone finding it, particularly of one of those big dragons out there finding it. They were strong. I tried to calm myself down by reminding myself that I wasn't defenceless and I could always fly home, if I was ever actually in danger. I could probably out-fly them. Possibly.

If they found it...

If they found it, I decided, I would tell them it was for jerking off. In fact, that's really what it was for. I wasn't exactly going to be hooking up with a string of men in their castle, was I?

I sat on the bed, feeling the relief inside me that I hadn't bought my dildo. Of course, I hadn't left it at home, either. I'd wrapped it up in a box and put that in a bag and then I'd taken it to the huge dumpster bin at the end of the drive and thrown it straight in there. The thought of my father finding it – ok, he would never have found it but one of the maids might have and then they might have told him – made me sweat even more. It was a good thing it was gone. It meant I had six months to get intimately acquainted with my fingers.

I got up. Sitting there thinking about missing my dildo was going to lead to thinking about who I might have imagined if I'd *had* my dildo, and that was all kinds of dangerous. I did not want to develop a fascination with dark eyes and muscles.

Instead, I stripped out of my clothes and went to wash so I could dress for dinner.

I tried on three shirts before having a word

with myself. It didn't matter what I looked like, as long as I was smart, and I was. I was wearing my evening suit, just like at home. If it was good enough for Lord Somerville, it was good enough for the Hoskins.

When the tap came at my door, I nearly tried to change my shirt again, but I resisted. Instead, I took a deep breath and opened the door. It was Lewis. And he looked incredible.

I blinked and tried to unstick my tongue from the top of my mouth. Seriously, his dark grey shirt stretched over his chest and clung to his arms to accentuate his muscles, *not* that they needed any help in that regard. And the grey made me wonder whether that was the colour of his dragon or not. I tried to picture him in dragon form but came up blank. He was probably ugly, anyway, I told myself. It would have been nice if I'd believed it for just a few seconds, even.

"Are you here to escort me to dinner?" I asked at last.

He opened his mouth to speak but nothing came out. I'd shocked him. Shit, it was probably because I'd made it sound like he was actually escorting me to dinner, like a date. I'd just meant showing me the way to the dining room. I braced myself, not sure what he'd do.

And waited.

After what must have been at least thirty seconds – though it felt much, much longer – he shrugged and said, "I'm here to take you down to the dining room. Dinner's ready. Uh, were you staying for dinner?"

"Yes. I understood that was the arrangement."

Was I meant to get my own dinner? I'd been told I would be living with the family, and I'd assumed that meant I was to eat with them as well.

"Yes, it is. I just- never mind. It's this way."

I closed my door behind me and followed Lewis along the hallway and down the stairs. He didn't speak to me, which was fine.

As we drew nearer to the dining room, I could hear the sounds of a lot of people gathered together. They were chatting and there was the sound of movement, footsteps, chairs being drawn back and glasses clinking as they were set down. I schooled my expression into one of polite blankness. It was the one my father preferred on me, and I tended to wear it as a habit.

When I walked into the dining room, I saw instantly what Lewis had started to tell me and yet had *completely failed to actually tell me.*

Nobody else dressed for dinner. They were standing around in the same clothes they'd worn earlier – those that I recognised – and there were others who were just wearing jeans and a t-shirt, a couple of women in summer dresses and cardigans, and one of the men was even wearing jogging bottoms and a t-shirt that had actual holes in.

With that in mind, I felt slightly over-dressed in my black tie and evening jacket.

Embarrassment washed up from my feet and I swear I felt it travel up my legs, my torso and into my face. I didn't tend to blush and I was never sure whether that was natural luck (which seemed unlikely) or my face had learned early on not to give anything away. I'd never been so glad for it, whatever the reason. I felt an utter fool.

Casting my mind back, I tried to remember accurately and I was *sure* the elder had told me to dress for dinner.

Turning tail and running was out of the question. I had to style it out.

So I kept my head up, my face politely blank and walked into the room like I wasn't the butt of the joke. It wasn't easy when I heard the titters from the other end of the room.

Beside me, Lewis – or *Traitor*, as I now thought of him – said, "I don't think you met everyone earlier. The kids have eaten already so it's just the adults here. We thought that would be best."

He introduced me by going round the table and saying the names of everyone there. I barely kept it together. No way would I remember who any of those people were in the morning.

By the time he'd finished, most of them

were sat down and I was standing stiffly to the side.

"Here," said Lewis, pulling out a chair for me. I eased down into it gingerly, since I half expected him to yank it away at the last moment so I fell over. He didn't. I sat at the table and looked around me in shock. It was a mess. There was no order. Some people were sitting and others were standing and two of them had already gone in for the bread rolls in the centre of the table, and most people were drinking, even though the elder wasn't even in the room.

"Can I get you some wine?" Lewis asked.

I didn't trust my voice not to give me away, so I nodded.

"Red or white?"

I looked up at him. He was standing beside me, looking down at me expectantly. Did he really expect me to answer that? I didn't know that unless I knew what we were going to eat. And even then, at home, the staff just poured the correct wine with each course so there was never a choice.

When I realised he was just going to wait for me to choose, I said, "White," and was pleased at how steady my voice had been.

Lewis was just pouring wine into my glass when I heard footsteps at the door and looked round to see who it was. It was the elder, and I shot up straight away and stood, hoping desperately that I wasn't blushing in shame at having been sat down already before she entered.

Her black eyes went to me, quick and appraising, and then she nodded at me. "Thank you, Morgan, you may be seated." That's when I realised that nobody else had stood at her entrance.

I sat, pulling my chair in from where it had scraped out, and decided that just keeping my limbs under control was about all I could hope for from the rest of the evening.

As the elder moved to the head of the table, I saw a man moving behind her and started in surprise. I could smell him. Granted, I was only a few feet away, since I was up near the head of the table, but still, no dragon I knew of allowed their scent out. I sniffed again. He was human.

His eyes were on me and I swear he saw the moment of realisation. He didn't look afraid, though – probably because he was surrounded by *curaidh* – and he didn't look insulted, either. He looked... if I had to take a guess at an emotion, I would have said *kind*. It seemed almost like he looked at me with understanding.

He gave me a smile. I'd never been smiled at by a human before.

"Good evening, Morgan, I'm pleased to finally meet you. I'm Gramps."

As he talked, I saw his jaw move and, just below that, the shiny flash of scar tissue on the side of his neck, reflecting the light. My eyes darted to it and I saw it was a series of round scars in a semi-circle. It was a mating bite.

"Gramps Hoskins?" I tried to say his name like it was a normal name and not like it was the weirdest one I'd heard in a long time.

"That's right."

The elder interrupted. She had stayed near him and I'd felt her black eyes on me the whole time, just like I could feel a dozen other dark eyes on me.

"His name is John and he's my mate."

I nodded. I thought if I held out my hand to shake, it would tremble, so I said, "I'm pleased to meet you, Mr. Hoskins."

"Dear god, don't call me that. It's Gramps. Everyone calls me Gramps."

"John, Morgan doesn't want to call you Gramps."

He folded his arms and looked like a stubborn child. I was near to laughing at it but that might have been hysteria. "It's Gramps or John."

I gave another nod. "Pleased to meet you, John."

"You, too. Now, has everyone got a drink?"

There was a chorus of agreements and a couple of *wait a minute*s and then Mr. Hoskins – John – raised his own glass and said, "Welcome, Morgan. I hope you'll be very happy here."

Everyone drank to me. I just sat there, utterly stunned. Nobody had ever toasted me before. The feel of tears behind my eyes was just me being overwhelmed, it was only to be expected. I watched John pull out the chair for the elder at the head of the table and then sit down beside her.

How had I not known she had a human mate? If my father had known, he'd never have left me there, I knew that for certain. A human mate? They must be fated mates, there was no other explanation.

When dragons mated, they joined souls. When they properly mated, that is, not just having sex or even having children together. Fated mates were rare, certainly for dragons. And mates shared a special bond that combined their power. I studied the human for a while before tugging my gaze away and trying not to look at him again. I didn't want to be caught staring, especially not by the elder. John must be her fated mate if she'd mated him and given him a share of her power, her very soul. She wouldn't have got anything in return, not from a human. No power, no strength, no magic, nothing.

I wondered whether any of the other dragons in the castle had mates. I wasn't thinking of anyone in particular, it was just that I'd never seen anyone with a fated mate before and I wondered if there were more.

Beside me, Lew reached across to the dishes of food that were being dumped very unceremoniously on the table and asked, "Would you like some of this?" to each thing he picked up. I couldn't do anything but nod, so I got a plate full of food that I couldn't even pretend to choke down and watched as he cleared two plates full.

Conversation was polite and formal, a bit stiff, and I felt myself retreating further into my training as the evening wore on. I kept my face blank and my scent masked so nobody would catch a whiff of my confusion. I was way out of my depth.

CHAPTER 5: MORGAN

When I woke the next morning, after a surprisingly sound sleep, I dressed much more casually. I didn't want a repeat of the night before where I stood out like a sore thumb and the curaidh all looked at me like I was an interesting specimen of another species entirely.

I realised I was up a bit early since I couldn't hear the bustling sounds of people awake in the castle, but I was also hungry. I hadn't eaten much the night before. The food had been unusual and I was too wary of the people around me, half expecting some form of attack. The fact that it hadn't come didn't help me relax. If I knew anything, it was that it would just be worse later when it did come.

Sliding out of my room quietly, I padded along the corridor and down the stairs, taking in the details of the castle around me. It was solidly furnished, which made sense since they were dragons and they needed things to be robust, but it wasn't badly decorated. Instinct made me keep my eyes peeled and my senses alert, which was how I managed to find the kitchen and why I heard the voices before they heard my footsteps.

"... leaving me to tell Nana you'd gone. By the way, if you think you had anyone fooled about checking the borders, you really don't know us very well."

"Leave it, Lew. I'll tell Nana I'm sorry."

Lew. I'd thought I'd recognised that voice. It was confident but not too loud, and I'd bet it was the sort of voice that could make men charge to their deaths. He spoke again.

"You know we- I'm here, you know, if you want to talk."

"Nothing to talk about."

I didn't recognise the other voice, and it was deep with a bit of a rumble in it, like the dragon inside was near the surface, straining to get out. That could just have been his voice, but it made me hesitate anyway and I stood outside the kitchen, not sure whether to knock and go inside or not.

Lew said, "I'm serious, Dane."

The other voice – belonging to Dane, apparently – said, "Drop it."

I wasn't imagining it: the rumble was worse.

There was a sigh and a door slammed closed. Sounded like Dane had stormed off in a huff.

Feeling that I could face Lew – he might be irritatingly handsome and not exactly my biggest fan, but at least I'd met him – I walked straight into the kitchen. And realised my mistake.

It wasn't Dane who'd left, it was Lew. Which left me face-to-face with a *curaidh* I'd never met before. Thousands of years of socialisation couldn't be undone in a couple of generations and we both tensed. I don't know about him, but I was tense because he was huge. Not just big but absolutely insanely massive. I was a dragon, I wasn't exactly weak, but this man's sheer size halted me in my tracks and made my dragon crouch warily inside me, ready to spring forward.

"Good morning," I said, proud of the even tone I managed to get out, even in my surprise. "I don't believe we've met."

We hadn't met. I would definitely remember him.

When he didn't reply, I added, "I'm Morgan Somerville. I'm staying as a guest of Edith Hoskins."

"Somerville," he spat.

I'd never heard my name said with so much venom. It was my first clue that I wasn't this man's favourite person. I didn't take it personally. I wasn't anybody's favourite person. I did, however, add a strain of pride to my voice when I said, "That's what I just said." It might have been foolish but I wasn't going to have this giant man think he could speak in that tone about my family, especially given that he was obviously a *curaidh*, with his dark hair and nearly-black eyes. Of all the people who could think themselves superior to Somervilles, this man was not it.

Dane took a quick step forward, and how I didn't stumble backwards is anyone's guess. Maybe my legs had frozen. And that was why I was there to learn to fight, because, seriously, freezing was not a great instinct when it came to staying alive. I just hadn't been in a situation where I was possibly going to be killed before.

On the other hand, freezing was what Somervilles were good at. I'd never seen Lord Somerville run or do anything to break a sweat because it was uncouth. He got everything he wanted by simply becoming cold and proud, and it was what my brother and I had been raised to do, as well.

It's what I did when faced with the enormous dragon, Dane, and that was possibly a mistake.

I stayed where I was and spoke cooly. "It's customary to introduce yourself in return. That is, if you have the manners for it."

Ok, maybe I was suicidal but at least my death wouldn't go unavenged, since my father would bring every ounce of his power to play if our family had been dishonoured. That didn't seem like such a comfort, though, when Dane's lips pulled back and he began to growl low in his throat.

I stood, watching as the massive man teetered on the edge of shifting, as though I was watching someone else stand there and provoke him. If it was a spectator's sport, I would have been shouting at the smaller man to run but, since the smaller man was me and I was frozen in place, calm and cool pride was all I had left to defend myself with. It was all I knew.

The door to the kitchen burst open and I twisted round so I could see whoever it was in my peripheral vision. No way was I taking my eyes of Dane.

Lew was half-way across the kitchen in a second and he slowed down, holding his hands up like he was trying to calm a wild animal.

"It's alright, Dane. Leave him. Just leave him."

I said nothing, which might have been the only wise thing I'd done since my father had said,

"You're going to train to fight, son," and I hadn't protested. It was all very well realising after the event that I should have thrown my brother or one of my cousins under the bus but, at the time, I'd said nothing and look where it had got me.

Lew edged forward, moving steadily between me and Dane, who hadn't taken his eyes off me. He looked about ready to kill me but his eyes were different from Lew's. Lew's had been intense and piercing, whereas Dane's looked unfocused and blindly angry. If he killed me, it wouldn't be pretty. He would trample me like a bull.

"Dane, look at me, that's right, look at me."

Lew's voice had gone softer, and my gaze flickered to him for a second before returning to the real threat. I could only see the side of his face but I could *hear* the affection in his voice as he said, "This isn't you, Dane. You're just wound up and you need to take a break. Go upstairs and I'll be up in a while. Leave him, Dane, and go upstairs."

Since I was between Dane and the door to the rest of the house, and I couldn't have actually moved my legs at that particular time, I was glad when Dane spun around and left by the back door, walking right out into the kitchen garden instead of attempting to get past me.

When the door slammed shut behind him, Lew breathed out.

I did, too, but I tried to do it in a way which didn't reveal that I'd been holding my breath for the entire time.

He looked over his shoulder at me.

"You ok?"

"Yes," I said, making sure I absolutely sounded like I was. The last thing I wanted was for this man to see me shivering with fear. That wasn't dignified.

"What did you say to him?"

I drew myself up proudly. Quite frankly, I was offended that he would assume *I* was the one in the wrong.

"I introduced myself."

Lew cringed. "Yeah, that would do it."

Seriously, how could he expect me not to be offended by that?

"I was under the impression that all of your... household knew of my arrival."

"Yeah, but Dane wasn't here last night when you arrived."

"I am aware of that."

"And he wasn't expecting to see you."

I had no idea why he would know I was in the castle and not expect to see me. Was I supposed to stay in my room the whole time?

"I was not informed that there was a restriction in my freedom." My voice was clipped, and Lew's eyes widened a little but my father would never have made such a mistake as

Edith Hoskins: everyone in the household knew exactly where they were at liberty to roam so there was no room for error.

"No, that's not what I meant. It's just- never mind, it won't happen again. Make yourself at home." He gestured around the kitchen. "Help yourself. I'll be back in a while, I just want to check that Dane got upstairs alright."

I thought it was bad manners to leave me to hunt around an unfamiliar kitchen just so he could go and check on Dane, but I was graciousness personified and didn't say so. Instead, I inclined my head regally – that was a trick I'd learned from my mother, actually, and she always did it when she didn't agree with something but didn't want to fight about it, either – and managed to get my legs to work well enough to step aside from the doorway.

As Lew left, it occurred to me to wonder what relationship he had with Dane exactly. I'd heard the affection in Lew's voice and I'd seen the brute calm down with his presence, not that that said anything other than the fact that they were close. And it was absolutely none of my business how close they were. They could be fated mates for all I knew or cared.

Absolutely not bothered in the least by Lew and Dane's relationship, I began to look in the cupboards for coffee, snapping the doors closed irritably as I searched. I didn't care about

Lew and Dane one bit. It wasn't any concern of mine.

CHAPTER 6:
MORGAN

When my father told me I'd be training, I hadn't hated the idea. I'd got pretty used to just doing what he said by then, so when he told me I'd be living with curaidh for six months to learn to fight so I could be of use to the family, I'd accepted it. I'd been nervous, of course, since I'd never lived away from home before. I was to live among so many new people, away from everyone I knew, which wasn't something that came easily to me. But I'd also been a tiny bit excited. There had been a little part of me that wanted to learn to fight. I wanted to leave the Somerville estate. I wanted to meet new people.

What a fool I was.

It wasn't even lunchtime on my first day

when I realised that I was going to hate every minute of living with the *curaidh*.

And, by hate it, I meant spend my time equally aroused and angry, which was an entirely new combination of feelings for me.

The reason? Lew Hoskins.

I'd thought he was handsome the night before but to see him wearing his jogging bottoms and a tank top I had to admit that yesterday's Lew was plain in comparison. The white top – which I began a passionate love-hate relationship with on sight – stretched over his broad chest and accentuated his wide, muscled shoulders. I swear I could see every muscle in his arms flex as he moved around and gestured and, when he picked up some weights to move them aside, I nearly whimpered at the bulging definition.

My out-of-control libido made listening to him difficult and he must have thought I was a complete idiot child who couldn't follow simple instructions. It hadn't occurred to me to pack any different work-out clothes than the ones I wore at home, so I stood there in my plain black leggings and long-sleeved t-shirt and tried to always face him head-on. I did not want him to see me in profile because, although I could mask the scent of my arousal, I couldn't seem to talk my dick down. The embarrassment, the tightness of my jock strap, and a feat of will-power that was, quite frankly, heroic, kept me from tenting the front of my leggings like a porn star but I kept sneaking glances down and the bulge there was definitely noticeable.

We started off with some stretches to warm up and I got a glimpse of just how flexible he was for a big guy and didn't that just put ideas in my head? I had to avert my eyes or get turned on enough that I started just rubbing myself right there in the training field at the back of the Hoskins' castle. That would have given them quite the show.

I knew there were enough of them watching me through the windows, trying to see what I was like and gossip about my abilities, no doubt. I saw their faces at the windows when I glanced that way. I made sure I didn't look outright, though – not like they were, just standing there ogling – because I had more dignity than that.

As I turned back to face Lew, though, I thought I saw where they were coming from. If he wanted to bend over like that to touch his toes, what did he expect? Hell, if I'd been anywhere else, watching anyone else that gorgeous, I would have just sat back and enjoyed the show. But I was there to train and I absolutely could not let my body get ideas about Lew bloody Hoskins and what it might be like to run my hands over the firm muscles of his thighs up to that glorious arse.

I seriously needed a cold shower.

When we'd stretched out, Lew informed me that we would go for a quick run, and set off before I could say anything. And I wasn't annoyed at all.

We went on what felt like a twenty-mile run and it was only the fact that I was determined not to give him any ammunition against me that kept me from reminding him that his great long legs could eat up the ground faster and easier than my short ones. I spent the entire run glaring daggers at his arse and wishing at once to bite it and to murder him for having such a biteable arse.

By the time we got back to the training ground, I was sweating and exhausted. It was only my pride keeping me upright – it certainly wasn't my legs, which had turned to jelly.

"We'll do some simple moves today, just to ease into it," he said, like that run hadn't been more exercise than I'd had in years.

I didn't trust my voice not to give me away, so I simply inclined my head in agreement.

"Just watch me do the movement and copy."

Right. I could do that. And I was starting to wonder whether he was standing in front of me deliberately, just to show off that incredibly broad back and tight arse. He didn't look like a show-off but he was definitely keeping his back to me. I should have been grateful, what with the unfortunate-boner situation, but I wasn't, I was tired and irritated.

I followed the movements as best I could and was concentrating so hard that I didn't hear the footsteps until they were half-way across the lawn. As soon as I did, my senses went on high alert. Not that I was expecting anything but one *uasal* alone in a whole castle full of *curaidh* was pretty much begging for trouble.

What exactly that trouble was, I didn't know, since nobody had told me. My mother had repeatedly warned me to 'protect myself' and 'make sure I was safe' and 'lock my door' but hadn't actually said what she expected to happen. I'd built up the courage to ask her just the day before I left, after weeks of 'watch them carefully' and 'never let your guard down' but she'd flicked her eyes over my entire form and said, "You're very young. Don't be afraid to burn them, if you must," which I found extremely helpful, obviously. Nothing like being clear about things to fill me with confidence.

It meant I was on edge and being outnumbered, even two to one, was not what I was comfortable with. The newcomer was larger than me and, even though he didn't have Lew's obvious muscles, he looked sort of solid and I decided I didn't want to find out how hard he could throw a punch. Otherwise, he didn't look remarkable. Fairly handsome, broad shoulders, dark grey eyes, all making him look nice – but nothing compared to the annoyingly sexy man beside me.

As the stranger approached, I eased out of the repetitive movement Lew was doing – some sort of slow punch thing – and turned to face the newcomer.

"Hey," he said as he approached. He was smiling, which not many of them had done up until then, and I found I liked that. Not many people smiled at me. Mostly because not many people were pleased to see me.

"Good morning," I said.

He chuckled, flashing straight white teeth. "Afternoon now – you've been going for hours."

I felt Lew shift behind me and he dropped to the ground, puffing out a breath. "That's why I'm knackered, is it?"

The newcomer laughed again and his eyes skimmed over Lew. "Probably. That, or you're just really unfit."

I glanced at Lew. He was sitting with his legs out in front of him, both knees drawn up, and was leaning back on his arms, looking like a bloody pin-up for gyms. He did not look unfit, as the definition in his arms attested, shining with sweat in the sunlight.

Lew smiled. "That'll be it," he said. "Brendan, this is Morgan Somerville. Morgan, Brendan, my cousin."

Brendan offered his hand, which I took.

He said, "Actually, I'm his second cousin twice removed."

Lew waved a hand in the air. "Whatever. Family."

Brendan's smile grew a little tense. "Family tree isn't your strong point, is it, Lew?"

Lew shrugged, not caring one way or another about his family tree. I didn't understand that. My entire family learned the family tree early on. We could recite the names of immediate family, aunts, uncles, distant relatives and ancestors like nursery rhymes as soon as we learned to talk.

Brendan rolled his eyes fondly and gave me a look that said *this guy, huh?* I didn't return it. I wasn't one of them. But I did incline my head slightly, a half-nod. I thought that was more than enough. The *curaidh* was behaving with a bit too much familiarity for a stranger.

"Why don't you come in and get some lunch?"

Lew hopped up again, saying, "Sounds great, I'm starving. You go ahead, Morgan, I'm just going to tidy this lot away." He gestured at the weights and mats we'd been working on.

"Very well."

Brendan said, "I'll help you, Lew."

"Nah, you take Morgan inside, show him to the kitchen."

I felt it was time to dig my heels in a bit. "I'd appreciate a shower before I eat, actually."

"Alright. Brendan, will you show him to his room? Be a while before he can find his way around on his own."

Brendan gave me a big grin and set off for the castle, talking. He chatted about the grounds we were walking through and I listened politely.

"Do you like the grounds? You must have seen a lot of it on your run earlier."

I hadn't. I'd seen a lot of Lew's arse earlier. I didn't tell Brendan that, though.

"Yes, it's quite charming." High praise indeed. I did not claim things were charming willy-nilly.

He was satisfied with that and continued to chat until we reached my room. I had already memorised the route but I didn't want to appear ungrateful for the effort he was going to.

"Here you are," he said. Then, to my surprise, he leaned a little closer and added, "Don't mind Lew – he's a bit grouchy but he means well. He's got a lot of responsibility and he's not used to training anyone so young."

I blinked at him. I was an adult. And alright, I hadn't been out in the world much and I hadn't been alive for half the years Lew had spent as a soldier but that didn't mean I was a snot-nosed child. Is that how they viewed me? I changed my mind about Brendan there and then, gave a tight, "Indeed," and let myself into my room, closing the door firmly behind me.

CHAPTER 7: LEW

I had expected to dislike training a uasal but I hadn't expected him to turn up to that training wearing a pair of leggings and long-sleeved t-shirt that was indecently moulded to his fucking body.

When we'd started doing our warm-up, I'd made the mistake of looking over at him to check he was doing ok and had gone light-headed from the way my blood had rushed south. I hated that he was so physically perfect. He was lean lines and barely defined muscle and those silver-blue eyes took me in with such composed judgement that I wanted to kiss him until he was panting and desperate, just to make him want me half as much as I wanted him. It didn't seem fair that my body could betray me like that. Not that I was a prude or anything; I'd had my fair share of casual flings, but I'd never out-right wanted someone I actually disliked before. My mind told me one thing – I didn't want to even be in the same room as him longer than I had to – and my body told me another – that I wanted to make him scream with pleasure and bury myself in his warmth. Those two things were hard to reconcile.

My lust had made me stupid. I had meant to take us on a gentle jog around the place, point out some of the landmarks so he could find his way around a bit later, and get our muscles working properly. What I ended up doing was running off at a pace that I realised later would have been uncomfortable for someone so much shorter than me, not talking to him at all and keeping us running for four times as long as I'd meant to. My body was tired. I hoped Morgan had been used to exercise or he was going to be sore tomorrow.

What made it worse was, half-way round, I'd realised I was going too fast but when I slowed down, he nearly caught up with me and I sped off again. If I'd allowed him to catch up, I would have had to talk to him and he might have jogged alongside me and I couldn't let him do that, not unless I wanted to traumatise the poor little nobleman with the massive fucking hard-on I was sporting for him.

I felt like the worst kind of pervert. He was young. Legal – thank god – even for a dragon, since we aged slower, but still, younger than me, and probably inexperienced. I'd heard that *uasal* kept their virginity until they mated, like they were eighteenth-century maids who needed to be pure for their husbands.

And wondering whether Morgan was a virgin or not was *not* helping my arousal.

At least I could see him and Brendan going into the castle, which meant nobody was there to see my predicament. I'd had to keep my back turned on Morgan while showing him some moves – which is famously *not how you instruct someone*, not if you're doing it right – because my damn erection hadn't gone down.

I'd been both thankful for Brendan's interruption and put out by it, since it meant I could finally stop doing the same fucking move over and over again, but the reason I was doing that was because I couldn't turn around to tell Morgan we were done, not without pointing my erection right at him. I'd had to sit down sharpish and draw my legs up to hide my crotch when talking to Brendan. We were pretty close friends but there were some things I didn't want the guy to see and that was one of them.

And I was never wearing light-coloured trousers again. I had an actual wet spot where I'd leaked pre-come at the sight of Morgan's slim body glistening with sweat. He was shiny and beautiful, and it gave me a glimpse of what he might look like in his dragon form with his silver scales. *Curaidh* were plain old grey. We could vary in tone quite a lot, and we had different markings, but we didn't shimmer like the *uasal*.

When I'd finished putting the equipment away in the storage shed, I faltered. Everyone would be running round the castle, going about their business. I didn't want to walk through the middle of them with an erection and a wet spot to draw attention to said erection.

There was only one thing for it. I turned my back on the castle – just in case anyone happened to be looking out the window, I didn't want them to get an eyeful – and stripped off my clothes, bundling them up into a ball. Then I shifted. It felt good to release my dragon after having so much pent-up frustration, and I reared up, stretching and flexing my wings. Then I scooped up my clothes with one claw and pushed off the ground, beating my wings.

I loved the feeling of flying and, normally, I would have circled the castle a couple of times just to feel the air rush over me, but I didn't quite dare. If I flew past Morgan's window, I wasn't sure I could stop myself from looking and that would lead to all kinds of trouble.

Instead, I took off straight for my window and landed on the large stone windowsill, shifting back with practiced timing. My window was unlocked and I slid my finger between the window and the sill and pulled, shuffling out of the way as it opened. The castle windows had been designed by dragons many, many years ago, for that exact purpose.

Slipping into my room, I breathed a sigh of relief. At least I was out of sight for a while. I'd have to stay there until my erection went away.

Naturally, when I got into the shower and felt the warm spray hit my back soothingly and reminding me of all the miles we'd run that morning, I was also reminded of just how fucking needy my dick was. The way the water ran down my body had it spraying onto my hard dick and just the feeling of the droplets landing on it was making it throb.

I tried valiantly to ignore it and wash my hair instead but, as I began to lather shower-gel over my body, my hand slid inevitably further down, over my stomach and groin and right along the length of my dick.

I groaned loudly. I was so hard it was going to take almost no time at all and, once I'd started, I couldn't have stopped even if the whole fucking castle had started to collapse around me. I gripped tight and ran my wet hand up and down my length, letting more moans spill from me. My other hand was braced on the tiled wall and I began to fuck my dick into my palm desperately.

The feeling was exquisite and I couldn't remember the last time I'd been so turned on. I'd had full-on sex which wasn't as hot as my own hand in that shower. And if what was making tingling pleasure ripple up and down my spine so quickly was the thought of Morgan's supple body moving beneath me, then I would accept I was a bad man but I'd take the orgasm, thank you.

And what a fucking orgasm. I leaned forward to bury my head in my arm and stifle the shout I let out as pleasure exploded in me and my balls drew tight to my body and released a thick stream of come against the wall.

I kept stroking, feeling the shock-waves ripple through my whole form and my jet of come seemed endless.

By the time I'd finished, I felt completely wrung-out and sagged against the shower wall, panting. I barely had enough energy to wash myself off, direct the spray at the tiles to wash away the evidence and then turn the shower off.

As I climbed out of the shower, I sent up a fervent prayer that I'd got Morgan Somerville out of my system.

CHAPTER 8: LEW

I had a serious problem and its name was Morgan Somerville. Unsurprisingly, I had not got Morgan out of my system with one wank. In fact, over the past week of him living with us, I had not got him out of my system with three hundred wanks.

I couldn't say for certain that's exactly how many times I'd touched myself to the thought of him but it felt pretty close and the amount of lube I'd gone through verified that I had an unhealthy obsession.

It wasn't like I helped myself, either, since I followed him around like a puppy. He'd asked me outright two days into his stay why I was there and I'd said, "It's my job to watch you and keep you safe."

That was a laugh. It was not my job to watch him. And it most certainly wasn't my job to watch him in the way I really was watching him, which is like he was a piece of living porn. If it had been my job to protect him – and our defences were more than adequate to do that without me constantly at his side – I'd probably have arrested myself, since I was the biggest danger to him. I couldn't stop myself imagining what it would be like to have him. And the fact that he was coldly indifferent to me should have put a dampener on my lust but, unfortunately, it didn't.

And then, after seven days of torturing me with his mere presence, Morgan decided to test my self-control by going swimming.

We'd told him about the private beach below the cliff that could be reached by the cliff path that zig-zagged down to the sand, or by just flying down there, but he hadn't shown much interest in it at the time.

So imagine my surprise when he set off towards the beach wearing shorts, t-shirt, flip-flops, and carrying a towel.

I had the decency to wait a few minutes before following him, and then I stood at the top of the cliff and looked down at the tiny human form I could see below me on the sand. He laid his towel out and kicked off his flip-flops but then he just stood for ages, looking out to the sea. I'd have given anything right then to hear his thoughts. And I don't think it would just be good for me, it would do him some good, too.

With how closely I'd been watching him, I'd noticed that he never actually spoke to anyone, not
really. He said what was polite and no more, and
if someone talked to him, he asked them a question and let them talk some more. I knew almost
nothing about him, about his past, about how he
felt, only that he must have felt pretty alone to
be among people he didn't know and not be able
to talk to anyone. I'd seen Brendan chatting to
him a couple of times and had smiled at him, glad
one of the family was going out of his way to welcome Morgan – the rest of them tended to keep
out of his way, like he was something they had to
accept was there but didn't want anything to do
with.

After several minutes, Morgan moved. He
stripped off his t-shirt and shorts to reveal swimming trunks underneath. I nearly fell off the cliff
leaning forward to see more clearly. I wanted to
see every detail of his exposed skin.

Morgan walked across the sand and hesitated when he reached the water's edge. I knew it
would be chilly but not too cold to go into.

It seemed Morgan hadn't decided on that,
yet, though. He dipped his toes in the lapping waves and stumbled backwards. I watched
in fascination as he did it again, like a sort of
dance, strangely graceful, testing the water like
he wasn't sure what to make of it.

Just watching him made my body tingle

with lust, and I knew that, if I stood there much longer, I'd get a semi. But I couldn't tear myself away.

Then I heard the high-pitched shriek of a dragon laughing and looked up to see four young dragons go flying over me, sweeping out to sea and looping back to land on the beach not far from Morgan. He tensed and I actually saw the cold hardness settle into his features. He never smiled. That bothered me. But he'd at least not been looking so frosty and unamused a moment before.

As the four young dragons settled and shifted into human form, Morgan set off at a swift walk up the beach towards his things. I was surprised to hear the growl emanate from my own throat, unaware that I'd been doing it. My dragon didn't like that. It didn't like that four young men were naked in front of Morgan and baring all, and it didn't like that Morgan was half-naked in front of them, either. It really didn't like it.

My dragon and I had always been in tune before and it was a new feeling to have it take over like that but I felt it stir below the surface, wanting to get out and rip the eyes out of all the young dragons on the beach. Which, obviously, was insane. They were my cousins. Well, two of them were my cousins – or second cousins – one of them was my nephew and the other was some relative of an uncle-by-marriage but I had no idea what that made him to me. It didn't matter. He was looking at Morgan like he was a treat, and my dragon was beyond cranky.

I saw what was about to happen about five seconds before Morgan did. The four young ones were just into adulthood, which meant they were big – especially compared to a lean little *uasal* like Morgan – but not yet mature enough to be responsible for all that raw strength. They fanned out along the beach, blocking Morgan's retreat. And that's when Morgan realised he was going to get dunked.

I saw his eyes go wide, even from where I was on the cliff. The four young dragons said something, and then attacked, bounding forward with youthful energy and gangly legs, and Morgan stumbled back and raised his hand in front of him like that would stop them.

"Stay where you are. I'm warning you."

He sounded panicked, and I let my dragon out. If I hadn't let it out, it would have burst out of me and then I'd have had no control whatsoever. As it was, I gave a warning shriek as I leapt from the cliff and shot down to the beach like an arrow, and it was only through a huge effort of will that I controlled myself enough not to spew fire all over the youths. It wasn't like it would have done them much harm, since they were fucking dragons, but it would have stung a bit.

They were stunned enough by my sudden

appearance and the warning in my voice that they stopped and looked at me as I landed directly in front of Morgan, my back to him, facing the youngsters.

"Uncle Lew, what are you doing?"

I swivelled my head in his direction and snorted.

"We were just playing," said one of my cousins and I growled. They all shrank back a little, looking much more like children than they had before. I nearly felt bad but my dragon was out now and it was fucking furious that they had their eyes on Morgan still. I fanned my wings, shielding him, and the four of them began to bunch together, not sure whether I was going to harm them or not. I would like to say that I wouldn't, but I honestly didn't know for sure.

For someone who'd made a reputation for being a good soldier, I'd botched my rescue up completely. It wasn't that I thought the four would attack me, and, seriously, if they did they'd just try to dunk me, which we did to each other almost every week anyway, the problem was that I couldn't get Morgan out of there fast enough. If I wanted to talk to him, I'd have to shift back and then I'd be naked, since I'd ripped out of my clothes when I shifted and, while I was ok at the moment, if I turned to look at him, I'd get hard and that would be awkward for everyone, especially me.

Also, if I told him to shift so we could just fly back to the castle together, he'd have to take his trunks off and I didn't think I'd handle that well.

In the end, I just spun around, lunged forward and grabbed him around the middle and practically threw him over my shoulder. He let out a grunt when his chest hit my hard frame and I released him, letting him slide along my back. He clung to my shoulders, where my wings joined my back, and I lowered myself down so he could settle there, which he did. He gripped hard with his legs and I felt his hand rest on my spine, right below my neck. I wanted him to stroke his hand along it but he didn't.

I took off and, in seconds, we were flying over the cliff and back across the huge lawn to the castle. I landed on my windowsill with a clatter and gripped on with my claws, taking up far too much space in my dragon form.

He slid off my back and moved into the corner, looking small and fragile standing there in just his swimming trunks with his arms wrapped around his torso.

I shifted and opened the window, motioning for him to get inside. He jumped down into my room and I followed.

He stood there awkwardly for a moment and then turned to me.

"Thanks."

"No problem," I said, twisting round and trying to get to my chest of drawers without him seeing my junk. I pulled some jogging bottoms on and only then did I turn around to look at him properly.

He'd always been pale but he was whiter than usual and his mask was hard in place. I had the urge to comfort him, but he looked like he'd absolutely hate any contact I would give him, so instead I said, "I'll go back for your stuff later."

"Thanks," he said again. He managed to say it in exactly the same tone as before, which was unnerving.

"Take a seat." I gestured at the bed, which was the only place to sit, and tried to conceal my surprise when he actually did. He looked relieved to sit down. In fact, the more I looked at him, the more I was convinced he'd gone through quite a shock.

"Are you ok?"

"Yes."

I wasn't convinced. I was also getting far too much satisfaction from seeing him sitting on my bed, in my room, and my eyes kept wandering down the deliciously smooth skin of his torso. A tiny shiver ran through him and he wrapped his arms around himself again.

"You cold?" I asked. I didn't even wait for an answer. I just pulled out another pair of joggers and a jumper and held them out to him.

He took them and gave me a strange look, one I couldn't interpret.

"You know, I could just have flown back to my room and put my own clothes on."

Ah. That would explain the look. It must have been a *you're stupid but I don't want to actually say it* look. He put mine on anyway, and my dragon hummed inside me in satisfaction. It liked to see him in our clothes, marked as ours.

That thought made me start. I hadn't thought that about Morgan before. Sure, I'd wanted to fuck him – seriously, the man was so gorgeous – but I hadn't wanted to mark him before. My dragon hummed again and strained to smell him. Of course, we couldn't. He masked his scent just like the rest of us and it wasn't like I could ask him to reveal his scent. Dragons only did that with people they absolutely trusted. It was rude to ask.

Instead, I eased onto the bed beside him, leaving a gap between us, and asked as gently as I could, "What's wrong?"

"Nothing."

"You're still shivering, are you still cold?"

"No. I mean, yes."

"Which is it?"

"Yes, I'm cold."

I pulled a blanket out from the trunk at the end of the bed – I never needed them, I was never cold at night – and draped it around his shoulders. He looked small under there, wearing my clothes that hung off him, several sizes too big.

"Did they hurt you?"

I was surprised by the emotion in his eyes when he glanced at me, but he looked quickly away again before I could identify what it was. At first sight, it looked like fear.

"No."

I tried to reassure him, hoping he wasn't afraid of my family. "They were just playing. They were going to dunk you."

"Under the water?"

"Yes."

"Oh."

"You've never been dunked before?"

His voice was tight when he answered. "No, I have not."

I might not know much about Morgan, but I'd studied him pretty well the past week and I knew already that, the more formal he got, the more he was trying to conceal something behind his mask. He did it when I made him do pull-ups, which he hated, and when Dane was in the room with him and he'd draw into himself and look proud. That also had the unfortunate effect of making Dane get even more pissed off because he thought Morgan was just the arrogant little *uasal* he'd expected.

I remembered what Jill had said about *uasal* not playing with their kids.

"You don't lark around like that at home?"

"No."

"Not even with your cousins?"

"No."

I was getting nowhere fast with that line of questioning. He was blocking me.

"What did you think they were going to do?"

His eyes flickered to mine, briefly, and then skittered away again. "I don't know," he said. "Drown me?"

"What? Why the fuck would they do that?"

He shrugged, like he contemplated being drowned every day and it had ceased to be important to him. "Because they don't like me."

"They—"

I'd been about to tell him they did like him, but they didn't. They didn't know him. And didn't that make me feel bad? He was young and unworldly and had come to our family home alone and been dumped there by his father, and instead of taking care of him and making sure he was alright, I'd lusted after him and used him as my own personal wanking fodder. Shit, I was a horrible, selfish man. And I'd let Morgan down.

That was going to stop right fucking then.

"They wouldn't have drowned you, Morgan." I reached out to put my hand on his shoulder, wanting him to look at me but not brave enough to take hold of his chin and bring his head round. "They're good boys, they're just young and high-spirited and they're used to people who play with them. They'd never have done that if they'd known you weren't used to it."

I didn't mention that, if I'd thought about it for two fucking minutes, I'd have realised that and could have told the young ones last week. I was so angry at myself. But me getting pissed off wasn't going to help Morgan, so I'd save that for later.

I gave a little smile, hoping to ease some of the tension out of his shoulders. I could feel it underneath my hand and it bothered me.

"So you've never been dunked under water? Have you ever had a water fight?"

"No."

"Have you ever built a raft?"

"No."

"Been diving?"

"No."

"What about swimming races?"

He swallowed. "No, I haven't done *any* of it, alright? I've never been to the beach before."

He looked so fucking young right then, swaddled in my blanket and confessing that like he thought it was something to be ashamed of. I could *feel* the defensiveness come off him in waves as he spoke, expecting me to... what? Laugh at him? Stand him up and route march him down to the beach again?

I wanted to grab him and hold him to me, pull him into my chest and tell him that everything was going to be alright. Because nobody else was there to do it and he needed to know. But he was hunched defensively and I thought I'd probably got as much physical contact as I was going to get with just my hand on his shoulder. Remembering the way his cousins (or had they been his brothers?) had shaken his hand when they'd said goodbye, I had a feeling that this was more physical comfort than he'd had in a long time.

I wanted that to change, too. And I was going to make it happen. If there was one thing my family was good at, except fighting, that is, it was hugging. And it was about time Morgan was introduced to that concept.

CHAPTER 9:
MORGAN

L ew had been strangely sweet after the beach incident. Normally, I got the impression that he barely tolerated me: he was brusque and watched me from a distance rather than come and walk beside me, and I felt bad that he was duty-bound to protect me when it was clear he would rather be anywhere else. But I hadn't seen him that morning when I'd gone to the beach and I'd thought I was alone to test out the sea for the first time.

I'd hardly even formed an opinion when I'd heard the joyful shriek of a dragon and seen the four young dragons land on the sand and shift. They were bigger than me, even though I'd put money on them being a fair number of years younger. Once we got to adulthood, it was often difficult to tell our age, since we aged so slowly. Still, they'd looked young and they'd looked big and they'd looked strong and it had looked like they were going to hurt me.

I don't know what I'd expected them to do to me. I'd told Lew I'd thought they were going to drown me but that had only been one of the nasty thoughts that surfaced in my mind when faced with the four of them, my back to the wide sea and nobody around me. The thought had flashed through my mind that this had been exactly what my mother had warned me against and I'd been stupid enough to put myself in that position, but then Lew had arrived.

I'd known it was him, even in his dragon form. He just looked like Lew. And he was so incredibly beautiful with his dark grey scales that faded to a much lighter shade underneath his belly. I kind of wanted him to lay on his back so I could rub it, not that I'd ever tell him that.

I'd never been so glad to see anybody and, when he'd thrown me across his back and let me ride him, I'd felt safer than I could ever remember feeling.

That was why I hadn't protested when he took me to his room. It hadn't done my crush any good – and, yes, I would admit I had a crush on the gorgeous hunk of a man – but I'd felt safe and he'd cocooned me in clothes and blankets until I was warm and safe.

I was surprised he hadn't noticed that those very same clothes and blanket were still missing from his bedroom, since I had them tucked away in my room. I hadn't stolen them! I'd just worn them out along the corridor and into my own room and forgotten to take them back. And, since they were in my room anyway, it seemed silly not to use them, which is the only reason I slept in the clothes and bundled the blanket into a ball to cuddle against. Because it was practical.

At that point, I was barely even fooling myself. I had it bad. And the fact that Lew continued to be sweet to me really wasn't helping.

The cold, analytical part of me wasn't fooled. It waited for the other shoe to drop and warned me I'd be sorry that I was ever suckered into this stupid fantasy. The warm, feeling part of me, though, that was swept along in the rush of dates I went on with Lew.

Ok, they weren't really dates. I wasn't *that* delusional. But if I quietly pretended that they were, I wasn't hurting anyone. And they felt like what I'd imagine a date would feel like.

I got to spend time with Lew when we weren't just training. He started walking around with me rather than hanging behind me, and he talked to me during training and he smiled at me and, I swear, every time he did, my heart have a little extra thud, just for him.

After training that morning, I helped Lew put all the equipment back in the shed and then he closed the door and bolted it and said, "So, Morgan, you want to head down to the beach?"

I hesitated. I wasn't sure about that.

He carried on.

"I thought we could paddle a bit. The others are still in lessons or they're busy so nobody else will be there until later. We'd have it all to ourselves."

The man sure knew how to tempt me.

"Alright." I tried to keep my voice even so he wouldn't think I was afraid. Actually, I was excited. I was a bit nervous about the sea – I knew dragons could drown – but I wanted to spend more time with Lew and, if I said no, he'd probably send me up to my room and I wouldn't see him until dinner time.

He grinned and my heart beat its extra beat.

"Great. I'll go get the stuff. You put your trunks on and I'll stop by your room on my way."

I hurried off to do as he said, slipping some shorts and a t-shirt over the top and sliding into my flip-flops that Lew had retrieved from the previous week's aborted session. When I stood by the door, I wasn't sure whether to wait outside or stay in my bedroom. I didn't want to look too keen.

There was a tap at my window and I

turned to see Lew in glorious dragon form hovering right outside it. He was bobbing up and down with each flap of his wings but his head remained still, undulating on his long neck. He had the same eyes in dragon form as he did in human. They were so intensely dark and piercing, I was half convinced he could read my thoughts.

Throwing the window open, I raised my eyebrows.

"Why did you tell me to put my trunks on if you wanted me to shift?"

He gave a snort and pushed nearer to me so his head was almost in the room.

"You want me to climb on your back?"

He snorted again. That wasn't an answer.

"Lew?"

His big head nudged me, and he was big enough in dragon form to knock me off balance so I had to brace against the push.

"Alright, don't get violent. I've never ridden on someone's back before. I thought last time was a one-off."

I tried to sound annoyed just so he wouldn't be able to tell how excited I was to get back on his back. He wasn't the biggest dragon I'd ever seen but he was big enough, probably twenty feet in length, nose to tail, and I climbed out carefully, thinking that flip-flops were not the best mountaineering shoes, all things considered. I slid over his shoulders and he twisted his head around so his neck followed me, making sure I didn't fall. It was sweet.

When I was settled, I was straddling his back and I reached forward to rest my hands in front of me. A quick image flashed into my mind of me straddling him when he was in human form, but I pushed it away. If I got a boner then, he'd definitely feel it and then I'd have to never speak to him again. That, or he'd tip me off his back in revulsion. I tended to affect people that way. My uncle had been driving us one day when I was seven and I'd got car-sick and thrown up. He'd slammed on the brakes, dragged me out so I could finish throwing up by the side of the road and then he'd told me to shift and I'd had to fly behind him all the way home. I have no idea how far from home we were at the time but I was exhausted by the time we got there and he'd had to have his car valeted anyway.

Unaware of my train of thought, Lew turned and dipped towards the cliff, sailing across the air smoothly. It felt strange to ride him. I hadn't been in a condition to properly enjoy it last time, since I'd been scared for my life and my honour – whatever, I'd thought I was going to be drowned or beaten or raped or something else horrible – and I'd clung to Lew like a lifeline. Perhaps it was instinct. He was one of the few members of the Hoskins family I recognised, even a couple of weeks in, and familiarity was comforting. Or maybe it was that he was a *curaidh* in dragon form and my *uasal* nature had seen him as a protector. Either way, I'd felt safe.

I felt safe with him all the time, I realised. And riding someone's dragon should have been a weird experience but that felt natural, too. It was strangely intimate. I'd never ride anyone else's dragon, certainly not outside of an emergency.

He landed on the beach gently and I slid off his broad back and then, because I had at least some sense of self-preservation, I turned to look out across the vast sea instead of doing what I wanted to do, which was watch him shift into human form and ogle both of his beautiful, naked bodies. But I knew I wouldn't be able to control my arousal if I did, so staring out across the sea it was, at least until he'd covered himself.

"Do you like it?" he asked and I tried to repress the shudder that wanted to take over my body at his voice so near to me.

"I haven't decided," I said.

He laughed, and I felt a flash of triumph. I'd made him laugh, and it was a beautiful sound. Then I realised he was probably laughing *at* me more than anything, and my elation dimmed.

Looking over my shoulder, I raised my eyebrows and tried to look cool in the face of his bare chest and long, muscled legs revealed by his dark swimming trunks. God, how could one man be so beautiful?

"Hard to please?" His lips were quirked up in a half-smile, so I didn't think he was mad at me for it, which would make a first. I hadn't realised I was so hard to please. Compared to the rest of my family, I was as laid-back as they came.

"Perhaps."

He laughed again and moved to stand beside me. "You want to paddle?"

I swallowed. "Sure. Let me just take my clothes off."

Retreating a bit further from the water's edge, since I didn't know how far the waves would reach and I didn't want my clothes to get wet, I stripped them off and folded them onto the towel he'd laid out. Either he'd been carrying a bag in one of his claws earlier and I hadn't noticed, or he'd brought it down to the beach already.

When I went back to him, he looked tense and his arms were held rigid by his side.

"Are you alright?"

"Yes, I'm fine."

His voice was a little husky and I wasn't convinced. I looked around me, trying to see anything that would have disturbed him. "Is there something wrong?"

"No, it's fine."

His body relaxed with a visible effort and he shot me a smile, and, even though I was worried, my heart still did that stupid little beat at the sight of it.

"Come on," he said, back to his normal self. "Let's do this."

He reached out his hand for mine and I took it out of pure surprise. I had to admit, though, that it felt wonderful to have his warm hand wrapped around mine, and I revelled in the feeling of his strong fingers with their calloused skin against my soft palm.

We waded into the water, and I felt the same strange sensation as the last time, of my feet slowly sinking into the wet sand like it was trying to envelop me and the water washing over my feet as though I wasn't even there.

I stopped and looked down and, when the next wave washed over me, I stumbled backwards, sure I was sinking that time.

Lew laughed and gripped my hand tighter.

"Does it feel strange?"

"Yes."

"Good strange or bad strange?"

"I'll let you know."

We walked out again and I was so close to him that our arms brushed, too, where I was holding his hand close to me. It made me feel better and I waded into the water right up to my middle.

The waves tried to knock me over and I struggled against them. Lew, being taller than me, was only in up to his hips, and he moved right in beside me until his broad chest was pressed along my arm.

"Let yourself float for a second. I've got you, you won't float away."

Tentatively, I followed him deeper out to sea and the sceptical little voice in my head told me that he was probably going to hold me under the water and drown me, but the sensible side of me couldn't see what he would get from that, and so I mentally shrugged my shoulders and trusted him.

With Lew so close to me, I didn't panic when my feet first left the sea bed, and instead I just bobbed there and felt his hand press against my back, reminding me he was there. The waves swelled and I floated around, always with Lew's hand on me. When he took his hand away, I was unanchored and my arms and legs thrashed in the water, instinctively trying to find some purchase. I couldn't feel any. One glance back at the shore told me that I'd gone way out of my depth and there was no way I'd touch the ground beneath me. As I struggled to keep my head above water, a wave washed over me, pulling my body along with it wherever it wanted me and I sank under for a moment before thrashing my way to the surface again.

I felt my arm collide with Lew's hard body, though I have no idea where, and then I felt his strong arms around me. He encircled my chest completely and pulled me back against his chest and I gripped at his forearms, just in case he was thinking of letting go of me again.

I'd splashed water all over the place in my panic and my hair was dripping wet. It meant I felt his breath in a cold breeze against the back of my throat.

"You're safe, Morgan, I've got you. I've got you."

The softness of his voice was strange. He never shouted at me – and I was incredibly surprised by that, in itself – but sometimes he sounded a little impatient and sometimes exasperated and more and more he talked to me like he would anyone else, but I'd never heard that soft, fond voice directed at me before. He'd used it when he was calming the giant Dane down, and when one of the children had fallen over and skinned her knee and he'd held her gently for ten minutes until her skin had grown back over it, but he'd never used it on me before.

"It's alright, Morgan," he murmured, and I realised the tug of water against my body wasn't entirely from the pull of the current, it was because he was moving us slowly back towards shore. "You'll be able to stand soon."

I stumbled when my feet hit the sand but he kept me pressed against him and we walked further up the beach until the water was only pooling around our legs, and then he stopped, halting us.

I was incredibly embarrassed, now that we were out of the water, because it occurred to me that I could have shifted at any time and my dragon, even if it wasn't as big as Lew's, would have been able to touch the ground.

Lew still held me to his chest and I was grateful, since it felt nice, and since I didn't want to look at him right then.

He chuckled and I felt it vibrate through my body.

"It's different from a swimming pool, huh? With the waves and the current pulling you out of your depth."

"I don't know."

"What do you mean?"

"I've never been in a swimming pool before."

He stilled, which I thought was ominous. And then his arms tightened around me, pulling me so close that it began to feel uncomfortable.

"You've never been to a pool? And you've never been to a beach?"

"No," I ground out. Surely we'd been over my inadequacies enough, did he have to repeat them?

"Morgan, can you swim?"

"No."

"Shit," he said, and spun me round to face

him. His grip on my arms was hard and unyielding, and I prepared for a fight. Not a physical fight, obviously, but I knew that people getting angry with me was not fun.

He looked me in the eyes and glared. "You can't swim?"

"No."

"Why did you go out that far then? It's dangerous."

I glared back. It was *his* fault, why was he blaming me?

"Because you said you had me."

See, *he* was the one who'd made me think it was safe in the first place.

"Shit," he said again, and yanked me forward. My whole body went stiff, not sure what he was doing. It took me several long seconds to realise that he wasn't hurting me. He was holding me in his arms and pressing me against his warm chest. His face was buried against my neck and, slowly, I relaxed into the hug. I couldn't remember the last time I'd had a hug. In fact, I couldn't remember *ever* having a hug, though I was sure I must have had one once.

"I'm sorry, Morgan, I should have asked you that before I took you out there."

"It's ok."

"Stay here with me for a while longer?"

To be honest, I was just so glad that he wasn't angry with me, he could do almost anything right then and I'd have been ok with it.

"Ok."

CHAPTER 10: LEW

I'd had the fucking fright of my life when Morgan had said he couldn't swim. I have no idea what I was so worried about, since I'd been right there beside him the entire time, but my brain couldn't help but speculate: what if I'd wandered off and he'd been left there alone? What if a huge wave had separated us? What if I'd suddenly gone mad and flown away and he'd been left out of his depth in the ocean?

None of them were likely scenarios, but I was unusually afraid by the prospect of having accidentally drowned the *uasal*.

And then, when he'd said, *"Because you said you had me,"* like it was obvious, I'd felt a rush of power and protectiveness and pride that was way out of proportion. But it proved he trusted me. The man couldn't swim and he'd gone into the sea with me, completely trusting me to keep him afloat.

I wanted him so much then. Not just to fuck him – though, obviously, yeah – but to really be *mine*. I wanted to be the one he trusted more than anyone else and who would look after him and protect him and hold him like I was doing then.

My dragon rumbled in my head, proclaiming that it felt the rightness of it, just like I did.

I pulled back from our embrace and looked into his gorgeous silver-blue eyes. "You want to lie in the sun for a while and dry off?"

"Yes."

I grinned and let go of him just enough to take his hand and drag him up the beach to the towel I'd laid out. It was a big towel but it was still only one and, yes, that might have been my subconscious at work earlier, making sure we were going to have to share it. It was just that, at that moment, I didn't know whether my subconscious was a genius or a vindictive bastard.

I flopped down on the towel, shuffling over to one side so he could lay next to me, and looked up at Morgan standing over me. I could finally study his entire exposed body, see his pale skin gleam in the sunlight and track the water droplets that ran down his smooth chest to the slim blonde happy trail that started just below his belly button and drew my eye down to the waistband of his trunks.

I yanked my gaze away and rolled over, reaching for the bag I'd carried everything over in and pretended to rummage through it. I hadn't meant to ogle him so obviously. He was still standing at the edge of the blanket, probably wondering whether to leave or not. *I* wouldn't stay with me after that.

I felt the blanket pull beneath me as he stepped onto it and eased down beside me. Despite how close I'd held him in the water, he made sure he didn't brush against me as he sat down.

Grabbing a bottle of water for each of us, I rolled back and offered him one, smiling when he took it. I sat up to take a gulp of mine and then lay down again, drawing my leg up and settling my foot on the blanket to try and conceal the beginnings of my erection.

I had decided: my subconscious and my conscious were idiots together. Whatever part of me that had had the stupid idea of taking Morgan Somerville to the beach, where he would wear little trunks and get wet and look at me with fucking trust in his eyes, was a complete idiot. What was I meant to do?

To cover the fact that I was getting horny lying next to him, I talked. And talked. In fact, I must have bored him stupid by telling him about the times my family had been down to the beach, the games we'd played, the competitions we'd run and the celebrations we'd had. He nodded along like I was the most interesting person on the planet and that really didn't help at all – it didn't help me get my lust under control and it didn't help my dragon settle inside me, either. My dragon was practically preening under the undivided attention Morgan was giving me.

It meant I had mixed feelings when I heard the shout above us from the cliff.

"Hey Lew!"

I looked around to see Brendan waving and raised my hand in return. He grinned and began to wind his way down the cliff path. Behind him, Nadia sauntered along like she hadn't a care in the world.

"Hey, we wondered where you'd got to," said Brendan, dropping down onto our towel beside Morgan. I felt a spike of irritation, which wasn't like me. My dragon was annoyed and I tried not to think about why that might be. I hoped desperately that it wasn't because it had been starting to think of Morgan as *ours* and didn't want to share. That would be a fucking disaster.

"It's a nice day, we thought we'd enjoy the beach."

Brendan turned to Morgan and asked, "So what do you think? Do you like it?"

I listened to Morgan's reply carefully. He

was always friendly to Brendan, and Brendan was sweetly kind to him, too, and I liked that, I really did, but I wanted to judge exactly how friendly they were and my dragon was listening pretty intently.

Morgan's voice was back to normal, somewhere between friendly and indifferent whereas it had been just a little bit warmer with me earlier. My dragon sank its head down onto its paws inside me, content. Yep, that was going to be fucking difficult to deal with.

I felt a sudden blow to my ribs and grunted in pain, already in motion to defend myself before I even saw who'd kicked me. I'd forgotten Nadia was there. And my ribs had paid the price.

"Shit, Nadia, I think you cracked one of my ribs."

She shrugged. "I don't have shoes on."

"I wasn't complaining that you'd *only* cracked one, dearest, darling Nadia. I was suggesting that you refrain from fucking fuck fuck!"

My sentence was cut short with a string of expletives as Nadia's nimble, vicious little fingers pinched my nipple and twisted. I swear she was going to twist the whole thing off.

"Jesus, Nadia, what the hell?" I gasped as soon as I had breath in my lungs again. My hand was clamped protectively over my nipple while it throbbed with pain.

She didn't even spare me a glance as she

sat down on the towel where I'd been laying and placed her flip-flops beside her, fussing with them and showing me that her shoes were far more important than I was.

"You were in my spot," she said at last.

"You only just arrived."

"And a gentleman would have offered me a seat."

I knelt on the only corner of the towel still available and glanced at Morgan. He was looking down and I worried he was overwhelmed.

"Hey, Morgan?" I leaned closer to him, ducking my head slightly to try and see his face.

"Yes?"

When he glanced up at me, I saw the amusement in his eyes. It was such a small difference to his expression – it barely changed at all, really – but his whole face just radiated amusement and it was so fucking beautiful that I didn't even care that the joke he was laughing at was at my expense. I'd let Nadia bruise my nipples every single day if it could make him look like that.

Instead of calling attention to it, which I knew would make him shut down, just when he'd started to relax a little, I grumbled, "You know, I'm your trainer, you're supposed to be on *my* side."

He gave me a coy look and said, without missing a fucking beat, "Unfortunately, Somervilles are always on the *winning* side."

I stared in amazement, my mouth actually hanging open and making me look probably the most attractive I ever had, if he had a thing for guppies.

"Did you- did you just-?"

Nadia cooed, "*Ooh*, good job your dragon can heal that *burn*, Lew." She turned her black eyes on Morgan and gave a grin that made even my dragon cringe back with how evil it was. "I had no idea you were going to be my new best friend."

And then my dragon huffed in displeasure as I was totally dismissed as Nadia focused her attention on Morgan.

Brendan listened for a while and then caught my eye. He gave a small jerk of his head, indicating that he wanted me to walk with him, so I stood and stretched out and thanked my lucky stars that being around my two cousins had killed my erection.

When we were far enough away that they wouldn't hear us if we spoke quietly, Brendan asked, "How's he doing?"

I was reminded then of what good people my family are. They wanted Morgan to feel at home just as much as I did.

"He's doing ok, thanks. I think he's settling in. How's he been around you?"

"Fine, he's been fine. I mean, it's weird that

he has one facial expression but, if you ignore that, he's ok."

"One expression?"

Brendan nodded. "That's right. I know *uasal* are meant to be stuck up, so it's not surprising."

"So you don't know if he's ok?"

"He says he is. He looks healthy. You're training him hard. That's what he's here for, right?"

"Yes, it is." That was a bit of a punch to the gut, to be honest. I don't know what I'd started to think Morgan was there for but it had been a while since I'd thought of him as a duty I'd rather not have. "But he should be happy, Brendan. He's going to be here for six months, away from his family. That's got to be hard. We need to make it as easy on him as possible."

Brendan stopped walking and looked at me. "You're a good man, Lew." If he'd had any idea of what I'd been fantasising about doing to the innocent little Morgan Somerville while he was under our family roof, he wouldn't have said that.

"You too, Brendan," I said, not sure what else I could say. Brendan was only a few inches shorter than me and he was sturdily built, but I still felt protective towards him. He was family and we'd grown up together, more like brothers than whatever-it-was he said he was to me.

"Thanks for looking out for him, even when nobody else was."

He gave me a long look and then nodded. We turned back towards the couple on the towel and I cringed.

"Of course, now Nadia's adopted him, he probably won't need either of us."

Brendan snorted. "That or he'll need *more* help."

CHAPTER 11: MORGAN

Lew looked over at me as the sun began to sink below the horizon. It cast a red-pink glow that lit everything up and made it seem magical. Lew's hair was shining with red light, like a halo. I didn't want to go into why I thought that.

"So, Morgan, what do you think of the beach then?"

"I like it."

"And did you decide whether you liked the water or not?"

"No, not yet."

Lew waggled his eyebrows. "We'll just have to come back again so you can decide then, won't we? We'll bring a picnic and play some games."

"Don't threaten me, Lew Hoskins."

He looked startled for a moment and I felt a flash of worry that I'd crossed a line with my joke, but then his face broke out into the most gorgeously big smile I'd ever seen and he said, "That's not a threat, it's a promise."

Nadia squealed excitedly. "It's been ages since we've got everyone together at the beach."

Brendan raised his eyebrows. "That's because it's been winter – it's been cold as fuck."

"Stop nit-picking, Brendan! The point is, we're entering a new season now. There's no excuse."

Lew nodded in agreement and I found myself getting caught up in his enthusiasm. He'd told me all about the times his family had spent there together, and it sounded like something you'd read in a children's book – picnics and games and laughter and lashings of ginger beer and all that. I hadn't been able to help but wonder whether he was exaggerating to make it sound better than it was, because it *sounded* idyllic.

I asked Nadia, "Does the whole family fit on this one beach?"

It was a private beach, essentially, accessible only by boat and air and the cliff behind us that came from the castle. It was surrounded on either side by tall cliffs and sharp rocks.

"Of course! We have to squeeze in a bit

sometimes, especially if Daniel stays in dragon form – he doesn't like to be in human form much – but at least the children get a kick out of using him as a boat, don't they Lew?" He just had time to nod before Nadia carried on anyway. "Unless Nana insists, and then he turns back. Maybe we can get him to come out with us next time."

Brendan interrupted. "I don't reckon we'll get everybody to come with us this early in the year. It's too cold."

"A lot of the cousins will," said Lew. "You, me, Nadia, Morgan... Daniel... Guppy... Laura... Prince... maybe even Dane."

I had no idea who most of those people were. And I had to wonder what their parents had been thinking when they named them. Guppy? Prince? Were they nicknames?

Brendan gave a forced grin that looked painful. "We're not cousins, Lew."

"Whatever."

"Second cousins *twice* removed." He sounded insistent about that, and it was the second time he'd said it in front of me. He definitely had a point to prove.

As Lew waved a hand and said, "The point is, the oldies won't come to the beach this early but some of the younger ones will. Do you think Dimpy would come? That would make it five-a-side for games."

I was very nearly distracted from Brendan's glare by that name. Dimpy? That was worse than the others.

However, I wasn't totally distracted. I saw the burning look that he gave Lew then and, unless I was mistaken, it was a lot to do with lust and not a lot to do with family. I wasn't claiming to be an expert, since my experience of lust was limited, to say the least, but I had never seen any of *my* cousins look at *me* that way. That was probably a good thing, all things considered. Still, I hoped Brendan was right and he wasn't actually related to Lew by blood.

Lew bent down to gather all of our things together, cramming the towel and water bottles into the bag and barely shaking the sand out first. As he bent down, he accidentally gave us all a glorious view of his bubble butt. I looked quickly away – which wasn't what I wanted to do, but I really, really didn't want to get an erection in my swimming trunks and in front of those three – which meant I saw Nadia gazing serenely out over the water, looking much more relaxed than I'd ever seen her, and I caught Brendan's eyes glued to Lew's arse.

Yep, I was right. Brendan had the hots for Lew.

The realisation didn't bother me as much as I'd thought it would. In fact, I actually felt warmer towards Brendan than I had before. Maybe he would win Lew's affections, in the end, and that would be a bit hard to swallow but, for the time being, he and I were actually the same. We both fancied Lew, and neither of us had him. I sympathised with him. I mean, where were we *meant* to put our eyes when Lew displayed his glorious body for us to drool over?

From the corner of my eyes, I saw Lew straighten and looked away from Brendan as he turned abruptly, obviously realising he was about to get caught ogling his *not*-cousin's butt.

I set off for the cliff path quickly. No way did I want to get stuck behind Lew waking up there, with his arse right in front of my face. Whoever I ended up walking next to would definitely notice the way I looked at it. Not that I was obsessed with it, but I did want to squeeze it every time I got near, so there was that.

Brendan caught up with me and gave me a huge smile. "You don't live near the sea, do you?"

"No."

"Is it just fields around your castle, then?"

"There are some woods, too."

It wasn't that I was reluctant to share that information – he could look it up easily enough in any number of places – but I got the feeling he was leading up to something and I got a prickly sensation all over my skin.

I was right. Brendan leaned in towards me as we walked, and asked, "So you can't exactly see people coming, then? From your castle, I mean."

"Yes, we can."

"Except from behind the trees."

I shrugged. "We have defences in place."

"But no natural protections? Not like our cliff?"

I looked at him. Was he trying to brag about their beach or was he trying to get information about our defences? In the end, I said, "No." Well, it was true.

Brendan snorted. "Sometimes I wonder how your lot survive."

"My lot?"

"Yeah, *uasal*. You're not exactly equipped to deal with any attacks, are you? Land wide open, castle you can surround, no fighting skills..." He trailed off.

Perhaps he was trying to provoke me by insulting my family. Or perhaps he was just one of those people who spoke without thinking. Either way, I wouldn't get riled. Besides, I knew something about the Somervilles that he didn't.

I felt the glow of satisfaction inside me and my dragon blinked and looked up, almost like it was awoken by the thought of *uasal* having to defend ourselves. My dragon wasn't particularly aggressive, but the first thing any dragon did – what any animal instinct did – was to protect itself.

I smirked a bit and said to Brendan, "Oh, I think we'll manage."

We reached the Hoskins' castle just as the sun sank below the horizon. It had been a nearly perfect afternoon. In fact, the only thing that could have made it better was if I'd been able to bring Alfie with me and show him the beach. He'd never been on one, either, and I wanted to chuckle to myself at the thought of how he would react to the feel of sand underneath his feet. He'd definitely scream. I had to clamp down on my desire to giggle at the image in my head. I didn't want to look bonkers. But I did decide that, if I could persuade my father to let Alfie visit, I'd definitely ask Lew to take us back to the beach.

When I got back to my room and checked my phone, I saw that I had a missed call – I'd left it behind because I didn't want to lose it on the beach or get it wet or, if I'm more honest, to ring and distract me from spending time with Lew. My stomach dropped. It was my father.

I rang him back straight away, standing by the side of my bed and staring at the thing as though it would give me answers.

"Yes?" he snapped by way of greeting.

"Father, it's me, Morgan."

"I know that, I saw your ID on the screen."

"Oh. I'm sorry I missed your call earlier. I was... training."

"Don't miss it again."

"I won't, Father. What did you want to speak to me about?"

"I don't have time to talk to you now. You should answer when I ring you. I'm not available at your beck and call, you know that."

"Yes, Father."

"Just make sure you work hard. I won't have you embarrass the Somervilles."

"No, Father, I won't. I *am* working hard."

"Good."

The call ended abruptly. I sat in the gloom of the evening, staring at my phone, my good mood completely gone.

For a while there, I'd forgotten what I was at that castle for. I was there to train, to work hard, to learn how to fight. I was not there to make friends and enjoy myself and paddle in the sea with handsome men.

I put my phone back on the nightstand. As I turned towards the bathroom to shower the sand from me, I tried to cling to the relaxed, easy feeling I'd had all afternoon. I might have to report my week's activities to him, but Lord Somerville didn't need to know everything.

Which was just as well, because he would not be pleased.

CHAPTER 12: LEW

I was pleased to see Morgan settle into life at our castle more and more each day. Nadia adopting him was a blessing and a curse, just as I'd thought it would be. I got grouchy when she took him away from me for 'girl time' and completely ignored my protest that he wasn't a fucking girl. But, even then, I couldn't be too upset because he began to practically glow with happiness. I swear there was an aura around him that just radiated peace, and that definitely hadn't been there before. I was prepared to overlook some pretty serious offences on Nadia's part for putting that look of contentment on Morgan's face.

I saw them eating popcorn together in her room as they sat on the floor leaned back against the bed together, watching a film, and I saw him brushing her hair in long, gentle strokes, and I saw them play snap and, yes, it might have been creepy for me to fly by her window quite as often as I did but I just needed to check he was ok.

The weather turned chilly with an unexpected reminder that it wasn't actually spring quite yet, and so we put any further beach adventures on hold. I still took Morgan outside to train, though. I liked it outside and we could be louder and not worry about breaking anything if we got carried away. He was starting to build more strength, which I was pleased about, and he was also starting to let me touch him a little, which I was absolutely thrilled about.

The first time I'd tried it during training, he'd locked up completely like he'd turned to marble. He was so obviously uncomfortable with it that I'd backed off and changed tack, getting him to run circuits with me, but he hadn't lost the tense mask across his face for the rest of the day.

Hence it was a bit of a thrill to know that he trusted me enough to touch him. It was like our little swimming session had loosened something in him. I didn't try and wrestle him or anything. Firstly, that wasn't what we were training for, secondly, he definitely hadn't built up the strength to even attempt to match me, and thirdly, if I got that much of my body in contact with his body, I'd probably spontaneously orgasm.

All in all, I thought it best to stick to some rather basic self-defence moves for the time being.

We were repeating the same movement again and again, where I would grab his arm and he would bring his hand down sharply on my wrist to break my hold – and he was getting good enough at it that I no longer had to just let go when I felt contact, he was actually breaking my hold – when I heard Nadia's voice.

"Lew, put Morgan down or I'll have to maul you."

I sighed. "Afternoon, Nadia."

She ignored me and talked to Morgan. "You're getting good at that."

He was pleased with her praise, looking happy and bashful and not quite sure how to take the compliment, which is why, when she grabbed his arm and began dragging him away, I didn't rip her whole hand off.

"Where do you think you're going?" I asked.

"You ask such obtuse questions, Lew. We're going inside."

I focused on Morgan. "Why haven't you broken her hold on you yet? That is literally what we've just been practicing."

He gave me a shuttered look and I cursed

myself. He was never sure whether I was joking or not. I'd worked out quickly – yes, all on my own, because I was that much of a genius – that the Somervilles didn't joke around that much and he was absolutely not used to it. I gave him a wink, to let him know it was fine.

Nadia, facing where she was going and dragging Morgan along with her, with me trailing behind, didn't see the wink.

"Dearest cousin, he's not breaking my hold because he doesn't want to. He wants to come with me instead of doing punchy-punchy things with you."

"Is that an inuendo?"

"Only if you're a moron."

Just went to show, I was a moron.

Rallying, I asked, "What exactly are you going to be doing with him instead?"

Nadia rounded on me and put her hands on her hips, letting Morgan's arm go so it fell to his side.

"He's going to paint my nails."

Considering Morgan looked as shocked as I was, I didn't think she'd warned him about that.

"He doesn't want to paint your nails, Nadia."

"Shows what you know. He hasn't tried it yet. When he does, he'll love it."

"He's supposed to be training."

"And you've trained him."

"We weren't finished."

"You'll never be finished, Lew, because you are a perfectionist."

It also just went to show that Nadia was unaware that I already thought the man beside her was absolutely, horribly, detestably perfect.

"Nadia, you can't just—"

"I need someone to paint my nails, Lew, because I can't hold the brush steady enough to do my left hand. It's either Morgan or you." She narrowed her eyes. "And if I get any nail varnish on my fingers, I won't be happy."

At that point, I was willing to sacrifice Morgan. Nadia was terrifying.

"Alright, you can take him. *If* he wants to go."

We both looked round at Morgan, and he blinked at us like he couldn't believe it. "You want me to decide?"

It broke my heart a little that he'd never expected to be able to decide on such a stupid matter. Nadia must have felt the same because she nudged him with her shoulder gently. She always touched him, but it was never enough to make my dragon growl since it was always fleeting and not intimate, just enough to get him used to being touched without crossing a line. That's when I realised why she'd suddenly been so keen to have someone paint her nails when I was sure she'd always done it herself before: it would require some physical contact, but not too much. Everything she'd done with Morgan had been the same. My respect for my cousin went up drastically at that realisation. She was going to be a great head of the family.

Morgan looked at me from under his lashes and it was like he knew that would get him anything he wanted.

"I'd like to paint Nadia's nails. When we're done training."

I sighed and Nadia gave a victorious, "Hah!" and took his hand again, already dragging him away by the time I said, "It's fine, we're done."

He'd been looking back over his shoulder, not sure whether to resist Nadia's lead or not, and, when I gave him permission to go, relief broke out over his face and he turned to walk beside my cousin.

"You know I've never painted nails before, right?"

"You'll be fine, you're a natural."

"You have a lot of faith in me."

"Yes, I do. You'll do great, trust me. And I have nail varnish remover in case you do turn out to be appalling at it, so don't worry."

My heart clenched at the quiet, "Ok," Morgan gave.

Turning back to the mats we'd been using, I decided to do some more training. I needed to keep up my own strength as well as develop Morgan's. And, if I didn't keep busy, I just knew I'd spend the next hour fidgeting and flying past Nadia's window to sneak peeks inside.

I worked hard and was sweating hard when I heard Dane approach. He had kept away from me for weeks, hardly talking to me, but I knew, really, he was keeping away from Morgan and I just happened to always be with Morgan.

"He skiving?" he asked as he reached the mat. I saw he was wearing training gear, so he was there for a purpose and he probably meant to be friendly but I didn't like the little needle at Morgan.

"He's been here more than you, especially given you're meant to be one of his instructors."

Dane's face closed in a frown, which made me realise – belatedly – that he hadn't actually been frowning before, which was like a world record or something. Which I'd just ruined. Great.

"You seem to be doing fine. I watched you from the castle."

That was worrying. I was used to hiding my random erections at the sight of Morgan's skin or his muscles or his soft gold hair getting darker with sweat and flopping forward over his forehead or his beautiful silver-blue eyes... but I only hid them from Morgan, I didn't think to hide them from any creepers studying us from the castle.

I grunted in response, which was a very Dane thing to do, so I figured it was fair.

He said, "If you want me to train him, I will."

It sounded like a threat.

"No, it's fine."

I should have been more insistent but it didn't occur to me that he'd want to do it.

He said, "No, you're right. I should do my duty. I'll come out here tomorrow."

That surprised me and had me scrabbling around for a way to put him off.

"I don't think he's ready. I mean, I can keep training him."

Dane gave me a dark look which I wasn't sure whether it was for me or for Morgan or for every *uasal* out there. "He's been here a month already. He's only here for six months – he needs to start training properly or he won't learn enough."

Unfortunately, I couldn't argue with that.

"Yeah, ok then, if you say so. But- he's only small and you're massive. Just stick to demos, alright?"

I didn't want to examine the feelings in me that made me revolt against the idea of Dane touching Morgan. I didn't want him to get hurt, I knew that, because Morgan had turned out to be surprisingly innocent and kind, and I wasn't even going to think about Dane touching him in a way that wasn't combat because it made my dragon rear up and roar, and then it took me hours to calm down again. I knew that from experience. I had completely stopped thinking about the possibility of other men touching Morgan, and I'd done it for my own sanity.

I knew I had a problem. For fuck sake, I'd only known the man a month and we hadn't exactly been the best of friends for the first week, but I felt closer to Morgan than I did to a lot of my family, which was... unheard of.

He grunted, which, I noted, was neither an agreement or a disagreement.

Dane didn't go in for raised eyebrows. His only facial expression in the past four years, since I'd retired from the Fife Army, had been nothing at all or a frown. Those were the two extremes. Nothing. Frown. I knew why but I was also starting to think that Dane was taking his hurt a bit too far. He'd been completely torn up by the selfish prick who'd dumped him out of nowhere and hadn't even bothered to give Dane a proper reason as to why. I didn't understand why Dane still let the man affect him, if he was that much of a dickhead. I wasn't one to say something as trite as 'get over it' but it didn't look to me like Dane was even trying to move on. He seemed to delight in wallowing in his own misery and hatred.

I tilted my head.

"Dane?"

He sighed. "Let's just fight, ok, Lew?"

"You don't know what I was going to say."

"Yes, I do. You were going to tell me that you're here if I want to talk. Well, I don't want to talk. I want to fight."

"You know, it's not healthy to keep things bottled up."

Dane took a swing at me and I only just ducked in time. It was pure reflex and I was still processing what had happened when I raised my hands to block the next swing. He took a few jabs at me and I parried before backing off. He'd gone easy on me, just letting me know that the talking part was over and the fighting part had begun.

But I was nothing if not foolish, so I said, "See, you're ignoring it."

"I'm not." He attacked with a flurry of blows that I easily blocked but felt like sledgehammers against my forearms. Thank god for dragon healing. "I'm angry. And I'm letting that out quite nicely, thank you. Not bottling it up at all. In fact, I'd say I'm doing the complete opposite of bottling it up."

I couldn't really argue with that. He was angry, and he didn't hide it, not around me, anyway. When he was around the elders and the children, he tried to rein it in, and that was when he slipped into neutral mode. Not happy, just neutral. No matter what he said, it wasn't healthy.

"Have you—?"

That was all I got out before I had to use all my concentration to keep myself in one piece. Dane fought like a tank – he just ploughed right through you and, if you were caught by one of his blows, you were flattened. He was my favourite person to spar with because he showed no mercy and he expected none, either. There were only about four people I knew who I could completely let loose with, and Dane was one of them.

We fought until we were panting and pouring sweat and the grey clouds above began to turn darker with the dusk.

"Let's just say I won and call it a day," I said.

"If you want to tell yourself that you won, you go ahead and do that, Lew."

"Pft, I don't care what your tone says, you're just bitter that I won."

"That's right," he said, dryly.

I put my arm around his massive shoulder and it felt weird that he was taller and broader than me, not petite and perfect like Morgan. Fuck, when had I got used to having my arms around Morgan?

"Don't worry, Dane, I won't brag about it," I promised.

He grunted.

We walked into the castle ten minutes later, after putting the equipment away, and several people were filing down towards the dining room.

Even among the crowd, my eyes went straight to Morgan. I don't know what it was about him that drew them there, it was like that aura shone so brightly that it caught my eye. He was with Nadia, who was talking.

"Hey," I said, walking up to them and stopping their progress. I was like a fucking puppy begging for attention.

Nadia pulled her lip back in a cringe. "Ew, Lew, you're sweaty and gross. And if you even think about touching me, I will ruin my new manicure by burying my claws in your thighs." That might have sounded like a hollow threat but I'd felt Nadia's claws in my thighs and it was painful. The woman did not make idle threats.

I held up my hands placatingly. "I wouldn't dream of it. And, for your information, I'm not sweaty and gross, I'm sweaty and victorious. Because I just beat Dane. Who is a loser. Poor Dane, who I beat up because he's weak. And unskilled. Just can't compete with a soldier from the Fif—"

I was surprised he'd let me go on that long, to be honest. If I'd been baiting Nadia, I'd have had the aforementioned claws in me after the first sentence. But Dane had always been slow to anger. It was unfortunate that he tended to burn there longer when he was.

I felt Dane's huge arm wrap around my head like a boa constrictor and I held my breath, not willing to breathe in his sweat any more than I had to. He dragged me away a few feet and then released me.

"Get upstairs," he said. "It's nearly dinner time."

When I looked back at Morgan to give him a smile, he was looking straight ahead, not at me. I followed his gaze but it was just a plain wall which, I have to be honest, I didn't feel should hold his attention more than me. I might not be the *most* interesting or the *most* handsome but I was better than a fucking wall. Wasn't I?

"Save me a place," I said to him. He didn't respond or look round at me, like he couldn't hear me, and I frowned.

Dane gave me a shove in the back.

"Get," he growled. I knew that he thought Morgan was being standoffish, and I suddenly didn't have the heart to argue.

As I trudged up the stairs, Nadia called, "I wouldn't rush, if I were you – it's Aunt Brenda's turn to cook today. You should have had the foresight to spend the afternoon eating chocolate chip cookies like me and Morgan."

I groaned. Fucking great.

CHAPTER 13: MORGAN

Well, that would teach me to get my hopes up. I'd wondered right at the start what Lew's relationship with the muscle-bound Dane was, but then Lew had spent so much time with me and had given me such attention and praise and understanding, that I'd stupidly forgotten all about Dane. But it made sense. They were both incredibly attractive, both warriors, both confident, and maybe Lew's beautiful, happy personality threw some light on Dane's dark moods. Maybe they were happy together.

I adjusted my sympathy levels for Brendan. Fancying Lew was one thing, and I could totally understand it, but knowing he was happy with someone else felt like a kick in the nuts.

Poor Brendan had suffered that feeling longer than I had. I determined to be much nicer to him next time I saw him. I'd been polite before, hardly friendly. That should probably change – we rejected men should probably stick together.

I groaned. I felt like a complete fool. What had I been thinking? That Lew would start to fall in love with me? The chances were slim to begin with, but since I couldn't compete with the sort of strength and confidence that radiated off *Dane*, it looked like those chances were practically nil.

I rolled my eyes at myself. I was an idiot. It wasn't like Lew and I could be together anyway, so there was no point in even thinking about it.

It was just that, even knowing that, I hadn't been able to stop myself from dreaming. Like an idiot. Like a stupid, stupid idiot. Like a stupid idiot who lit up at the sight of a man all sweaty and hot and energised only to realise that he was all touchy-touchy (I'd been hanging out with Nadia too much) with the muscle-man, and that said muscle-man had his hands all over Lew like the treat he was and sent him *upstairs*. Dane had told Lew to get upstairs, which wasn't a big deal, but he'd sounded like he meant it and if his thoughts were even in the same universe as mine, he wanted to send Lew upstairs to strip naked ready to be licked from head to toe. Or maybe I was just weird. It wasn't like I had any experience playing out sexual fantasies. Maybe Lew's skin would taste disgusting. Maybe he would smell bad. I'd wondered a lot over the past couple of weeks whether Lew would reveal his scent during sex. Theoretically, I knew people did that, because it was intimate, but it required a level of trust. I couldn't help that I'd wondered if Lew usually did that when he had sex, and I certainly couldn't help wondering whether he would do that if he ever had sex with *me*.

And all of my wondering had been completely pointless because Lew wasn't mine and never would be, no matter how much my stupid, stupid heart beat its little extra beat for him. Stupid heart. Who asked it, anyway?

It was only my pride that saved me as I sat down to eat dinner. I was so not hungry and I put very little on my plate and proceeded to push it around rather than eat it. Luckily, Brenda was a notoriously bad cook and the burnt smell that permeated everything – even the things that weren't actually cooked, and I had no idea how she did that – meant nobody ate much and so I didn't stand out.

There was a tense moment (tense for me, anyway) when Lew looked at me from across the table to my left where he'd ended up sitting, and said, "Morgan, are you ok?"

It made several people look round at me and I felt my insides squirm with their attention. I hadn't had that sort of attention directed at me in what felt like a long time.

I kept my face neutral. It wasn't Lew's fault that he was so attractive and he'd been snapped up by *Dane*. I didn't want to be a dick about it. I also didn't want to draw attention to my stupid little crush crashing and burning right there in front of everyone. So I tried to speak pleasantly and said, "Yes, I'm perfectly fine, thank you."

He frowned. "You're not eating."

"I made the mistake of indulging in some sugary snacks a little earlier and it ruined my appetite." I turned round to find Brenda sitting across to my right and added, "It's such a shame that I can't enjoy more of this delicious meal. Would you mind if I boxed up any leftovers in case I get peckish later?"

Brenda flushed, probably because nobody had ever asked for more of her cooking, and said, "Yes, you can take anything you like. I'll put a selection together for you."

"That's very kind of you, I do appreciate it." Then I added, "Could you make sure it includes a few of these roast potatoes? How do you get them so crispy?"

I had two reasons to keep talking to Brenda. The first was that she seemed so surprised and pleased that anybody liked her cooking, which, for the record, I didn't. I had no intention of eating any of it later. I was simply going to throw it in the composting with the rest of the leftovers when she wasn't around to see it. But she didn't need to know that. The second reason was that, if I looked at her, I practically had my back to Lew and therefore I couldn't see his face and he couldn't expect me to talk to him.

If I had been forced to talk to him, I'd either have blurted out my feelings or burst into tears, which would have been beyond humiliating. I needed time. I could cope with anything, if I was given time to prepare for it. As it was, I was clutching at my cold indifference, trying to draw it back to me. I had no idea how it had got so far away from me, but it was a struggle to keep my composure in the middle of so many people as the realisation dawned on me that I'd been imagining that I had a special connection with Lew and, all that time, he'd had that special connection with someone else. I felt incredibly small and foolish as I asked Brenda polite questions about this and that and tried to reason with myself:

I only felt that bad because the wound was new.

It wasn't my fault that I'd developed feelings for Lew, given that he was all kinds of sexy and kind and talented.

It wasn't Lew's fault that he hadn't told me about Dane, either. He hadn't realised he was leading me to believe I was special. In fact, annoyingly, what made me like him so much was that he was so kind, and he'd obviously been treating me to special attention since I was new there and he was the one training me.

It wasn't like my father would allow me to become involved with a *curaidh* anyway.

I was only there for another five months.

Unfortunately, none of my extremely reasonable, rational arguments made the squirming sickness in my stomach lessen. I continued to talk as well as I could and hold myself tightly together and swallow down the acid that kept rising inside my throat.

I'd shot myself in the foot by asking for a doggy bag. Brenda took me at my word and I was whisked off to the kitchen after dinner to claim my 'prize' when all I wanted to do was retreat to my room and lick my wounds. I was convinced that, if I could have a good wallow in my self-pity and self-disgust at my own idiocy for a night, then I would be fine again by morning. It wasn't like I'd actually lost anything. At least then I could carry on as normal for the next five months.

That was not to be.

I returned to my room only to find Lew leaning on the wall beside my door, waiting for me to get there.

"You get your snacks for later?" he asked, nodding at the Tupperware in my hand.

"Yes, thank you."

I opened the door and Lew levered himself off the wall and followed me in like he was invited, which he most certainly wasn't.

"Morgan?"

"Yes?"

"Did I do something wrong?"

"No."

That made me feel pretty bad, actually. I'd not been that subtle in my jealously. He'd noticed. The question was: had he realised why?

"Are you feeling ok?"

"I'm just tired, Lew. I didn't mean to be unpleasant."

"That's not a problem, as long as you're ok. I just wondered if Dane was making you feel—"

What he thought Dane might be making me feel, I never established because my phone rang. I'd left it in my room to go down to dinner, since it was terrible manners to have it at the table. My father would never have allowed it, that was for sure.

"Hang on," I said to Lew and picked my phone up from the nightstand where I'd left it. It was my brother's number. "Hello, Alfie?"

"Finally! I've been ringing you for an hour."

"I was at dinner."

"Really? That's early, isn't it?"

I gave a small cough instead of answering.

I was certain that Lew could hear Alfie's voice on the other end of the phone and I didn't want to agree in front of him.

"What was so urgent?"

"Oh yes! I thought you should know – Lord Somerville said nobody outside the house needed to know but I was getting worried about you all the way over there on your own with the *curaidh*, and I wouldn't forgive myself if something happened to you, so I thought I'd give you a ring and if I just happened to tell you, that's not disobeying, is it?"

My brother Alfie was a rambler, especially when he got nervous. We were basically opposites like that. I went tight and silent, and he splurged all the words. All. The. Words.

"Wait, Alfie, something's happened?"

"Yes, we had a- wait, did you say I *was* disobeying or I wasn't?"

"You can tell me," I tried to reassure him.

"Are you sure? Because Lord Somerville said we weren't to tell anyone. Do you count as someone?"

I was torn. Normally, I would like to say I did count as someone, though sometimes I had my doubts. But that would mean I wouldn't get to hear the news, whatever it was.

"I'm family," I said, in the end. That was true, at least.

"Ye-es." My brother didn't sound sure.

I began to get impatient.

"Alfie, did you just ring me and tell me something had happened and now you're refusing to tell me what it is?"

"Um.... Yes? I'm sorry, Morgan, I didn't think. I just got worried that nobody had told you and then you'd be all alone and you could be vulnerable. I mean, what do we know about those *curaidh* anyway? Are *they* going to protect you? Lord Somerville should have sent somebody else with you to keep you safe."

He gasped at the end of that little rant and I could actually picture him with his hand over his mouth and his eyes wide, like he couldn't believe he'd just said something so disrespectful about Lord Somerville.

I rushed to reassure him, because he was my little brother and he needed it. "It's alright, Alfie. Don't worry. I'm safe here. Are *you* alright? Not hurt or anything?"

"Me? I'm fine, they didn't get me. I just worried that, since you're on your own, and since, you know, I don't know what those *curaidh* are like and maybe they would- they might hurt you, or they might let someone else hurt you."

I tried turning my back on Lew, who was still standing in my room, just inside the door, which he'd closed behind him. Not that it would do any good to turn away from him, since he could absolutely hear the whole conversation anyway.

"I'm perfectly safe. Where else is a *uasal* safer than with a load of *curaidh* to protect him?"

"True," he said, but he sounded reluctant to agree. "But that was when they were dutiful."

I tried to move towards the window, as though that would keep Lew from hearing my brother. I dropped my voice.

"Alfie, they're not undutiful. Look, I think we got off topic."

"You're right. Are you sure you're safe, Morgan?"

"I'm safe."

"Good. Look, I don't want to worry you and it's probably nothing and Lord Somerville said nobody was to know but... if you could just be a little extra careful for the next few weeks?"

"I will, Alfie. What kind of thing am I being careful about?"

There was silence at the other end of the phone. He was thinking.

"Um, maybe nothing?"

"Ok. Or maybe...?"

"Maybe someone breaking in."

"To a *curaidh*'s castle?" I couldn't keep the surprise out of my voice.

Alfie was offended by that, as all of the family would be. Probably rightly. He said, "If they're foolish enough to break into a *uasal*'s castle, they'll go for a *curaidh*'s too. They've got to be suicidal."

That was the truth. People didn't trespass on Somerville land twice.

"Wait, if someone was in the castle, why are you warning me about them now? Aren't they dead?"

"Oh, um," said Alfie. I could hear him tapping something nervously and I wanted to tell him it was ok, but I also wanted to know the answer. "Um, I'm not telling you anything."

I sighed.

"I'm sorry!" he blurted. "I'm sorry, Morgan, I can't. Lord Som—"

"I know, I know, I'm sorry, Alfie, I didn't mean to sigh like that. I'm not annoyed with you." I was a little annoyed, but it was unfair so, I left it. "You did the right thing," I assured him. "You haven't told me anything. You just rang to see if I was ok, and I am. And I'll be watchful, because I always am."

The sigh of relief he gave went to my very soul. "Thanks, Morgan."

"Thanks for ringing. Look, I have to go now. Can I ring you tomorrow?"

"Yes. Yes, that would be good."

"Ok, bye Alfie. Take care."

"Bye, Morgan."

I hung up and looked out of the window, trying to will Lew away. If I did it hard enough, he would be gone by the time I turned around.

He wasn't gone. He said, "Are you ok?"

"Yes, I'm fine."

"I couldn't help but overhear," he said.

"Unless you'd left."

He cringed. "Yeah, that wasn't really going to happen, though, was it? Are you alright, though? You've got to be upset."

I studied him. He was looking at me with concern, but I couldn't work out why.

"I'm not upset. Nothing's happened."

"Oh, ok, you're going with that, are you?"

I shrugged. My brother was fine. What was there to be upset about?

"Right, well, I'm just saying that you can talk to me if you want. I won't tell anyone."

"I appreciate your discretion. Especially given that I haven't actually told you anything."

He cringed again but I wanted to drive that home. If he went around telling people that something had happened to the Somervilles, Lord Somerville was going to be angry and that would be directed at me, which I didn't want, and then he would work out that it was Alfie wo told me and his anger would turn that way, and I really didn't want that, either.

"Yes, well, ok. I'll leave you to it, then."

He left, and I stared at the door he'd closed behind him. I was a bit fidgety, and I felt like I had too many feelings squirming around inside me. I wanted to go flying but, considering the very generic and unspecified warning my brother had just given me, I decided against that. Normally, at that point, I would have got my lube out and relieved a bit of tension that way, but I couldn't bring myself to do it. I knew I'd end up imagining Lew's body over mine and his face in ecstasy because that's what I'd imagined every night since I'd got there. Seriously, I was down to the very last of my very big bottle of lube and too embarrassed to ask to leave the castle to buy more. Not that I would, anyway, since I couldn't picture Lew any more and I knew I would do exactly that the second I touched my dick. It just wasn't right to imagine myself getting fucked by a man who was in a relationship with someone else. It would be like I was making him cheat or something. And, yes, maybe I was weird but still, it wasn't going to happen.

I left my room and went to find Nadia. I liked her and she was ideal for distracting me from my own thoughts. I needed that.

CHAPTER 14: LEW

I left Morgan's room and went straight to Nana's. Morgan might not seem bothered by a potential break-in at the Somerville castle but I was. Firstly, Nana needed to know, and secondly, if anyone could find out the details I wanted, it was her.

I knocked and waited for the, "Come in."

I opened the door and went inside. Gramps was there reading to two of my young cousins, Hannah and Ed. He smiled at me and lowered the book to his lap.

Nana was sitting at a desk, tapping away at a laptop. The whole desk was turned towards the room so she could see everything going on in it, and I'd often wondered whether that was so she could keep an eye on the children that ran around the place or so she could watch Gramps. I'd never mention it to her face, but I'd seen her eyes flick over to him a lot when I'd studied her before.

"Hi Nana, hi Gramps."

"Hi Lew," said Hannah, obviously annoyed that I'd missed her in my greeting.

"Hi Hannah. That's a pretty dress you have on."

"Thank you." She smoothed it down and looked smug.

"Hi Lew," said Ed, eager to get his greeting, too.

"Hi Ed. I love your bracelet."

"Thanks, Hannah gave it to me. We match."

He held up his wrist and lifted Hannah's too, so I could see their matching orange bracelets. Ed had a bit of hero-worship going on there, I knew.

"That's cool. I wish I had one, then I could match as well," I said, more for something to say than because I wanted a plastic-bead bracelet. "Nana, can I talk to you?"

She flicked her eyes over me and seemed to see what I wanted.

"Hannah, Ed, it's time for you to go downstairs and get ready for bed."

They groaned but didn't protest – even they knew better than that.

"Can Gramps come and tuck us in?"

Nana's eyes flicked over to her mate. "You go and get your pyjamas on and brush your teeth, and Gramps will be down to tuck you in."

They scampered off and Gramps put a bookmark in and set the book aside. I wasn't surprised that he was staying. He and Nana were a pair. They were mates. She didn't like to be away from him too long.

"What is it you wanted to talk about?"

Ah. I hadn't quite planned how I was going to go about telling her that.

"Well," I began, and she waved a hand to stop me.

"You're going to beat around the bush, aren't you, Lew? I've told you before, take a seat, you tower over me."

I sat, and Nana and Gramps moved to sit on the sofa opposite me.

"What's it about?"

"Morgan."

"His training or him as a person?"

"Uh... I'm not sure."

Nana pursed her lips and I blurted, "It's about his family."

"What about them?"

"I just wondered... whether they were ok."

"In what sense?"

"In the sense that they... I don't know."

Shit, I really hadn't thought through what I was going to say.

Gramps came to my rescue, because he always did.

"There's no need to treat this like the Spanish inquisition, Lew. You like Morgan, don't you?"

"Yes." I could just hope they didn't realise how *much* I liked him.

"You want him to be safe and happy?"

"Yes."

"Is there something you're thinking of that could make him safer or happier?"

"Um, yeah. I mean yes," I amended when Nana's hand rose.

"Excellent. Why don't you tell us what you were thinking and we'll muddle through it together?"

"Ok." I took a deep breath and began. "I overheard Morgan on the phone to one of his family. Someone called Alfie – you know who that is?"

Nana frowned. "They don't have any Alfies. Maybe his brother Alphonse?"

"I don't think so – this Alfie kept referring to 'Lord Somerville'. Wouldn't he call him 'Dad' or something?"

Nana pursed her lips. "They all call him Lord Somerville, even his children. I've even heard our Morgan say that sometimes."

"Ok, yeah, that would explain it," I said

"Explain what?"

"Uh, the phone call." I was making a mess of that whole conversation. The trouble was, what I'd meant was it had explained the warm affection in Morgan's tone as he'd talked to this Alfie. My dragon hadn't liked that. It had padded inside me like it wanted to get out and pin Morgan underneath us and rub against him and release our scent until he was covered in it and smelled like us, so there would be no mistaking who he belonged to. That had scared me. My dragon was starting to become a possessive bastard and I wasn't sure I could stop it, mostly because I didn't really *want* to stop it. I wanted Morgan to belong to me. I wanted to feel him beneath me, moving beneath me. I wanted that warm tone to be mine, only when he was talking to *me*. My dragon had been spitting with fury when it had heard the... *love* in his voice directed at someone that wasn't me.

·   Nana raised her eyebrow. "And when you say you overheard this phone call...?"

"He knows I overheard it; he took the call in front of me. I was in his room. I mean, I was just standing there. I'd gone to see if he was alright since he was so quiet at dinner. I wasn't doing anything."

Great, I sounded like a guilty teenager.

Gramps smirked and I knew he'd got the wrong end of that stick. Nana said, "You think he was quiet at dinner? Didn't he talk a lot?"

"Yes, but they were only questions. That's what he does when he wants to deflect, he gets someone else to talk."

"But he was still talking."

"Yes, but he wasn't..." I struggled to find the right word. "Bright," was the word I settle on in the end.

"Bright?"

"Yeah, he was dull. Like... lifeless?"

I was not explaining that well at all.

"Is that because of this call from his brother? Did it upset him?"

"No, that was before the phone call. I don't know why he wasn't bright, that's why I went to his room to ask him."

I was sure I was blushing every time I said the word 'bright' then. Could I sound any more lame?

Nana and Gramps exchanged a quick look, then. It was just a glance but I was sure they had a whole conversation with just that one look.

Gramps cleared his throat.

"I think there are two things going on here: the fact that Morgan wasn't as *bright* as usual today, and the phone call. Which one do you want to talk about?"

"The phone call." Fuck, yes, could we talk about the phone call already? If we dwelled on my mourning Morgan losing his 'brightness' for another minute, I was going to enlist in the fucking Fife Army again and not come back for ten years.

"Ok, let's focus on that. You were in his room when he got a phone call?"

"Yes."

"And it was his brother, Alphonse?"

"Apparently. Morgan called him Alfie."

"What was it about the phone call that made you worried?"

"Uh, it was that Alfie said something had happened at the Somervilles' castle."

Nana and Gramps exchanged another look, but that one was sharper. They both sat up straighter.

"What happened?"

An attack on a dragon's castle was rare but it was always taken seriously, and other dragons liked to know about it because it often heralded a spate of attacks. They needed to know to guard their own family more closely.

"I don't know. Alfie wouldn't say."

"So how do you know?"

"That's the problem, it was all over the place. He wasn't making any sense. First he says something happened and he's worried for Morgan's safety, then he says he's not sure Morgan's safe with us and kind of heavily implied that we would do something to hurt Morgan, not that I'm bitter about that. And then he says Lord Somerville doesn't want other people to know whatever-it-was that happened, and then he says nothing happened at all and Morgan stands there agreeing with him, saying nothing happened and Alfie didn't tell him anything but he's still going to watch his back."

My explanation also made no sense, but I figured it was actually pretty accurate.

Nana sighed. "Somerville. He's a piece of work."

"What do you mean?"

"If something has happened at their castle, he would want it covered up. It wouldn't surprise me if he'd told his whole family not to let on that they'd been attacked. Thinks it makes him look weak or something ridiculous."

I huffed. Nana and I agreed on that one.

"Anyway, if there *was* an attack, it stands to reason that Alphonse would be worried about his brother and try to warn him."

Realisation dawned and I nodded, "Without actually warning him. So he couldn't get into trouble for it."

"Sounds like it."

"But we need to know."

"Yes. I'll have to have a word with Somerville."

"Uh, there's a problem," I said, and it was incredibly brave of me to say that to Nana.

"What problem?"

"Since I basically eavesdropped on the

whole conversation, I sort of said to Morgan I wouldn't tell anyone. But you don't count, Nana," I added hurriedly. "You have to know."

"Yes, I do. Alright, I'll talk to Somerville without letting on where I got my information. That should keep Morgan's secret safe."

"Thanks, Nana."

If there was a woman who could do that, it was Nana.

I left and went with Gramps to say good-night to Hannah and Ed. At least that kept me from wandering the castle like a lost puppy, wondering where Morgan's fucking *brightness* had gone.

CHAPTER 15: LEW

The next morning, Morgan was no warmer towards me. I didn't know what I'd done, but clearly I'd done something to make him pull away from me. He didn't tend to smile, I would have to admit, but he did at least show his emotions in his face, or maybe that had just been me reading too much into things. Whatever it was, it was gone. Morgan was completely shut down.

I tried to talk to him at breakfast but he ate a slice of toast the quickest I've ever seen him eat anything and gulped half a mug of tea before grabbing his plate and taking it to the kitchen. I was still wolfing down my breakfast when he disappeared and, by the time I followed him out of the dining room, he was nowhere to be seen.

I thought about trying his room and then realised that was going to get creepy quickly if I kept turning up there and trying to talk to him when he didn't want to talk, so I wandered the castle for a bit. I couldn't settle to anything, though, and I was twitchy and kept looking over my shoulder as though I would see him there. I didn't.

Deciding I needed a distraction, I went to Nana's rooms to see if she'd found out anything about the attack on the Somerville castle but she snapped, "What do you think I am? Of course I haven't found out yet, idiot child."

Nana didn't like to be interrupted and she especially didn't like it when she wasn't able to do something. Gramps had told me that, once. He'd said she was never in a fouler mood than when she was worried about protecting her family, so at least I kind of felt loved even as she swore at me and I backed towards the door. From across the room, Gramps laughed at me.

"I thought you were a soldier, Lew! You're not scared of one little old lady, are you?"

I eyed the said little old lady carefully and admitted, "Scared to my very bones, Gramps."

Nana rounded on him. "Old? Who are you calling old?"

Gramps smiled at her sweetly and said, "You, my love."

She walked over to him and rested her

hand on his head and stroked her fingers through his thinning hair. Nana's mood changed with the wind, but it always seemed Gramps could settle her.

He looked up at her and said, "Didn't I tell you I've got a thing for older women?"

She smirked and leaned down to kiss him. They were disgustingly sappy sometimes.

I groaned, "Ew, Nana, get your mouth away from him."

She rounded on me. "It's not my fault he's become a sexy silver fox, is it?"

I groaned again, seriously traumatised.

"The Somervilles, Nana? Didn't you find out anything?"

Maybe I had a death wish. I don't know why I brought that up again, just when she'd calmed down.

"I don't know anything yet. When I do, I'll let you know but until then you can get out and stop bothering me. In fact, you can organise patrols along the borders and around the immediate area. No fewer than two out at a time. Report back, don't engage. Check for magic, tracks, anything out of place, anywhere someone could hide – you know the drill."

"Yes, Nana."

I headed for the door before she could think of something else for me to do. Just before I closed it, I winked at her and said, "I'll let you get back to your toy-boy."

I heard Gramps laughing as I shut the door. At least he appreciated my sense of humour.

I hadn't realised until then just how much time I'd been spending with Morgan. Everywhere I went, people were looking over my shoulder expectantly and asking, "Where's Morgan?" By the time I'd walked into the fifth room and three people asked the same question, I was about ready to snap.

In order to avoid potential confrontation, I retreated up to my room and closed the door decisively behind me. I was basically standing there choosing between an angry jerk-off session to memories of Morgan's skin under my fingers or shifting into dragon form and flying around trying to spot anything on the borders, when the door flew open and crashed against the wall behind it, leaving yet another dent in my wall. That door tended to open that way far too frequently for its own good.

Nadia was pissed off. I could tell that because she stormed into my bedroom already shouting at me.

"—the absolute worst cousin in the whole family, and there's a lot to choose from. You know what, Lew? I would say you rank lower than Guppy. Don't you dare interrupt me," she warned when I opened my mouth to protest. But, seriously, worse than Guppy? That hurt.

She marched straight up to me and began prodding me in the chest with every point she made, and added a few extra jabs just for fun.

"Firstly, you've been hogging Morgan all to yourself for weeks and not sharing him at all."

I opened my mouth again but the glare I got persuaded me not to actually speak. I closed my mouth quickly in case I actually did start to look dafter than Guppy.

"And then, when I *finally* get some Morgan-time, you go and do something to make him clam up again. And it's taken me a whole week to be able to touch him without him flinching but he actually jumped out of his skin earlier when Daniel flew in to see Nana and didn't shift back, even though we were indoors and it was crowded and he spilled jam all over my favourite skirt."

She jabbed hard enough on that one for me to think she blamed me personally for it.

"And *then* I have to find out about an attack on the Somerville castle the day *after* you found out about it. A whole day. A whole day, Lew, and not a word from you. Not a gentle whisper in my ear, not a nice cosy little chat, not a text, not a post-it note stuck to my door... I didn't hear about it from you, Lew, because you are a dirty secret-keeper, that's why, and you can just stay in your room to do some serious thinking. You're going to stay here until you realise what a beastly-beast you've been and then I expect a full apology."

She stood back and I stared at her, half-dazed and backed against the far wall where I'd been jabbed into submission.

"Have you spoken to Morgan?"

"Weren't you *listening*, Lew? He wouldn't speak to me. He practically ran out of the room when I went into it. What did you *do* to him?"

I slumped back and rubbed my hand absently across my bruised solar plexus. "I didn't do anything."

"Then why is he acting so weird?"

"*Uasal* are always weird," I said. I admit, I was stalling for time and desperately scrabbling around for something to say. It wasn't my best answer ever.

Nadia gave me a mock glare. Not to be confused with her real glares.

"Is he alright?"

That stumped me. I wasn't sure if he was alright. I would say that, no, he wasn't alright but he might be fine and it was just that he'd gone off me – that didn't mean anything bad had happened to him.

"Um…. Yes?"

I was not subtle.

Nadia glared. A real glare. I flinched back.

"What did you do to him, Lew?"

"Me? I didn't do anything to him! And, believe me, I'd remember that."

She put her hands on her hips. "You totally did something."

"I didn't."

"Urgh, men."

"Hang on a minute, I don't think that's fair. Why am I lumped in with the rest of them? And Morgan's a man, too, are you lumping him in with us commoners?"

"No, Morgan's special."

I was pleased she thought so. I totally agreed. Morgan was precious and, the more time I spent with him, the more I saw that he shone with energy and life, and tried to conceal it behind his mask. I still couldn't for the life of me work out why he tried to conceal it.

Then I realised what Nadia had said and frowned in confusion. I held up a hand and said, "Wait, you're saying Morgan is special and I'm not? I'm your cousin, Nadia!"

She rolled her eyes. "Lew, just because I love you doesn't mean I don't think you're a complete ninny sometimes. We need to find out what you did so we can undo it."

I was torn. Part of me wanted to say that I didn't care, that if Morgan wanted to shut himself off from me, he could do that. But it was a small, proud part and it was being completely overruled by the rest of me, which ached to get Morgan back where he belonged, which was right beside me. I have no idea when that became his place, but it was. Or maybe my place was beside him. Whatever, splitting semantic hairs wasn't the point, the point was that my whole body felt restless being away from him and I didn't like it.

"I still say I didn't do anything," I muttered. I knew Nadia must have heard me, but she didn't acknowledge it. At least if Nadia was on my side, I might actually get something done. Nadia was a force of nature that way.

"Right, we need to talk to him."

"We can't just barge into his room and demand he talks to us, Nadia."

She looked round at me with her eyebrows arched up in surprise. "Can't we?"

"No."

"Oh. Well I'll do it on my own, then."

And she slipped out the door and was out of sight by the time I'd hissed, "No, Nadia, you can't do that," and run after her. I supposed she'd gone towards Morgan's room so I rushed along the corridor and headed up the stairs after her, taking them two at a time and still hissing, "Nadia!"

From the staircase above me, I heard her answering voice.

"What do you want *now*, Lew?"

I kept hurrying up the stairs but, unfortunately, so did Nadia. "You can't just barge in on him."

"I'm not going to barge in, I'm going to

knock."

"You'll make things worse than they already are."

I rounded the corner of the stairs and reeled back so quickly that I nearly tumbled down them again. As it was, I slipped down two steps and scraped my ankle and had to scrabble at the banister to hold myself up.

"What are you doing?" I demanded.

Nadia was standing with her hands on her hips. "You think I'll make things worse? Is that the thanks I get for trying to help you, Lew?"

"I—"

Ok, I felt bad about that but Nadia wasn't prone to subtlety and I had the feeling that she'd blurt out a lot more than I was comfortable with if she was able to get close enough to Morgan to tell him I was in love with him.

As she glared down at me and I clutched at the banister, I was suddenly grateful for that support because I'd just realised what my problem was: I was in love with Morgan Somerville.

Shit.

That was not going to go well.

"Why are you staring at me like a fish, Lew?"

"I- I'm not. I just…"

Clearly, I couldn't finish that sentence. Telling Nadia that I was in love with Morgan was tantamount to romantic suicide.

"Urgh, men. Why don't you go and talk to him, if you think he's upset?"

"He, uh, doesn't want to talk to me."

As I said it, the ache that had been in my chest all day came into sharper focus. I'd put it down to discomfort, heartburn, anything other than what it was. It was the place where Morgan should be inside me, and he wasn't there any more. Technically, I suppose, he hadn't been there at all. He'd never been mine. But I wanted him to be.

"That's because you won't tell him the truth," said Nadia. She walked down towards me, until she was on just the step above and we were practically eye level.

"I don't know what you mean."

Her voice was soft when she spoke, almost sympathetic, reassuring. "Tell him you miss him."

"I, uh, he knows I miss him."

"How does he know? Is he psychic?"

"Not that I know of."

"So you need to tell him. Tell him, Lew, and it'll make you both feel better."

"No, I can't- I don't want to, Nadia. Leave it."

She gave a huge huff and flounced past me, knocking into my shoulder as she went and shouting, "Don't be a cowardly-coward, Lew. I'll give you one hour to talk to him."

I stared after her. Was that a threat?

CHAPTER 16:
MORGAN

When I opened my bedroom door to find Nadia standing on the other side, I exhaled in relief. There had been a possibility that it was... someone else out there. Anyone else. I didn't have a particular person in mind, it's just that it was good it was Nadia there.

"You're either glad it's me or disappointed," she said, already walking past me into the room.

"Glad," I said. I was sure of that. "I'm always glad to see you."

She flicked her long hair back in a way that suggested she'd known all along that I would love to see her. I tried not to smirk at her. Nadia was one in a million. "Good. Now listen, I don't want to beat around the bush: I heard you were worried about your family, something about a trespasser that I didn't quite catch."

My stomach dropped. If everyone in the Hoskins' castle knew about the break-in, Lord Somerville would not be happy. In fact, it's safe to say that he would be very, very unhappy. The sort of unhappy that meant someone was going to get in a lot of trouble for blabbing family business.

"What makes you think that?"

My voice was a little scratchy and I swallowed, trying to ease my dry throat.

Nadia rolled her eyes like I wasn't trying to decide whether I would need to throw myself on that particular sword or not. If I told Lord Somerville I was the one who'd told the Hoskins' then he'd want to know who had told me. There was no way I'd be able to keep Alfie out of it.

Nadia sounded exasperated. "I told you, I didn't get the details. I was just told to send you along to Lew. Apparently, he knows more about it. You should go talk to him."

I was half-way out the door before I realised how rude I was being. Looking back over my shoulder, I gave Nadia a nod. "Thanks."

The door was almost closed behind me when she replied.

"It was a pleasure."

I didn't think about whether that was a

weird thing to say or not, I just hurried towards the stairs and along the corridor beneath mine. When I'd first found out where Lew's room was, I'd worked out where that was in relation to mine. Unfortunately, it wasn't directly below my room so I couldn't imagine him lying in his bed just one floor below me while I stroked myself to thoughts of him. Although, it was probably a good thing since he might have heard one or two things I absolutely did not want him to hear, so maybe it all worked out for the best.

His room was to the east, and I practically ran the length of the corridor, wondering what he'd found out about the break-in. I never thought to question that he knew something I didn't. I just accepted that he did.

I was so wrapped up in wondering what information he could give me about my family that I didn't even pause when I knocked on his door, which just went to show how worked up I was.

Lew answered the door with an impatient, "What?" and I blinked at him. When his eyes focused on me, his face softened a bit. It looked like he had been expecting someone else. I wasn't sure whether I was glad that the irritation hadn't been for me or annoyed that he'd been expecting someone else to turn up at his bedroom. And, yes, I was a complete hormonal wreck. My ability to think things through rationally disappeared in direct proportion to how near I was to

Lew bloody Hoskins.

My concentration was not helped by the fact that he was wearing low-slung jogging bottoms and one of those tank tops that was loose-fitting, with a big rounded neck and baggy armholes that revealed a large portion of his chest and moved around as he flexed. My brain tended to shut down whenever he wore those, since I spent most of said brain-power wondering whether it would move just enough for me to get a glimpse of his nipple. The one time it actually had given me a brief glimpse of it, I'd let out some kind of strangled noise and pitched my whole body forward like it had been trying to get nearer without my permission, and I'd fallen flat on my face in the middle of a round of routine warm-downs. But, seriously, it had been light-brown and pebbled and I swear I saw a smattering of dark chest hair just the other side of it. I still dreamed about that nipple. Shit, I really was weird.

And I proved that right then by glaring at his distracting nipple through the tank top as though daring it to make a fool of me again, while Lew said, "Oh, sorry, Morgan, I didn't know it was you. I wasn't, uh, expecting you."

He trailed off a bit and glanced down at his chest, as though thinking he had something on his top, and I shook myself out of my daze. I really, really couldn't let myself dwell on his perfect chest if he was seeing someone else. That was creepy.

"Although," said, sounding resigned, "maybe I should have."

He pulled his phone out of his pocket, lit up the screen and sighed.

"Yeah, it's been an hour. I should have known."

I blinked. "An hour since what?"

"Oh, nothing. Never mind, I'm just talking to myself. Did Nadia send you here?"

"Yes."

"What did she say?"

"That you knew something about my family. You have some more information about-about what happened."

I didn't want to say it out loud. That was the sort of thing that led to other people hearing all about it and it was also specifically what I'd wanted to avoid. I wouldn't have worried about it that much but everyone in the whole Hoskins household seemed to know my business most of the time. It was the complete opposite of my father's castle where I could go for weeks without anyone questioning me about what I'd been up to, as long as I hadn't made a nuisance of myself doing it. Here, almost everyone I passed asked me my plans for the day or invited me to join them. At first, I'd assumed they'd been told they had to ask me but I'd changed my mind about that in recent weeks. They were just really friendly people. Like *really* friendly. Over-friendly, even. Especially if, say, I wanted to run away and pretend I didn't exist and hibernate until I grew out of my crush on my sexy, sexy trainer. The trainer who was standing to the side of the door, holding it open for me to go into his room.

I walked in, head held high. I have no idea how long I'd stood there staring like a moron but I wasn't going to get embarrassed about it. The Somervilles didn't get embarrassed, not by things like that. We kept out chins up and reached for the cool ice inside us that could freeze our expressions and chill even the hottest cheeks. Therefore, I did not blush.

I didn't even blush when my eyes darted involuntarily over to the bed pressed against the wall. The duvet was rumpled, like he'd made his bed that morning but had been lounging on it since, all creased and rucked up. I did not want to think about what he'd been doing on it.

"I don't know much more than we did yesterday, I'm afraid."

"Oh. But Nadia said—"

"Yes, well, Nadia was wrong. And don't think I won't be having words with her about that."

"I see. Then I'm sorry to have disturbed you."

I took a step towards the door, clutching at my self-control to make sure I didn't show any signs of the mortification I felt. It looked like I'd barged into his bedroom for no reason.

"No, wait, wait," he said, and then his big bulk was blocking my way. "Stay for a minute and talk to me. We know a bit more."

"What do you know?"

"We know that none of the other clans have been alerted of an intruder."

I shrugged. "Why would they be told?"

He tilted his head to the side like he was confused. It was annoying and cute as hell. "Because attacks on dragons – particularly on their own territory – are rare but almost always incredibly dangerous. Nobody goes into a dragon's territory uninvited unless they're pretty confident they can survive it. Only incredibly stupid or incredibly deadly people would ever try it. If someone has the skill to get past a dragon's defences, it makes them dangerous to *all* dragons. That's why breaches of security are reported to other clans, to warn them to be watchful."

"Oh."

I hadn't ever thought of it like that. Actually, I hadn't thought of it at all. Lord Somerville always said that our family business was our own, and I'd just accepted that. It hadn't even occurred to me that a breach in security at our castle could be equally as dangerous to someone else's home.

Lew was studying my face intently and he gave a little smile, tentative and shy.

"Why don't you come and sit down for a minute and we'll talk about it. I'll tell you everything I know about it."

I knew I should say no. I knew it was the right thing to do but maybe I was just a bad person because I nodded and said, "Ok, then," and allowed him to steer me over to his bed. He probably didn't realise it was intimate at all but, to me, it was. At home the only other bedroom I'd ever been in except my own was Alfie's, and at the Hoskins' castle the only other ones I'd been to were Nadia's and Lews, when he'd flown me back there from the beach.

I sat down and took a deep breath, trying to inhale Lew's scent. Some dragons released it when they were sleeping, especially if they felt comfortable and secure which Lew seemed to be in his own castle, among his family. But there was no scent there at all, except the smell of citrus shampoo and laundry detergent. Don't get me wrong, the smell of Lew's shampoo could do certain things to me and he'd basically ruined oranges for me since I got hard at the first whiff of them, my body responding like Pavlov's dogs, but I wanted *his* scent.

It wasn't to be. I couldn't smell him at all.

"Are you feeling alright?"

"Yes, I'm fine."

I hoped he couldn't see my disappointment. I had never had such trouble controlling my expression until I met him and his family.

"Is Alfie alright?"

My head shot round to look at him sitting beside me, half a foot of space between us. "What?" I demanded. "Why wouldn't he be ok? What do you know? Do you know something? Has something happened?"

I was already reaching for my mobile when Lew said, "Relax, Morgan, I don't know anything about Alfie. Nothing's happened. I just meant that he sounded upset yesterday and I wondered if he'd be ok."

"Oh." My shoulders sagged with relief.

"Alfie's your brother, right?"

"Yes."

There was a pause and then Lew said, "Is he your only brother?" as though he was prompting me to answer a question he'd already asked.

"Yes. I'm the eldest of Lord Somerville's sons. He had a son before, called Alexander, but he died about five years before I was born. I think that's why my mother had me. To replace him."

Personally, I always got the impression that I could never actually replace my older brother, which made sense, since I was a different person, but I also got the impression that I was a constant disappointment to Lord Somerville and he'd much rather have had my older brother back than the pale imitation I turned out to be.

"I think that's why they had Alfie, too," I added. "So they'd have a spare ready."

Lew's face grew dark, his eyebrows pinched together and his eyes were intense when they looked at me. His hand clamped down on my shoulder and gave me a little shake.

"You can't be replaced, Morgan. Nobody can replace you, and you're not here to replace someone else. You just need to be *you*."

I couldn't look away from Lew's eyes. I was sure he was closer than he had been, his face inches from mine. He was so handsome, with his dark eyes and strong features, and his lips looked strangely soft and pink surrounded by the dark, bristly stubble that covered his jaw.

My voice was barely a whisper and I admitted what I'd never said out loud before. "I don't think my father likes me very much."

Lew's hand on my shoulder squeezed comfortingly and his other hand reached out to cup my cheek. I felt the warm brush of his fingers across my temple and the way his palm was so close to my lips that it actually made them tingle in anticipation.

"Morgan, if that's true, your father doesn't deserve you. You're wonderful. Everyone in the whole castle loves you because you're *you*."

My whole body became warm and tense

with desire and I leaned towards Lew. I was so wrapped up in the sight and feel of him that I didn't hear the pounding footsteps along the corridor and I nearly jumped out of my skin when the door to Lew's room flew open.

I leapt backwards like my life depended on not being within ten metres of Lew and was pressed back against the wall by the window by the time the unexpected guest had even stepped into the room.

Lew was slower to respond, maybe because he didn't feel threatened by anyone in the castle, or maybe because he knew he could handle himself if anything happened. Neither of those things applied to me and I was plastered against the stone as far as I could go, with my hands held out in front of me like I could ward off an attack just like that.

The man who stood before us was Dane, and my heart jumped up into my throat and lodged there, threatening to choke me.

He'd been intimidating before, sure, and I'd been a little worried in an abstract way that perhaps he would kill me, but I'd never seen him look as deranged as he did right then. His dark grey eyes were wild and his huge chest rose and fell like he'd just done a marathon.

His eyes slid across me, making me flinch back like the gaze had been claws, and settled on Lew.

The voice that rolled out was more growl than words and it sent a shiver of fear through my body. "What happened?"

Lew stood and held out his hands, just like mine, as though he were trying to sooth an animal.

"Nothing happened, Dane. Nothing happened, everything's fine."

His voice was calming and carefully neutral. I held my breath, not wanting to disturb the delicate balance being maintained between them. Dane looked... I wasn't even sure what he looked like. I could only see the anger in his clenched jaw and his balled fists. As I watched, I could have sworn the skin along his forearms became darker and then patches of dark grey burst out and receded like flowers blooming and withering in the space of a minute. He was starting to shift.

"Dane." Lew's voice held a warning note. "I said everything is fine. I said nothing happened. Don't you trust me?"

Dane breathed deeply and the scales stopped rippling across his skin.

Shit.

If he was this angry to find me in their room, I really, really didn't want to know what he would do if he ever found out how close I'd come to kissing his boyfriend. And if ever there was a time to be grateful that dragons could conceal their scent, it was that moment, since the room would have been thick with arousal if I hadn't muted my scent.

"Sorry, Lew, of course I trust you."

"Good." Lew moved slowly closer to Dane and put his hands on the larger man's arms, and began to slowly run them up and down, soothing, calming. "There's nothing wrong. Everyone's fine. Morgan?"

I barely managed to take my eyes off Dane long enough to look at Lew.

"I think it's time you left."

And just like that, I was dismissed.

Dane turned his face to me and I felt the vicious slash of his gaze again. He bared his teeth when he spoke and they were longer and sharper than they should be in his human form. "No, he stays. I want to talk to him."

"No, Dane," said Lew, "I want him gone. I want it to be just us. We don't need Morgan here to talk."

"But he's the one—"

"Let him go, Dane. Come and sit down and talk to me."

He began to tug Dane towards the bed and I felt the simultaneous bubble of relief that the giant was no longer standing between me and the door, and the stab of bitter mortification that Lew was touching Dane exactly like he's touched me not ten minutes before, that he was sitting beside him on the bed and had his hand resting comfortingly on Dane's shoulder, exactly the way he'd sat with me.

"Morgan?"

I could take a hint. I fled before my composure cracked and walked stiffly to the door, not looking at either one of them as I left and closed the door gently behind me.

CHAPTER 17: LEW

Morgan ignored me as he glided out of the room, hardly seeming to move at all. He was as stiff as a statue, face blank, like the stone dragons on the ramparts whose faces had been made indistinct by the wash of rain and time. Dane had scared him, I knew that. And it looked like it might just have been enough to scare him right back into his protective shell and never come out again. If that was the case, I thought I just might kill Dane. As much as I loved him, if he'd closed Morgan off to me forever, I wouldn't be able to find it in my heart to forgive him.

I felt his shoulder shift under me and I clamped my hand down harder. I was digging my fingers into the thick muscle to try and keep him still, instinctively trying to pin him down. It was a battle, nothing like the soft touches I'd shared with Morgan just a few moments ago.

"Dane? You need to tell me what you heard so I can talk to you about it."

I saw his jaw work, and the flush of scales that spread across his skin like a blush. His dragon was near the surface and he was barely keeping it inside. That was why I'd sent Morgan out. He needed to get as far away from Dane as possible. More than anything, I needed Morgan to be safe and I knew, unfortunately, that Dane was a danger to him. He was too big, too strong, too angry, and I knew why, but I had to hear Dane say it.

At last he managed to get his jaw working, becoming human enough to speak.

"The Somerville castle was attacked."

"Nobody was hurt."

I thought I'd start with that fact. It was the only thing keeping Dane together. No way was I going to start answering 'yes' to questions like that without prefacing it with that statement and repeating it. "Nobody was hurt, Dane."

"But they were attacked?"

"No, they know there was an intruder, that's not the same thing. Nobody was attacked, and nobody was hurt."

"We both know what happens after that. Only a *ridire* could get past the layers of protection around that place. If they've broken in, they're looking for weaknesses, they're searching for something to use. And when they find it, that's when they attack."

"We don't know it's a *ridire*."

"No, it could be a whole bloody cult of them."

"Nobody's heard of a *ridire* in more than fifty years."

Dane's eyes were unfocused when he looked at me. He wasn't seeing me at all and I could only imagine what images were layered behind those grey irises: *ridire* in their black armour, crippling spells, poisoned arrows, blood, the slaughter of a whole clan of dragons in the night... We all knew what the dragon-hunters were capable of.

"Tell me who else could break into a dragon's territory and leave again undetected."

I answered without thinking, automatically trying to help, but when I opened my mouth and the words came out, I realised I hadn't helped at all. In fact, I had been incredibly, spectacularly unhelpful.

I blurted, "I don't know, another dragon could, if they were skilled enough."

I felt the scales form beneath my fingers, hard as armour and rough. I clamped my hand down harder as though I could force the dragon back inside Dane's skin like that, but of course I couldn't.

"Dane, everyone is fine, nobody was hurt. They're all fine, he's fine, Dane. Dane! Seren is fine!"

I might as well have saved my breath. Dane's skin shifted to dragon hide and he began to grow and fill my room. Considering he was so huge that he already seemed to take up more than his fair share of space, suddenly taking up more was an impressive feat.

"Dane!"

I don't know why I bothered. Even I knew that, at that point, Dane was well beyond hearing me. He had lost control.

A tight worry pinched my chest. I'd known for four years exactly why Dane was so fucking grumpy all the time, why he was so angry, and I'd thought I'd understood. But as time went on and he showed no signs of moving on, I had to wonder what was going on.

Dane was a warrior, yes, but he was a really, really good warrior, which meant he was skilled and controlled and patient, he took orders well, he showed initiative, he planned, he prepared, he was logical. And yet in four years he hadn't demonstrated much of any of those skills. He'd been more wild animal than anything else. He moved around, sat, ate, and talked if he had to, but there was always something in his eyes, a spark of fire that made me uneasy. It showed his dragon was near the surface. As I watched him start to shift in my room then, it occurred to me that his dragon was in control nearly all the time and his human side was a thin façade stretched over it to please the rest of us.

Shit, why had I not realised that before?

"Dane, you have to stay inside. Nana wants you to stay."

He was still growing, rearing up high and scraping the ceiling with his head, which became bigger and his mouth lengthened into a snout.

"Dane, that's an order! Shift back now."

That had been a risk, I grant. I actually had zero authority over Dane and was in no position to give him orders but he was a good soldier – he *had* been a good soldier, anyway – and I took a chance.

It didn't work.

He didn't even hear me.

"Dane, Seren is alive and well, I promise."

His head whipped around to look at me and I stared into the snarling jaws. Perhaps saying Seren's name again hadn't been my best idea, either. I couldn't get anything right.

"Wait," I said, but he was gone.

He flowed towards the window, still shifting and growing, and pushed through it with his head, sliding his shoulders through by tilting to the side. If he'd shifted any more, he'd be too big to get through. In fact, as he gave a push with his legs and forced his belly through the window, I heard the crack of glass and Dane gave a last leap, his wings burst from his back and he was off. He flew so fast, I wasn't even at the window to my room before he was out of sight, and it wasn't like my room was massive.

"Shit!" I swore to myself for a while, venting. I was angry and, at the root of that anger, was fear. My heart beat rapidly at the thoughts that tumbled through my heard. If Morgan hadn't left when he did, Dane might have attacked him; I knew where Dane was going and I really didn't think it was healthy for him; Nana was going to be pissed off when she heard about it and, since it was my window that was broken, there wasn't any way I could see out of telling her myself. "Shit! Shit!"

I walked towards Nana's rooms. I wanted to drag my feet but there was no point. I'd get there soon enough anyway. It felt like I'd spent the past three days constantly in and out of those rooms.

"Nana?"

The door snapped open and Nana asked, "What happened?" in just the way I hated. She already knew, she just didn't want to believe it.

"Yeah, Dane heard about the break-in at Somerville's castle."

"And?"

"And he left."

This time, she didn't ask me why I hadn't managed to stop him. It didn't stop me from trying to explain, though. "He wouldn't listen to me. I tried to tell him Seren was fine, but—"

"It's not your fault, Lew." I frowned. That sounded incredibly understanding.

"So...?"

I couldn't help my suspicious mind, I just expected there to be a follow-on from that, and I expected not to like it.

Nana sighed. "So nothing, Lew. I should have told Dane myself, but I was hoping he wouldn't find out."

"Why?"

"Because I knew if he found out, he'd go and do exactly what he is doing."

"And that is...?"

I'd feel safe betting my very life on the fact that Dane had flown straight to the Somerville castle to see Seren. The question wasn't where he was going but what he'd do when he got there.

"Probably nothing. He probably just wants to see him."

I asked the question that had been bothering me, nagging away at the back of my mind. "Why is he so obsessed with Seren? I mean, the *uasal* dumped him, I get it, he's sad, but... that was over four years ago. Why is he still angry about it? And why is it that the second he finds out the Somervilles were attacked, he flies over there to make sure the man is unharmed? Either he hates him or he doesn't."

That was the real bafflement for me. Dane hated *uasal*, hated the Somervilles and especially hated Seren. So why the fuck did his dragon practically burst out of his skin and streak off to check on the man at the first hint of danger?

Nana cocked her head at me. "You really don't know?"

"Know what?"

"Huh," she said, and I had to grind my teeth together. Snapping at Nana to spit it out wasn't going to do me any favours.

Instead, I asked very politely, "Nana, can you please tell me what you mean by that?"

"Isn't it obvious?"

"No."

"Hating being dumped is not the same thing as hating the person who dumped you. Dane has very deep feelings for Seren, and he can't just let them go because he wants to, trust me."

"If you say so, Nana. Are you sure he won't do anything stupid while he's there? Do I need to go after him and stop him?" I cringed a little. "And, uh, if so, can I have a couple of others to take with me?"

"Dane won't harm any of them. He's not stupid."

"You didn't see the way he looked before he left."

Fire glittered in Nana's eyes then, and she held my gaze. "Trust me, Lew."

There was nothing else I could do. I trusted Nana more than almost anybody else, especially where her family were concerned. To say she was protective was an understatement.

"I trust you, Nana."

"Good boy, Lew. Now, go and do some training. I want you young ones kept busy." I nodded and turned to go, and she added, "And strong."

It didn't reassure me.

CHAPTER 18: LEW

I don't know what he expected me to do, but Morgan looked surprised to see me when I hunted him down less than an hour after he'd left my room. It was like he didn't realise that I'd been practically plastered to his side for the past two weeks.

He was sitting with Brendan in the corner of one of the first-floor sitting rooms, their heads bent close together while they watched something on a phone. Their heads were almost touching and their shoulders just brushed together and they must have been breathing in each other's breath as they watched. I didn't even realise I was growling until Morgan looked up, alarm in his wide eyes.

"Are you alright?"

"Yes."

There was a pause which went on just long enough to be uncomfortable but I couldn't think of a damned thing to say. Morgan's face had settled into his placid mask again and I searched it for the slightest crack that would give me just a peek of the emotion underneath but I found none. I was no longer one of the people he let in, and that fucking hurt. Not just feeling upset, but an actual shooting pain in my chest that worried me. Dragons didn't tend to get sick and I hadn't heard of one having a heart attack but in that moment I wasn't sure whether that was what I was feeling or not.

Morgan broke the silence and I didn't keel over, so I ruled out heart attack.

"Is Dane well?"

"Uh... yes."

That was a lie. I felt bad for telling it but I didn't think Dane would appreciate me blabbing his business all over the castle.

"I'm very glad."

Shit, he'd slipped back into formality. How the fuck had I lost so much ground with him in such a short space of time?

I floundered for something to say. And, because I was the idiot Nadia accused me of being, I just said the first thing that came into my mind and what was uppermost in my mind at that particular point was my absolute raging jealousy that Morgan had been sitting so close and cosy with Brendan, leaning their heads together and sharing something.

"What are you doing?"

Also, I hadn't schooled my tone of voice, so it came out abrupt and basically screamed *possessive jealous bastard* but there was nothing I could do about it then.

"I'm conversing with Brendan."

Brendan butted in. "Watching cat videos, Lew. Did you know Morgan likes cats?"

"No." No, I hadn't known that and it pissed me off that Brendan knew something about him that I didn't. What was worse was, if he'd wanted a cat, he could have had one. I'd have taken him to the shelter to choose one and, when he left, he could take it with him or leave it here with me if he wasn't allowed to take it home.

"Yeah, he does."

I seriously had a problem. I'd never been jealous before. I'd never minded other people getting promotions over me, I'd never minded that there were smarter, better-looking people around me, I'd never even batted an eyelid when my boyfriends talked to other men, or flirted harmlessly with them, and if they wanted the other man more than me, well they were welcome to it because I wanted them to be happy. That's why it made no sense for me to have such an abrupt personality change where Morgan was concerned. I was so jealous that I was struggling to control my dragon, who wanted to rush out of me and between Morgan and Brendan. It wanted to encircle Morgan until he was safe and snug and *ours*.

It scared me.

As the realisation came to me, I did what I always did. I fell back on my training and followed orders.

"Nana wants everyone training. You have ten minutes to get ready and then meet me outside."

Brendan looked up, his mouth open in outrage. "What? Not me, right? I don't have to go."

I eyed him closely. He looked good, with his broad shoulders and stocky build, and I knew he could probably out-fight Morgan even with all the training Morgan had done, just by overpowering him with bulk, but I also knew that he should be fitter than he was. He did just enough to keep Nana from getting on his back and not a thing else. I also realised, as I thought it then, that I was going to have to focus on Morgan's defensive training a lot more than I had. If I was contemplating how easy it would be for a *curaidh*, who was heavier and larger, to overpower him, I hadn't been doing my job properly. Of course, it wasn't like he hadn't come a long way, he had. But he had a way to go yet and not long to get there, so this training session was probably for the best.

"Yes, you too. You've got nine and a half minutes now. Don't be late."

"What got you all bossy all of a sudden?"

"I'm always fucking bossy. And you don't have time to sit around giggling together like schoolgirls."

Morgan stood and blinked slowly at me, and my dragon prickled inside me at the utter calm he radiated. Without hurrying, he turned to Brendan. "Thank you for sharing those with me, Brendan. I enjoyed your company." Then he strolled past me like he didn't have nine minutes to get outside or be doing a hundred pull-ups, which he hated.

I couldn't even help the growl. It was quiet and low, barely a rumble, but I had to let it out or my dragon would have felt too enclosed and then it might have tried to burst out of me like Dane's had. I growled as Morgan walked out of the room and Brendan gave me a strange look as he caught the sound of it. I kept growling, even when he noticed. I didn't need to hide my feelings from Brendan and I wanted to commiserate with my dragon on how badly things were going.

To my surprise, Brendan studied me, tipping his head to the side.

"This isn't like you," he said.

"I know. Sorry."

"If I didn't know any better, I'd say you

were jealous."

It was a bit of a blow, being called on it so bluntly, but, since it was also true, it wasn't like I could deny it.

"I am."

"Huh. I never expected you to admit that."

I focused on his eyes properly, since I'd been staring in his general direction but hadn't actually seen him. He had a small smile on his lips and he looked up at me from under his dark lashes. I wasn't in the mood to deal with any more drama than I already had, and admitting my feelings for Morgan had been about my limit for the day on heart-to-hearts, so I said, "Eight minutes now," and left.

To be fair to them both, they were outside in eight minutes. As were six others that I'd rounded up on my way through the castle. Three of them were young – in fact, two of those were the ones who'd cornered Morgan down on the beach – and one of them was older than me despite the fact he looked to be in his early thirties – he was some sort of academic and spent most of his time in the library, which I hadn't been inside in years except when I was playing hide-and-seek with the children – and two of them were fully-grown adults who I trained once a week anyway.

They gathered round as I hauled out mats and shouted, "Pair up!"

As soon as I said it, I realised that Morgan

and Brendan were likely to pair up together and, since I'd just been thinking how easily Brendan could crush Morgan with his bulk, I amended that statement swiftly. It had absolutely nothing to do with the fact that my dragon would probably go nuts if I saw Brendan's hands on Morgan right then.

"Brendan, I want you to work with Laura, she's been training for months so you'll make quick progress."

He shot me a weird smile and batted his eyelids. "If you say so, Lew."

Well, yeah, I did.

"Morgan, you can team up with Dimpy. Dimpy, Morgan – Morgan, Dimpy," I said by way of an introduction.

Dimpy was the academic and I didn't think there was much risk of him squashing Morgan. If I expected a smile from him, I was disappointed. Ok, I *was* disappointed, but at least Morgan was cooly polite to Dimpy, and I was glad – the man was a bit shy and coming out to train with me was unusual for him. I didn't want to scare him off.

In order to try and stop myself from sounding like a total drill-sergeant-dick, I modified my tone a little and tried to smile at him.

"I'm glad you decided to come – it's good to see you."

He gave me a shy smile, beaming and then

looking instantly down at his plimsoles. The first thing I noticed was the totally adorable dimples in his cheeks and the second thing was those plimsoles. Who the fuck had plimsoles any more? I didn't want to even guess how old they were.

Brendan moved close beside me and said, "Dimpy hates running circuits more than I do," and I saw the dimples flicker and fade.

Dimpy said, "I heard you were doing some training. I've been thinking I should get out a bit more and do some exercise, you know, toughen up, lose a bit of weight, all that jazz. So here I am."

I glanced down at his stocky form. He was... plump. It wasn't unpleasant, it's just he also wasn't exactly a killing machine. Which is why, I suppose, it was a good idea for him to get some training in before whoever-it-was that broke into the Somerville castle decided to give ours a try as well.

"Good thinking," I said. "More the merrier."

I don't know who the fuck I thought was merry – it certainly wasn't me. I was still smarting from Morgan's cool dismissal and unsettled from Dane's behaviour and basically not feeling at my sociable best.

Luckily, I wasn't there to chat, I was there to train, and *that* I could do in my sleep.

"Alright, we'll start with some warm-ups."

CHAPTER 19: LEW

I began to lead them in some easy warm-ups and then started with some self-defence moves. I really wanted Morgan to learn them and, if I could get the others to learn as well, I'd feel even better.

They were doing pretty well and my dragon was surprisingly calm inside me considering another man had his hands on Morgan, but Dimpy was so gentle that I didn't worry in the slightest that he would hurt him, even though he was taller and heavier.

I kept them in my peripheral vision at all times, but never looked directly at them. I knew from experience *not* to look at Morgan in his skin-tight training clothes unless I wanted to spend the next hour with my back to him, trying to conceal my erection. I'd finally learned to wear compression shorts under my joggers but still, there was only so much they could do for me.

"You're doing good," I said to Brendan and Laura. "Brendan, use your weight against her, she'll struggle to compensate. Laura, you're smaller but you're faster, so try and use your speed to disable him before he moves."

Brendan shot me a strange look then. I wasn't quite sure what to make of it. On anyone else, I would say it was sultry but, since it was Brendan, it couldn't be that. Maybe Laura had hit him too hard in the balls earlier and he was still suffering.

"Why don't you show me?" he said.

"Alright." That was fair, since it was my job and all. I went over and, since he didn't move out of the way, I walked around him and drew Laura a few feet away. "Use your weight advantage. Go for height and bring it down on her, that way she's fighting you and gravity, and you don't waste energy."

I gave a nod to Laura and she flew at me, but I grabbed her arm, spun her round and brought her steadily down to the ground, nice and controlled.

I looked back over my shoulder at Brendan and said, "You get that?"

He gave a one-shoulder shrug and said, "I meant demonstrate on me."

"Oh. But that will help Laura, not you."

He rolled his eyes and I blinked in confusion until Laura's muffled voice came from where her face was pressed into the mat beneath me. "Are you done demonstrating yet? Are you giving a speech?"

"Sorry."

I climbed off her where I'd been straddling her hips, using my weight to hold her down and keeping her arms and legs pressed into her side. She gave me the finger but, since she smiled when she did it, I assumed we were still ok. To be fair, she was used to me doing that kind of shit in training anyway.

Brendan was at my side again, crowding me and he reached up to brush something off my chest – what, I didn't see – and then rested his hand there on my pec. It was like he hadn't noticed he was basically fondling me right there in the open.

"Ah, right, well, get on with it then, I'll go and watch the others."

Brendan slid his hand down and I cringed backwards. He kept his eyes on mine when he said, "You can watch me, I don't mind."

That made no sense. Of course I could watch him. How else was I going to instruct?

I gave a confused nod and went to look at some of the other pairs, dishing out some general advice but not feeling at all on top form. It was too much to hope that we'd get through the training without anything else being weird, and I was right. I froze when I heard the voice and barely restrained a groan. I recognised that voice, and it was nearer than I'd like.

"We heard you were doing some training."

It was Dee, which meant it wouldn't be long until—

"We thought we'd come and support you."

Yep, there it was, the second voice. I never heard one without the other.

"Dee," I said, turning. "Dum."

I gave them both a nod. And, yes, they were called Dee and Dum. In fact, they *weren't* called that but they were always together and somewhere along the way, they'd been nicknamed Tweedledee and Tweedledum, and then it had been shortened to Dee and Dum and now nobody could remember their real names. If they were to be believed, not even *they* could remember their real names. Of course, they weren't to be believed. Believing either of them was a very bad idea.

"That's... kind," I said, thinking even as I said it that it definitely wasn't kind. In fact, I really wished they hadn't bothered. It sounded ungrateful but then I'd had to clear up a lot of the messes they left lying around and it wasn't pretty.

Dee and Dum had an alarming penchant

for 'retrieving information'. I had long ago decided that I didn't want to know what Nana meant when she said that. All I knew was that they would not make my training session any easier.

Sure enough, they walked right into the middle of the mats we were using and stood to either side of me. It meant I couldn't keep my eye on both of them at the same time and it was a deliberate tactic they used to unsettle their victims. I took a step back so I could just about see them both, and said, "Stay where I can see you."

"Aw," moaned Dum.

"You're not fun," said Dee.

"We're not here for fun, we're here to train." I felt pretty confident saying that. Of course, when they both gave wolfish grins, showing far too many teeth, I wanted to take it back.

"That's why we're here," said Dee.

"To train," said Dum.

They were dressed exactly the way they always were. Both wore thick black lycra that was somewhere between sports wear and biker gear. I suppose that was deliberate. At least they'd taken their jackets off, since they had an array of 'trophies' that made my stomach turn to see, sewn into the black leather.

Their physical similarities were distinctly noticeable: both were lean for *curaidh*, even verging on slim, and Dee was tallish for a woman while Dum was average for a man, bringing them both in at 5'10" and they both had short-cropped black hair and the same merciless stare of a shark.

They brought my skin out in goose-bumps.

"Alright, well," I said, only just keeping it together. They had that effect on me. Even though they were standing there being perfectly nice, they made me feel like my throat was too exposed. I was beyond grateful that they were Hoskinses and therefore on our side. "Let's get to it, then, rather than waste time. You two aren't working together. Split up."

Dee gave me a look a venomous snake would be proud of and hissed, "If you say so, Lew."

When she turned her sights on Dimpy, I felt kind of bad about it. Poor Dimpy stammered, "Oh, yes, I see, well, I'm sure I'm more than happy to, er, oblige?" He definitely went up at the end of that sentence, as though questioning his own sanity in offering to do anything with Dee.

I let a little dragon slip into my voice when I growled, "Dee?" I waited until she looked around at me before carrying on. She had 'not heard' my instructions before and nearly crippled her training partner. What? She was just really good at hitting where it did most damage. It was actually kind of creepy that she could hone in on the most vulnerable spots with so much accuracy. "No permanent damage, no blood, no broken bones. Play nice."

She pouted and repeated, "You're no fun."

"I'll live with that."

She turned back to Dimpy and I just heard her mutter, "Spoilsport," while Dimpy shot me a grateful look.

Then Dum turned his snake-eyes on Morgan and said, "I guess that leaves me to work with you."

My blood froze. My whole body froze. He said that with *way* too much glee.

"No!"

Everyone stopped and every head slow-panned towards me. I scrambled for something to say.

"No, you can't, Morgan's not good enough."

I knew that was a mistake even as the words left my mouth. Morgan's face was already cold and fixed in place, a perfect mask, and it bugged the hell out of me that I couldn't tell any more whether he was afraid or just not bothered. He'd blocked me and I could no longer read his eyes. At my words, though, his eyebrows rose gracefully up his forehead.

"Don't worry about me, Lew. I can handle myself."

"That's not what I meant."

Why did I get the feeling that everything I said would make the situation worse? Probably because it would. Admittedly, Dum didn't help –

and I was pretty sure it was deliberate not-help-ing, as well – when he said, "I'll take it easy on him, Lew, you don't need to worry that he's no good."

I ground my teeth. "I didn't say he was no good."

"But not good enough?"

Seriously, could he say anything else to make me look like a complete dick-head? Or had I done that myself?

"Just get on with it, Dum."

It seemed I couldn't stop myself from say-ing stupid things.

"Pleasure," he said, and began to circle Morgan.

"Dum, you can pair with me."

Morgan was the one to stop me. "It's ok," he said, utterly calm, like he didn't have a nat-ural predator circling him and sniffing for weak-nesses. "I'll partner him."

Dum's lips slid over his teeth in a feral grin. "Don't worry, I'll go easy on you."

The haughty glare Morgan sent him would have frozen the blood of anyone else. I was proud of him for managing it in the face of Dum's chilling presence – the man had an energy that radiated cold-blooded killer and I'd seen actual soldiers stare into his eyes for ten seconds before bursting into tears. Morgan, though, held himself with dignity and sounded nothing short of fucking regal as he said, "I don't think that will be necessary."

"Excellent," hissed Dum. He shot forward, struck quickly and retreated. Morgan raised his hand to his face and slowly wiped the blood that was running from his nose. My dragon roared in my head and began to fill my body, pushing against my skin. It wanted out. It wanted to protect Morgan, since I was doing such a shit job of that myself.

"I see we're not simply practicing the routine Lew set us, then."

I was about to push in to strangle the bloody life from Dum when a snake-like arm slid around my neck and Dee's voice hissed in my ear, "Stay still, Lew."

I felt the press of the dagger against my abdomen and the sharp graze of her teeth against my ear, right above my very vulnerable throat.

I groaned. Dee hissed with laughter. "Just let us work, baby brother. We'll do no lasting harm. Unless you struggle."

I knew better than to test her, and the word 'brother' actually soothed me. I was actually only her half-brother and she'd already been grown-up when I was born, so it wasn't like we were that close. People tended to assume she and Dum were twins, but Dum was only our cousin. Or uncle? The point was, I tended to forget Dee and I were siblings at all on a day-to-day basis, lumping her under the same generic term 'family' that I did the rest of the castle, and her reminder was calming. She wouldn't harm me and I was 95% sure she wouldn't harm Morgan, either.

Just to make sure, I raised my hand to the knife that had pricked my skin and clenched her fingers, though I didn't try to direct the blade away just yet. "Play nice."

She pulled her arms tighter around me and I wasn't sure whether it was a threat or a hug.

Dum was still circling and Morgan moved with him, graceful and light on his feet, but hopelessly out-matched by the experienced *curaidh*.

"Tell me, how do you *uasal* defend yourselves these days, now you no longer have *curaidh* to protect you?" The mocking twist to Dum's mouth made me growl and Dee's arms tightened around my middle, squeezing like a boa constrictor.

Morgan gave Dum a look of utter disdain. "We don't resort to violence unless we have to. It's so uncouth."

To me, it looked like Dum actually lit up at the barb and he cooed, "Oooh, uncouth, am I? Would you like me to teach you some rough and tumble, *uasal*?"

Morgan's hands were in front of him, holding them palm out, uselessly trying to ward off any attack. When Dum moved, he was quick, but Morgan was quicker. Dum was almost on him, practically nose to nose, and then blue light flared between them and blinded everyone for nearly thirty seconds. I moved forward, even though I was blind, totally forgetting about the knife pressed to my ribs, and luckily Dee decided not to slice it into me. I stumbled towards the blue flash and shouted, "Morgan!"

The light faded and bright spots danced around my eyes, clouding my vision and I tried to blink them away.

Morgan stood exactly where he had been, his hands raised exactly as they had been, and his fingers glowed faintly blue with residual... magic? Dum was on the floor about five feet away, sprawled on his back and arched in pain. As my vision cleared, I stared at Morgan's hands and saw a flash of blue spark across his wrist and then another tiny bolt dance along one slim finger.

Until then, it had never occurred to me that Morgan had any kind of magic. He'd certainly never given me any reason to believe it.

"You—" I began, but couldn't think what to say. I'm proud of you? Congratulations? Holy shit? I thought them all but couldn't get the words out of my mouth.

He turned his icy blue-grey eyes on me. "I presume that will be all for today."

With that, he turned to leave, not sparing any one of us a single glance. I watched him as he walked all the way back to the castle, stiff and upright and dainty and totally confusing. It was only when he'd disappeared behind the thick stone wall that I even turned to Dum.

CHAPTER 20: LEW

"**A**re you alright?"

Dum was laying back on the grass by then, with his ankles crossed and his arms folded behind his head. I'd watched Morgan for a long time. Dum looked pretty relaxed for a man who'd just been knocked the best part of two metres backwards with a blast of magic – and I had no idea what kind of magic it really was. He opened his mouth but it was Dee who answered first.

"Yeah, he's fine."

"What the hell *was* that?"

I wasn't the only one who wanted to know, apparently. Behind me, everyone on the training mats murmured their own questions.

Dum answered. "I don't know what *he*

thought it was, but it felt like lightning punching me right in the gut."

"Are you sure you're ok?"

He shrugged. "Still talking, aren't I? No sign of permanent damage, all body parts working as they should- wait!"

He sat up and yanked his hands from under his head and pressed them down on his crotch. One hand worked under the waistband of his trousers and I saw the disturbing image of Dum's fist gripping his own junk through the flexible material. He used the other hand to pull his waistband out so he could eyeball his dick and then he sighed and flopped back down on the grass.

"Phew! Yeah, all good."

Dee moved past me and grabbed him under his armpits, hauling him up and slinging one of his arms around her shoulder so she could support him.

"Glad you established that. Now maybe we can see if you hit your head when you fell."

"Hey, my head is less important than my dick."

"You use it less than your dick," she agreed, and I gagged. I did not want to think about Dum's dick.

Dee rolled her eyes at me and said, "Thanks so much for an interesting training session, baby brother. I'll be sure to repay the favour."

I shuddered. Was that a threat?

Brendan sidled up to me and slipped his hand into the crook of my arm. He leaned against me in a way that was unfamiliar.

"I suppose we're all done, then," he said.

"There's still training to do."

"You let Morgan go. Besides, I was hoping to spend some time with you alone."

"What do you mean?"

"You know, to talk about what you said earlier."

My mind was half on what Brendan was saying and half on what Morgan had done. I didn't know what the fuck kind of magic he had, but it was a new development. I wanted to laugh hysterically that I'd spent weeks worrying how small and breakable he was when he could knock Dum – Dum! – flat on his back with one blast of magic. I also wanted to shake him until his teeth rattled for not telling me that. And I wanted to curl around him in dragon form and be assured that he was fine, that Dum hadn't hurt him and his poor delicate nose was properly healed.

Yep, when it came to Morgan, I had a lot of feelings and they all warred inside me, making me a complete and utter loon.

I looked down at Brendan, who was smirking up at me like we were sharing a secret and couldn't remember what the hell I'd said earlier.

"What did I say?"

"That you wanted me."

"What? No, I didn't."

The smile slipped from his face. "What? Of course you did. You admitted you have feelings for me."

"I- I like you, Brendan, I've always liked you. We're cousins."

"We're not cousins, Lew."

"Maybe not, but we're family."

"We're not even related."

"Whatever. Family. We're like brothers."

He pushed away from me, shoving so hard that I actually stumbled a step. I was a big guy. I didn't normally stumble.

Brendan was breathing heavily. "Are you kidding me?"

"I—"

To be honest, I was more confused than anything. Where had this come from?

"What did you mean earlier then when you said you were jealous?"

"I meant—"

I didn't really want to say what I'd meant, since we were standing in front of six other people and they were all watching us avidly like we were the latest show in their favourite drama. Besides, if I was going to tell someone how I felt about Morgan, it should probably be Morgan that I told.

Brendan's eyes narrowed. I'd never seen him look like that before. He always looked bright and happy to see me but, right then, he looked ready to kill. My dragon pushed forward instinctively, which had *never* happened when confronted by any of my family before. Seriously, I'd pissed off Nadia and Nana and got not a peep from my dragon, and Dee and Dum had circled me like sharks before and, sure, I'd got the heebie jeebies but my dragon had stayed low inside me. When Brendan looked at me like that, it skittered over my skin as though it was trying to protect us from the look.

"It's him, isn't it? *He*'s the one you want."

"Bren—"

His hand shot up to his neck and his claws burst through his skin and he shredded the t-shirt he was wearing, just in time. He shifted and his t-shirt fell away and there was a rip from his trousers and they fell away in tatters.

I was shifting before I even realised it. One moment I was watching Brendan start to shift and the next, I was leaping up after him when he bounded away and into the sky. He gained height slowly and I was right behind him. I gave a shriek – a warning – and he put on a burst of speed. He was heading towards the castle and the only thing that ran through my brain was: *what if he heads for Morgan's room?*

I pushed myself faster, caught him up,

drew level with him, and called, trying to sound less angry, but I was scared for Morgan and confused, so I'm not sure how successful I was.

Brendan spun much faster than I'd ever seen him do anything. His head whipped around and his jaws aimed right for my neck. I barely twisted out of the way in time, and it cost me some flight as I fell and had to pump my wings quickly to keep to the air. I felt a sting in my neck, though, so I knew he'd drawn blood.

After all the years we'd known each other – all our lives, in fact – and the way we'd become close after I'd retired from the Fife Army, Brendan had bitten me in anger. And he was almost at the castle.

No fucking way was I going to let him reach Morgan.

I gave a final warning and too bad if he didn't heed it. He swerved off to the side, round to where Morgan's room lay in the north, and I rose above him. That was so ingrained in me by then I couldn't tell if it was instinct or training, but he who has the height, has the advantage, and I dropped onto Brendan like a stone. He shrieked, and I pinned his wings to his side, and we fell together. Just before we hit the ground, I let go and gave a huge flap of my wings, keeping me from landing on him with my full bulk.

He hit the ground with a crack. But dragons are hardy, especially *curaidh*, and he wiggled round like a worm and faced me. Behind me, I heard two other dragons land and they fanned out so we surrounded him.

He shrieked, anger and resentment spewing out at me, and I readied myself. If I'd known at the start of the day that I'd have been prepared to rip out the throat of one of my best friends, I'd never had believed it, but I absolutely was prepared to do it. He didn't give me the chance. He ran across the grass and took to the sky, heading out across our territory towards the south.

Beside me, one of the dragons shifted back and Laura said, "Prince, go after him and see where he goes. Lew, come with—"

I wasn't going to wait around to hear what she said. I took off and flew like an arrow straight for Morgan's window. Behind me, I heard Laura sigh and say, "I'll tell Nana, then."

At least I knew Nana would protect Morgan. Not that I planned on letting him out of my sight any time soon. Any time ever.

CHAPTER 21:
MORGAN

There was a thud right outside my window and I looked up just in time to see Lew shift back into his human form from the glorious dragon that had smacked its paws down on my windowsill.

I was sitting slumped on my bed, trying to get up the energy to take a shower or something, but using magic always took a lot of energy and I'd barely made it back to my room without my legs collapsing underneath me.

Lew pushed his fingernails into the window frame, prised the window open and slipped into the room, jumping down from the windowsill and standing in front of me entirely naked. His dick was hanging right there in front of my face and I couldn't help that my eyes kind of snagged on it and couldn't move on. It was flaccid but, even then, impressive. And, as I stared at it, it began to fill with blood and grow before my eyes.

Lew cleared his throat and I jumped, darting my gaze up to his face and blushing at my own stupidity. When I finally got my eyes north of his nipples – there was no need to dwell on my little problem with them, either – I saw that his whole neck and shoulder were covered in blood.

"What happened?" I asked, leaping up and going straight over to him, automatically reaching out to touch him and then snatching my hand back at the last moment. Lew was not mine to touch. That had become abundantly clear.

"Oh, this?" He reached his hand up to touch his neck where I could see the wound already scabbed over and healing. It was like he'd already forgotten about it.

"Yes, that," I said, still wanting to know, even if he didn't care.

"Brendan bit me."

"What?" I staggered backwards and my knees hit the edge of the bed, making me sit down with a bump. "Like a mating bite?" I don't know why, but the thought of it sent a cutting feeling right the way through my body, as though I was being hacked at from the inside by a tiny man with a sword.

"No! No, not like that. Nothing like that. I

think he was trying to kill me."

"What?" My voice had gone up to a pitch I never knew I could achieve, but that was not exactly comforting, either.

"I didn't die, though," he said, and he smiled tentatively, stepping forward and then crouching down in front of me. I was grateful, since I didn't think I had the will-power to keep my eyes off his body if he kept standing right in front of me in the nude. "Breathe nice and slowly, Morgan, that's right," he said, his voice calm and soothing, just like it always was. Lew's voice made me feel safe in a way I've never felt before, even in my own family castle. He kept talking and I did as he said and, as I did it, I realised he was telling me to breathe instead of hyperventilate. Which meant I'd been hyperventilating. Great. Why did my dignity go straight out the window where Lew was concerned?

"What happened?" I asked, mostly to get his attention on something that wasn't me, although I admit I was curious about it. You know, since he and Brendan had been good friends when I'd left them not ten minutes ago.

"Oh, it's a long story."

I sat up straighter, forcing my back to hold me up in the face of my embarrassment. "Forgive me for asking, I didn't mean to pry."

His hand on my leg sent a shock wave through me. He was warm and I felt tingles all up my thigh from where his palm rested on the thin layer of my trousers.

"No, that's not what I meant, Morgan. Shit, I'm making a mess of this, too, aren't I?"

It took me a second or so to catch up with what he was saying, since most of my brain was taken up with the feel of his palm still resting against my thigh and what little attention I could spare was desperately willing my cock not to respond to the touch. It meant I didn't answer him quickly enough.

"Morgan, please, don't shut me out. Please, talk to me."

"You're naked." It was not my most brilliant conversational repartee, but it *is* what I was thinking. My voice came out stiff and distant because, if I hadn't kept control over myself, I would have launched myself at him and tried to kiss him. And then I would be one of the worst people on the whole planet, someone who tried to kiss a man they knew was in a relationship.

The memory that Lew was with Dane cleared my head better than anything else could have, and I reared back from him, crawling backwards across the bed to press my back to the wall, and Lew hung his head for a moment, gathering himself.

"Morgan, please, talk to me. If I cover up, will you talk to me?"

"Yes."

By that point, I'd do almost anything to get him into clothes – totally the opposite of what I really wanted, which was to see him gloriously naked sprawled out on my bed – because I didn't trust my eyes and my hands not to wander if given the temptation.

He stood and I closed my eyes. I just couldn't resist one tiny peek and my eyes caught on the blood that had dried over his shoulder and dripped down his chest as he stood there.

"Is your neck healed?"

"Yes."

"Jump in the shower and wash the blood off. I want to check the wound."

Like he wasn't the best person to tell if he was healed. What was I going to do about it if it wasn't healing like it was supposed to? That tiny bastard swordsman inside my chest got a second wind and began carving into my lungs.

Lew went into the small bathroom, I heard the shower run, and then two minutes later he came out with a towel wrapped around his waist. The smug show-off had let it sit low on his hips, though, showing off how trim they were and letting me get a good eyeful of his amazingly hard abs and the dark happy-trail that cut from his belly-button down his abdomen and disappeared below the towel. No way was I going to be able to concentrate if he was wearing that. Couldn't he have put my dressing-gown on or something? Admittedly, I wasn't sure it would fit him. None of my clothes would stretch round his broad shoulders and firmly-muscled thighs – not that I'd noticed them, but they were thick and shapely and were speckled with dark hair. Then I had a brainwave.

"Here, put these on." I scrambled over to my dresser and grabbed the jogging-bottoms and jumper Lew had given me weeks ago, after the beach incident. They were rumpled and, as I handed them over, I realised it would be totally obvious that I'd been wearing them.

Thankfully, Lew was gentleman enough not to question me about them. I turned around so I had my back to him while he changed. I really didn't need to do anything else stupid that day; I'd basically had my fill of humiliation for the time being.

"Ok, I'm dressed."

I turned and looked at him, standing in my room, and couldn't help that my dick twitched at the sight of him. It had been at half-mast since he'd arrive, and I hadn't managed to will it down completely but I'd tried.

With my best impression of someone brisk and efficient, I checked Lew's wound. It was almost completely healed, just a light-pink scar that would fade well within the hour.

"Why did Brendan bite you?"

"Oh, he was upset." Lew began to fidget,

shifting from foot to foot. "Apparently he might have been hoping that he and I could... I don't know, get together, maybe?"

I didn't know what to say to that. If the man didn't know that Brendan had the hots for him, there was hope for me yet. Maybe Lew was one of those people who didn't notice people drooling over him, in which case there was a very, very small chance that he hadn't noticed *me* drooling over him.

He raised his eyebrows when I didn't say anything. "Aren't you surprised?"

"No."

"Do you think he *did* fancy me?"

"Seriously?"

"Oh," was all he said to that. It looked like it was a genuine shock to the man.

I was curious. "So all those times you kept calling him your cousin and he kept correcting you, that wasn't you trying to turn him down politely?"

He looked devastated. "No. I didn't- I mean, we're cousins. Who thinks that way about family?"

I very carefully did not mention that Dane was his family, too. I didn't know exactly how they were both part of the Hoskins' family, and if they were anything like my family, there was a strong chance that fewer than a third of the people in the castle were actually related to anyone by blood, but still.

"Anyway," he said, gathering himself. "He got a bit upset and we had a row. I told him I liked- someone else."

"And he tried to kill you for it?"

"Well... yes, but he was just upset. He'll probably feel terrible when he calms down. I know I would."

Yes, I knew *he* would, but I wasn't sure about anyone else. Other people didn't have Lew's capacity to be kind and forgiving. Under the circumstances, I didn't feel I should say that, though. Instead, I dived straight in, ripped the plaster off, and asked, "What will you tell Dane?"

"About what?"

"About Brendan?"

He was watching me like I was talking another language and, in the end, he said, slowly, "I guess I'll tell him the truth."

It was probably best. I'd heard that honesty in relationships was important. It was just that the dickhead little knight with his sword who had taken up residence in my chest was back in action and I was kind of angry that someone had dared to harm Lew, had tried to kill him, even. If I felt like that, I could only imagine how Dane would feel. He didn't seem the sort to hold back on his homicidal urges.

"Are you sure that's wise?"

Lew sighed. "I'll wait until he's calm. He

might not care."

I spluttered, "Not care? He'll tear the castle apart looking for Brendan."

It might have been my imagination but Lew seemed closer, then. We were still a good few feet apart, but he wasn't pressed back against the wall by the bathroom the way he had been a minute before.

"Brendan's not here."

"He'll still be angry, though."

"Maybe. But Dane's angry about everything these days, I doubt he'll do anything."

Frowning, I couldn't help but give a tart little response to that, which meant I was basically turning into my mother. "I would think learning that another dragon tried to tear your boyfriend's throat out would be cause for concern."

Lew blinked at me. It was not my imagination, he was standing nearer, just three feet away.

"I don't have a boyfriend."

"What?"

Hope surged forward in my chest, knocking that little tiny knight over. Lew was single? That meant I had a chance – even just a really, really slim chance – that he and I could—

I stalled that thought. He and I could what? It wasn't like he'd want me and, even if he did, we couldn't be together. A *uasal* and a *curaidh*? Lord Somerville would never allow it. That tiny knight was scrambling back up and digging his sword into my heart as leverage.

"What made you think I did?"

The stabbing in my chest was distracting me, and I didn't think before I answered. If I had thought about it, I would probably have lied and I'd have been really good at it, too. I could tell myself that.

"You and Dane—"

Lew gave a bark of surprised laughter. "Me and Dane? Shit, Morgan, Dane's my cousin."

I frowned. "You realise you say that about everyone and some of them *aren't* your cousins." Picking a totally random example: Brendan, who was not Lew's cousin and very much wanted to be his boyfriend.

"Yeah, but Dane really *is* my cousin. Like my actual aunt birthed him. As in, we share blood."

"Oh."

"What made you think Dane was my boyfriend?"

He was much closer, and this time there was no mistaking it. He was barely a foot away and I was breathing in the sweet puffs of air he exhaled and wanting to press my whole body against him and beg him to hold me. I resisted that urge, though. Just.

"He was really angry to find me in your

bedroom," I began.

"He was angry and you happened to be in my bedroom. The two were unconnected."

"You, um" I swallowed, trying to swallow down the urge to cry. "You threw me out when he arrived."

The feel of his hand on my arm was like a brand, and I looked down at where he was touching me as though I needed visual proof that I wasn't just dreaming the touch.

"Morgan, I wanted you out of the room because Dane was angry. He- he wasn't in his right mind and I didn't want you getting hurt."

"Oh." I was so articulate. "Well, you were very touchy-touchy," I added, struggling to think of things now that Lew's fingers were burning through my sleeve and warming my whole arm.

He chuckled. "You've been hanging out with Nadia too much."

He wasn't wrong. I had never said anything like that before I met her. Nobody did. When I spoke again, my voice was a whisper. "So you aren't going out with anyone?" Was I a bad person for being pleased about that?

"I'm not going out with anyone," he confirmed. "I'm definitely not going out with Dane, my cousin, who is related to me."

I got the feeling he was kind of mocking me with that.

"So when you touched him…?"

Little frown-lines appeared on Lew's forehead. "Have I touched Dane? We were fighting the other day, but I don't see how that could be misinterpreted. He hit me pretty hard." I flinched at the thought and he reached up his free hand to press his palm against my cheek. It felt wonderful. "And when he came barging into my room, I had to practically dig my claws into his shoulder to stop him shifting."

"Oh."

The frown was replaced by a tentative little smile. "Are you glad I don't have a boyfriend, Morgan?"

That sounded like a trick question and I absolutely wasn't going to answer. "Yes." Ok, my mouth answered for me while my brain was still trying to take control of my body.

"Do *you* want to be my boyfriend?"

"God yes." Wow, I sounded desperate. Why he would ever agree to it now, I had no idea.

"Good."

My mind blanked out in shock and it meant I didn't say anything, which was probably a good thing considering Lew slowly moved closer to me, lowering his perfect lips down to mine.

I felt the first brush of them against me and something in my chest eased. The sweet sensations of his lips gently brushing mine were agonisingly beautiful and I felt too full of emotion. To my utter mortification, a tear leaked out of my closed eyes and then another, and another, and Lew kept pressing his lips gently against mine like he would never stop.

He must have felt my tears on the hand that was still pressed against my cheek and tasted them on his lips because he pulled back. I wanted to kick myself for doing something so ridiculous, something that made him stop kissing me, but he just brushed his fingers over the tracks of the tears and whispered, "Do you want me to stop?"

I couldn't force any words out of my throat, so I shook my head.

"Good," he said again, and kissed my cheeks, my eyelids, my temples, my nose and finally my mouth again. When his lips landed on mine, I pushed into him, wanting to be closer, to feel more. The hand still resting on my arm slid around my waist and pulled me to his body. I felt the hardness of his chest pressed against me, his solid warmth, and his prominent erection digging into my belly.

As though feeling his arousal suddenly made me aware of my own, I pressed my hips harder against his leg, pushing my hard dick into his thigh. He groaned and I felt the vibrations. I wanted more.

Parting my lips, I wasn't sure what to do. Did I just stick my tongue into his mouth? How was that supposed to feel good? I needn't have worried. Lew's tongue slid out of his mouth and brushed over my sensitive lips, and then dipped inside my mouth to slide against my tongue. The feeling of it was incredible and it took me a split second to realise that Lew had frozen. Just as I realised it, he moved again, pushing into my mouth harder and dragging his tongue against mine exquisitely. His taste was amazing and my whole body sparked with energy, practically humming with the glory of it.

He pulled back abruptly and my mouth tried to follow him, but he was too tall for me to capture his mouth unless he bent his head to let me. At least he kept me pressed against his body. At that point, if he didn't, I'd probably have just collapsed in a puddle.

"Mate," he growled.

"What?"

He didn't answer, just ducked his head down and claimed my mouth again. I stopped thinking about anything, then, and just felt the way he worked his hands over my skin, the way his lips felt pressed to mine, the way his tongue massaged mine and drew me out, into his own mouth. His flavour was stronger there and I pushed in, desperate for more, desperate to taste and taste and taste. And that's when that one little word clicked with me. Mate.

CHAPTER 22:
MORGAN

Yanking my mouth back, I panted, "You're my mate?"

I almost wanted to giggle at how dazed he looked right then. His pupils were blown wide and he had the air of a man who'd been totally stunned. Then a slow smile spread across his lips, drawing his mouth up and making my heart beat hard.

"Yes."

I couldn't believe it. "How can that be?"

He ran his fingers over my cheek and down to my jaw. "You don't think a *uasal* and a *curaidh* can be mates?"

"I don't understand how you can be my mate. You're..." I trailed off, flapping my hand feebly, trying to encompass all of him. I couldn't describe him. How could anyone describe the sheer physical perfection, the kindness, the protectiveness? And did I mention his arse? I still wanted to bite it.

He had a teasing tilt to his mouth when he smiled. My heart beat its extra little beat just for him.

"Is that '*you're*'" and then he flapped his hand in imitation of me, and I have to say it wasn't flattering, "a good thing?"

I hit my hand against his chest. "Don't tease me. And, yes, it is good. I can't believe I'm your mate."

"I can believe it." He sounded so certain and I looked up at him, pressed tightly against him so that there was no space at all between us, and it still wasn't close enough.

"You can?"

"Yes." He ducked his head to kiss me again, but it was too brief, and he pulled back after just a few seconds. "It feels right. To belong to you."

"You belong to me?" That also sounded like a trick.

"Of course. That's what it means to be a mate. You belong to me and I belong to you. Don't you want to be mine?"

I did want to be his. I just had never thought of *him* as belonging to *me* before. The idea that I could possess him was a little too intoxicating. I hadn't even realised I'd begun to roll my hips against his thigh, grinding my erection into his firm muscles, until he pulled back a little and held me away so I couldn't reach him. I whimpered.

"Morgan? Don't you want to be my mate?"

"I want to. I want you. I can't believe you're mine."

The look of relief that washed over his face seemed strange and I almost paused to consider it, wondering what he'd been worried about, but then he pulled me against him again and I forgot all about it.

Lew slid his hands down my back to my arse and gripped it firmly with both hands, pulling me into him and pressing my dick back against his leg. His big hands worked me against him and it was almost too much.

I gasped his name, not sure what I was asking for. I just wanted more and I didn't know how to get it.

"It's alright, Morgan, I've got you. We're going to take this nice and slow."

I didn't want slow, I wanted more, more, more.

He chuckled as he pulled back and I tried to follow him, dragging myself up his body to capture his mouth again, and I felt the chuckle against my lips.

"Have you ever been with anyone before, Morgan?"

That stopped me in my tracks. Was it that obvious that I didn't know what I was doing? I felt myself freeze up and my voice was tight and hoarse when I answered. "No."

"God," said Lew, and reached one hand down to grab his dick. He gripped the base tightly and screwed his eyes closed. "Does it make me a shitty person that I'm glad about that? It does, doesn't it?"

"You're... glad?"

"That nobody else has touched you, baby? Yes, I'm glad. I can't help it; I just don't like the thought of someone else with their hands on you."

"So you don't mind, then?" I just wanted to be clear about that.

"No, of course not. Why would I mind?"

"Um, no reason."

"Have you- have you got any lube?"

My whole face flamed and Lew actually laughed. At least it broke the tension in the air and I could begin to breathe easily.

"Um, maybe," I said, totally playing it cool.

"Maybe, huh? Well what would I have to say to make that a yes?"

"Um."

"Morgan? Look at me."

God, he was beautiful. His face was strong and square, perfectly handsome, perfectly formed, perfectly perfect.

"Morgan, I'm not going to claim you right now. That's a big step and it's too important to rush, and I can't think straight at the moment. I want to get us both off. Do you have any lube?"

"Yes."

He watched me and I watched him, wondering what he was going to do. Eventually he raised his eyebrows and asked, "And where *is* your lube?"

I blushed again and walked over to the drawer where I'd hidden it. As I got it out, it suddenly seemed like a ridiculously large bottle of lube. He was going to think I was a sexual deviant or something if he thought I'd got through all that on my own. Which I had. And I'd had quite a few little sessions in the shower, too, after training, when he'd driven me to it by being so big and muscular and touching me. I definitely wouldn't tell him about those.

When I turned around, Lew had his hand out to take the bottle and I tried to keep my face neutral as I handed it over. He held it up and said, "You're nearly out."

"It wasn't full when I got here! I've been here weeks! I just have a normal, healthy sex drive."

At least I hadn't embarrassingly over-shared or anything.

Lew smirked at me and said, "Oh, baby,

you have no idea how much lube I've got through thinking about how much I wanted to touch you."

I started. "Really?"

"Yes, really. I was starting to worry I'd wear my dick out."

I nearly chuckled at that, my lips twitching into a smile and Lew's whole face lit up like the sun.

"Shit, Morgan, you're so fucking beautiful. I love it when you're happy."

If he didn't stop talking like that, I was going to start crying again. "What- what are you going to do?"

"I'm going to strip you naked and run my hands all over you."

To be honest, that sounded incredible. I nearly came in my pants just from the promise of it.

"And then I'm going to work your dick until you come all over me."

I hadn't meant to throw myself at him, but I did. He stumbled under my attack, more from surprise than because I was particularly troublesome as an attacker, and then he hooked his hands under my thighs and lifted me. I wrapped my legs around him and wound my arms around his neck.

We kissed for a long time, and the friction of his hard abdomen under my dick was almost too much. When I was panting and gasping and seconds away from spilling in my pants, Lew suddenly leaned over the bed and dropped me onto the covers. I groaned like I'd been stabbed and my hips arched up, desperately seeking relief on my dick. I didn't get any and Lew loomed over me, holding my hands at my sides when I moved to touch it.

He was panting almost as hard as I was. "Don't touch yourself."

He released me and knelt on the bed, and I got a glorious view of his chest as he stripped the jumper off and threw it aside. He had to scramble off the bed in order to shuck his trousers and then he was naked and, this time, I could look. I sat up to get a better view and my eyes were everywhere, trying to see as much of him as I could.

His hand went down to his dick again and squeezed the base. His dick was thick and standing to attention. The tip was red and it looked angrily aroused. As I watched, a bead of pre-come rose up and spilled over the head, trailing down the shaft to his fingers.

"I'm not going to last long."

I looked up into his eyes, wanting to tell him that I didn't care, I just wanted to feel him pressed against me when he went over the edge, but I couldn't get any words out. My throat felt thick and I bucked my hips involuntarily at the sight of him.

He took that as an answer. All I had to do was lay there and let him slide my clothes off me, peeling away my tight trousers which had been doing nothing to hide my arousal and running his hand slowly up my chest as he worked my top off. When he was finished, and I was naked, he straddled me and looked down at me writhing below him.

"You're mine, Morgan," he said, and his voice was thick with gravel and something else I couldn't identify. He sounded sincere.

"Yes," I said, and my back arched, pushing my hips off the bed, trying to brush against him.

The feeling of Lew's naked skin pressed against mine was the most erotic experience of my life. Admittedly, I didn't exactly have that many experiences under my belt, but still, touching Lew like that had to be the most amazing experience of anyone's life, right?

He lowered himself onto me and kissed me, grinding against my leg and pressing his hips down hard so I got delicious friction on my dick. I couldn't help the sounds that came out of my mouth and Lew drank them all in, absorbing them in his kiss.

Then his hips lifted and his hand slid between us. I gave a huff of disapproval at the sudden lack of contact, but then his slick fingers wrapped around my aching dick and I gave the most lascivious moan I'd ever heard in my life. I hadn't even been aware I could make such a noise.

It sparked a groan from Lew and he pushed his hips forward, lining our bodies up so his hard cock rubbed against mine. It was too much to feel all at once, with the heat of his body, the hardness of his length, the softness of his skin, the easy glide up and down my dick, the way his thumb circled my head and made my balls draw up tight. I was sweating and panting and whimpering, trying to buck my hips up into his grip, but his weight held me down and he worked me in his own time, slow and steady and sweet and too perfect. It broke me.

My orgasm came from my very soul and burst up through my body with such force that I wasn't at all sure I hadn't been split completely in two. My dick spurted ejaculate all over Lew's hand and his hard dick and my own chest. I thought I would orgasm forever, but at last the shock-waves began to diminish and I was only shaken by ripples of pleasure as I settled, and that's when Lew grunted and stiffened above me, and I felt his hot semen join mine. I got a weird satisfaction out of looking down and seeing both our releases pooling together on my belly, indistinguishable, proof of our pleasure.

Lew collapsed, rolling to the side so as not to squash me, and, strangely, that made me feel safe beside him, tucked into his side, still trembling with aftershocks. He pressed kisses to my head, my temple, my jaw, and I just lay there, revelling in the feeling until I could co-ordinate my limbs enough to move them somehow.

"I never realised sex could feel like that," he murmured into my hair.

"Mmm hmm," I said, not even able to get my tongue to work properly.

Concern crept into his voice. "I didn't hurt you, did I?"

"Nuh uh."

"You're just super talkative after an orgasm, right?"

"Mmm," I agreed. I was getting sleepy and I wanted to slip away while I could still feel the tingles in my fingers and toes, and while he was pressed the length of my side.

He chuckled and whispered, "Can I stay with you, Morgan?"

"Yuh mmm."

The sweet kiss he pressed to my cheek was the last thing I remember before sleep took me.

CHAPTER 23: LEW

A sleepy and sated Morgan was one worth seeing, I knew that. He looked so peaceful, with his face relaxed and open and it made my chest swell almost painfully to be there with him, so close to him after I'd thought he was lost to me, unreachable and closed off. Shit, it hurt to think of that, so I concentrated on the sight of him beside me. His lips were slightly parted and his breath came out in little bursts. I wanted to breathe in his scent so much, but I didn't want to push him too far too soon. Having what I'd already had was more than I thought possible, and definitely more than I deserved. I was still reeling from the discovery that he was my mate. I should have felt surprised – I definitely wasn't expecting to get a mate, and certainly not one who was so perfect, but then maybe that should have been my first clue that he was my mate. More than surprised, I felt the rightness of it and my dragon rumbled with satisfaction in my chest, perfectly content to be laying next to our mate with our combined releases smeared over him.

As I noticed my dragon's satisfaction, it occurred to me that maybe my dragon had known, that *I* had known it, somehow, deep inside, and just hadn't recognised that knowledge for what it was.

I also noticed that our come was cold and was going to become irritating and sticky on Morgan's sensitive skin, so I reluctantly eased away from his sleeping form and climbed out of the bed.

When I found a flannel in his bathroom and soaked it in warm water, wrung it out and brought it over to the bed, I took a moment to look down at Morgan's body before wiping up the mess. I couldn't deny the satisfaction I got from seeing him covered in our come. He'd looked so spectacular as he came apart beneath me, all traces of the stiff, reserved Morgan completely gone. It had been the most incredible gift.

When he was clean, I threw the flannel into the shower and went back to the bed, lifting Morgan so I could manoeuvre the duvet out from under him. I did take just a moment to take one last look – maybe it was more of an ogle – at his body before I slid into the bed beside him again and pulled the duvet up to our chests.

His shoulders and neck were visible and I traced one finger over the join, right where his shoulder met his neck. That would be where I marked him, if I ever claimed him. My dragon pushed forward slightly, wanting to mark him, and just for a second I felt my teeth grow sharp, but I pushed the urge down. I wanted to claim Morgan – fuck, did I want to claim him! – but that was something he needed to decide and we hadn't talked about it at all. I had no idea whether it was something he'd want. For me, it was an easy choice. I'd claim him in a heartbeat if he'd let me, but I knew him well enough to know that he would need to think it through, and I hated to admit it but I was aware there was a possibility that he would decide he didn't want that.

My dragon prickled and I shuddered. I turned away from those thoughts. They didn't have any place in this bed, with Morgan naked beside me.

I hope it was romantic, rather than creepy, but I couldn't keep my hands off him. While he slept, I slid my hand beneath the duvet and rested it on his chest, stroking my fingers across his soft skin occasionally.

I don't know how long I lay there, watching him sleep, but I wasn't in the least bit tired and I didn't mind at all just existing in the peaceful moment.

When he began to stir, I stilled my hand on his chest, not wanting to freak him out, but I left it pressed to the centre of his chest and waited to see if he would move it off him. I knew he'd liked it at the time, but I'd had quite a few partners who enjoyed fucking me right up until the point they were done, and then they couldn't get away fast enough. It was a bit of a blow to my self-esteem each time it happened, but I'd never cared about any of them the way I cared about Morgan.

He stretched and the duvet slipped down his body, revealing more of it to me. I caught a glimpse of his nipples and realised I hadn't paid them enough attention earlier. In fact, if what we'd had was all I was going to get of him, I really hadn't had enough of a chance to explore his body the way I wanted to.

He still hadn't opened his eyes but he turned towards me, snuggling further into my side. The feel of him there made my dick perk up and I took a deep breath, wanting to smell him and only getting a whiff of his conditioner. It was frustrating not to be able to catch his scent and I realised my dragon had been itching for it for weeks, always twisting this way and that, trying to catch the faintest trace of him.

"This is the best dream," Morgan said, mumbling against the side of my pec where his face was smooshed against me.

I chuckled and stroked a hand down his back. "Glad to hear it."

He stiffened in my arms and slowly raised his head. His eyes were wide and he looked nervous as a rabbit. "It's not a dream, is it?"

"No."

"Was any of it a dream?"

Shit, it sounded like he was kind of hoping it was a dream. I'd be the first person ever to be dumped by their mate as soon as the sheets cooled. "Um, no, it wasn't."

"So you really are my mate?"

"Yes." Honesty was the nest policy, after all.

"Thank God!"

Morgan flung himself across me and buried his face in my neck, and I felt the warm softness of his skin all down my chest and my legs and my hard dick nudged against his thigh. My arms wrapped around him automatically, holding him close to me, feeling his weight pressing me down, and I was glad my body was still capable of responding because my brain had completely shut down.

"Are you glad I'm your mate?" I asked, when I got it together.

"Of course I am, who wouldn't want you as their mate? I can't believe I'm this lucky." He pressed his nose into my neck and inhaled, then huffed. "I want to smell you; I want your scent."

My heart soared and I gripped him tighter. If he was ready to exchange scents, he must be serious, he must believe we were meant to be together forever.

Slowly, I released my scent. It was like undoing a knot, working it open little by little. Dragons masked their scent so naturally that I had to concentrate in order to *un*mask it. As I felt my body release it at last, Morgan moaned against my skin and pressed harder against me, breathing deep over and over again. His dick grew harder against my abdomen and it dug into me like it was trying to drill a hole. He breathed in again, his dick twitched, and he began to hump against me. I doubt he even realised he was doing it, but the fact that I had Morgan Somerville sprawled naked on top of me, breathing in my scent and rubbing off on me, was the most surreal and amazing experience.

He began to pant, his grinding became more desperate and I reached down to try and take hold of his dick, wanting to work him, and, when I pushed my hand between our bodies, I found it soaked with pre-come.

Pushing him off me, rolling him onto his back and looming over him, I looked into his eyes. They were glazed and shiny, and his lips were pink from where we'd kissed so much earlier, and his cheeks were flushed with red. He looked debauched and I'd never seen anything so hot in my life.

"Let me smell you," I said. My dragon shivered at the thought of it and I waited for Morgan to answer me. He didn't say anything, just writhed and pushed his hips up, pressing his dick against me and gasping at the slick glide.

At first, I didn't realise he was releasing his scent. All I knew was that my nose began to tingle, like there was something there I couldn't quite catch, and then I caught the faintest snatch of a scent that made me rock hard in seconds. It was the most delicious thing I've ever smelled; sweet and warm and musky all at once. It was the smell of sex and comfort, and I couldn't work out how it could be both at the same time.

My dick became so hard it hurt and I pushed my hips forward, driving it along his skin. I wanted to get off so badly. I felt the pre-come spill from my slit and leak over Morgan's thigh, and then more spilled out, and more. I was leaking like a tap and surrounded by Morgan's scent and I could feel his lithe body beneath me and I was half out of my mind with need.

My brain latched onto one image and then my body began to move of its own accord. Sliding down his torso, I breathed in Morgan's scent and licked his skin and tasted the saltiness of his sweat and all it did was drive me higher. I pushed his legs apart and settled between them.

I was so far gone, I barely even registered that I was growling, and the only sound I could hear was Morgan begging, "Lew, Lew," chanting my name like a prayer.

When I reached his groin, I pressed my nose against the crease between his thigh and his balls and took a deep breath. His scent was stronger there and I almost came from it, the sharp smack to the back of my nose with the one scent in the whole world that was made for me. My dick throbbed and I felt the pre-come spurt from me, soaking the sheets.

Morgan had a beautiful dick. It was long and slender, pink and tipped with red, slick with pre-come and, as I pulled back to take a look, it bobbed in front of my face and more ran down it in rivulets.

"Lew," he moaned, and I heard the desperation in his voice. He sounded frantic, more so because he didn't quite know what to ask for. I hadn't been lying earlier when I'd said I was glad nobody else had touched him. I know it made me a bad person, but it was true. But his inexperience meant Morgan didn't know what he liked and what he didn't. I suddenly felt a huge responsibility to make this good for him, to push him to the greatest height without pushing too far. It sobered me in a way nothing else could have.

Slowly, so he could stop me if he wanted, I slid my hand up his thigh to his balls. I ran my fingers across them, touching gently, but not tugging on them or rolling them the way I wanted to. I was testing his reactions. He responded so beautifully to me, throwing his head back and panting my name. I was close just from the smell of him, the sight of him, and the incredible sounds he was making.

I ran my fingers down his taint and he whimpered.

"Morgan, have you ever touched yourself here?" I brushed my finger lightly across his hole, feeling the tight pucker and barely resisting the urge to push his legs up and dive into it with my tongue.

"Yes," he cried, and it was somewhere between a confession and a plea.

It was too much for me. I wanted to ask him more questions, but none of them were as urgent as my need and I rose up and took one last look at his flushed face and panting chest before I focused on the angry red stiffness of his length. It twitched before me and I settled myself comfortably and reached for it, encircling it with my hand and running my fist up and down twice.

Morgan gave another whimper and begged, "Lew, please," and I gave him what he wanted. I licked up the length of it, wanting to get a taste of him, and groaned as the flavour burst across my tongue and filled my mouth with the most exquisite taste. My own cock throbbed and I ground my hips down into the mattress, barely getting the friction I needed.

I only allowed myself another couple of long licks and, as fast as I lapped up his pre-come, more spilled from his head. My scent and my touch were doing that to him, and I let my dragon growl out its satisfaction. Then I took him into my mouth and swallowed half his dick at once. My mouth felt uncomfortably full, which just went to show how long it had been since I'd sucked cock, but the exquisite flavour drove me on and I sucked hard, laving with my tongue and working him further into my mouth. I wanted to draw out all his flavour and, for a moment, we stayed like that, both thrusting our hips and panting, right on the edge. The feel of him driving into my mouth was almost too much.

If he'd had a little more experience, I might have pushed a finger inside him, felt the tight heat of him, massaged his prostate until he came, but I didn't want to hurt him and I had no idea where I'd chucked the lube earlier after pumping enough of it into my palm to ease the glide as I'd worked us together. I wasn't going to breach him without it, and I wasn't going to stop what I was doing to look for it, so I contented myself with sucking his taste into my mouth and running my finger along his taint, around his hole, and back to his balls, which were drawn tight to his body.

He thrust again, I responded by grinding my hips into the mattress again, and groaned around his dick. The vibrations must have tipped him over the edge, because he gave a shout and his hips bucked uncontrollably and his cock throbbed inside me and spilled his seed in my mouth. The taste of come had never done it for me before – I'd always swallowed it quickly and then rinsed out – but Morgan's taste was salty and earthy and sweet all at once and I greedily sucked it out of him, lapping at his dick until it was completely spent. Then I thrust my hips down, groaning at the friction, and Morgan's soft, dazed voice said my name again as he rested one hand gently on my head and I came hard, shooting my load between his legs and wishing I was filling him up with my seed.

I floated on a cloud of euphoria and rested my forehead on his hips as I recovered. As I came to, I realised Morgan was gently stroking his fingers through my short hair and I could still smell him. His scent was sex and come and contentment and Morgan, and I felt my dick try to twitch back to life again.

"You smell incredible," I murmured, not even bothering to lift my head to talk. I just said the words directly into the soft skin stretched over his hipbone.

"So do you. I've never smelled anything like it."

I smiled, feeling, I have to say, just a little bit smug. Morgan thought I smelled good, which meant I didn't stink of sweat and come.

"I'm starving, it must be nearly dinner time. Come on, let's get cleaned up."

CHAPTER 24:
MORGAN

The shower was nice, since Lew took hold of my hand and led me into it, pressing himself close in the confines of the stall. It was a tiny bathroom and there really wasn't room for both of us in the shower, but he made it work and we spent more time pressed against each other, bumping together and sliding our wet skin across each other than actually washing. Which just went to show that Lew was a genius for putting us both in there at the same time.

The only bit that was disappointing was the fact that he gradually withdrew his scent and I tried to smell him, taking deeper breaths and pressing closer, but it was gone. I'd been breathing in the heady aroma of Lew's body without even realising it, delighting in the uniqueness of it and the way it surrounded me. When I'd first caught the faintest trace of it, my heart had sped up and my dick had filled rapidly. I hadn't even known what I was doing until Lew had me on my back and I heard his sex-gravelled voice demanding to smell my scent, too. I'd only been aware of his smell and his skin, and the blinding lust coursing through my body.

When Lew withdrew his scent, the water washed it off and I could no longer smell him on either of our bodies. It made me feel bereft.

He pressed his nose into my neck, just below my ear and inhaled, before murmuring, "Cover your scent again. I don't want anyone else smelling you."

I couldn't believe I'd even allowed Lew to scent me. My mother had always impressed upon us the need to conceal it, and we'd had dire warnings about what others would want to do to us if ever they caught our scent. I had always felt hunted because of it, like releasing my scent would be dangerous. There were only a handful of people who'd ever scented me in my life; I hadn't even allowed most of my family that degree of trust. As quickly as I could, I gathered my control and masked my scent. The shower water quickly smelled duller and the only thing between us was water and soap, not a rich bouquet of our mingled releases.

"I wish I could keep smelling you," Lew

murmured, and my skin broke out in goose-bumps. "Are you cold? Let's get out."

He turned off the shower and reached out to grab a towel, which he wrapped around me and rubbed against my skin to dry me off.

It wasn't the water that had made me cold, it was the thought of not concealing my scent. The idea of anyone else catching my scent was strange and intimate and my dragon prickled below my skin at the thought that they might be able to track me. I rarely got any interference from my dragon inside me, but I noticed it lifted its head occasionally, usually when I was thinking of doing something that put us in danger. The last time had been when I'd come to the Hoskins' castle and had walked into the territory of a whole clan of *curaidh*. My dragon had not been happy about that decision, and I had agreed with it at the time, thinking it was just begging for trouble. But I hadn't been given a choice and so my dragon could prickle against my skin all it liked, it wouldn't have made a difference. Nothing I could do or say would have made Lord Somerville change his mind.

For the first time since Lew had landed on my windowsill, I thought about my family. Specifically, I thought about what Lord Somerville would do if he ever found out about me and Lew. He'd be furious that I'd engaged in any kind of sexual act with anyone, let alone a *curaidh*. We'd had that lecture often enough: do not trust them, do not allow them to touch us, do not lower our guard, etc. If we allowed a *curaidh* any intimacy, they would try to claim us. That was what we'd been told. It was fact, one of those things that we knew almost from birth, like it was ingrained in our psyche from generations of *uasal* having to defend themselves from the unwanted attempts to claim us. But Lew hadn't claimed me. He hadn't even tried. And it wasn't like I could have stopped him, if he'd decided to do it; I had been completely beyond reason and desperate to have him in any way I could; I'd have welcomed it.

The realisation struck me hard. Two questions circled around my head, and I didn't know how to answer either of them, and I didn't know how to stop the stabbing pain that dug at my chest with each one: What would Lord Somerville do if he ever found out about us? Why hadn't Lew claimed me when he had the chance?

Lew was quiet and that suited me fine. We dried off and dressed, and Lew dragged on the clothes that I'd returned to him earlier. It annoyed me, since that would mean he'd wear them back to his room and then I wouldn't get to have them any more. I knew I should have kept my ideas to myself, and then I'd still have his clothes to wear.

As we walked down to dinner, Lew took hold of my hand and held it all the way down the stairs. Just before we turned the corner to the corridor that would lead to the dining room, he leaned close and whispered, "Is this ok? We don't have to let anyone know if you're not ready."

I didn't know what to say. I wanted to hold Lew's hand, I wanted to act like a couple, just like some of the other members of his family. But I wasn't sure how. Nobody in my family did things like hold hands. It was weird. Nice, yes, but weird. And if anyone saw it, there was a chance it would get back to Lord Somerville. Those two questions circled round my head again, mocking me: What would Lord Somerville do if he ever found out about us? Why hadn't Lew claimed me when he had the chance?

"Um," I said, not sure how to answer.

His face fell and he dropped my hand. "It's ok, we don't have to if you don't want to. We don't need to let anyone know."

It was the most sensible thing to do, and it didn't matter that my heart felt like it shrivelled up a bit when he let go of my hand.

I had to say something, though. "Um, I'm just... not ready yet," I said, which was both true and not true. I *wasn't* ready, but I also wasn't sure I ever would be.

"That's alright, Morgan," he said, and leaned down to press his nose briefly against my neck, just below my ear. "You don't have to do anything you don't want to."

That was a laugh. I'd spent my whole life doing things I didn't want to, from the moment I could remember. Lessons, drills, training, tests, parades, dinner parties, talking, not talking, all of it had been inflicted upon me. I'd become practically a wooden puppet to get through it all.

"Sorry," I said, wanting to say more and not sure what exactly that should be. I wanted to ask him what he'd do if Lord Somerville ever found out about us. I wanted to know why he hadn't claimed me when he had the chance.

I felt the soft kiss against my neck and then Lew stood upright and walked confidently round the corner. I caught up with him after just a few steps and tried to keep my composure in the face of what seemed to be the entire household gathered for dinner. Every pair of eyes that looked at me seemed to have a knowing glint to them, but surely they couldn't know what we'd just been up to in my room, and they definitely couldn't know that Lew was my mate. I tried to wrap myself in calmness. The years of training to school my features in front of my father helped. If I hadn't had that practice, I felt like I would have just screamed in the middle of the dining room, "Yes, I've seen Lew Hoskins naked and he touched my dick!" Needless to say, that would have been a little embarrassing.

Instead, I sat down with as much composure as I could and gave polite greetings to the people around me. Lew sat next to me and I felt the press of his leg along the length of mine under the table, warm and solid and comforting.

Other than that, he didn't do anything different. It was like we'd never been in my room together, like I'd never felt his hands all over my skin and never tasted his mouth and we hadn't just been a panting, sweating mess not half an hour earlier. It was surreal.

"Carrots?" he asked.

"Yes, please."

He served them onto my plate and then added some to his, and reached for the next bowl in the middle of the table. The Hoskinses always served a dinner that I thought should feed a thousand, and everyone just helped themselves to what they wanted. I suppose I had noticed, but I just hadn't thought it strange before that Lew would sit beside me more often than not, and he would dish a little of everything I wanted onto my plate. Was he serving me dinner? Was that unusual? I looked around, wondering if people noticed. Nobody was looking at us, so maybe they didn't care either way.

When the elder arrived, I fought my usual instinct to jump to my feet. It had taken a lot of re-training not to jump up when she entered the room and, each time I did it, I reminded myself not to get used to it or I'd lapse around Lord Somerville. I glanced at her and her human mate who followed her. She met my eyes and I gasped, looking quickly down at my plate.

"You alright?" Lew murmured beside me.

"Yes, thank you."

He didn't question me further and I didn't dare to look at the elder again. The blackness of her eyes was deep and dangerous. I was sure she knew.

The possibility churned my stomach. If she knew what Lew and I had done, she could tell my father. Or perhaps she would convince Lew to claim me. It would be a boon to her to have a *uasal* in her clan.

After that, I lost interest in eating. I pushed the food around my plate until Lew had finished and then we stood together. It was only then that I realised I didn't know what I was doing. I'd waited for him as though I expected him to spend the evening with me, but he hadn't given any indication that he would.

"Lew?" The elder looked up at him, her nearly-black eyes sharp and assessing.

"Yes, Nana?"

"I want a word with you. Are you free now?"

He glanced at me but I ducked my head, so he shrugged – I felt the movement against my arm since I'd somehow moved close enough to touch him – and he said, "Yeah, why not?"

Watching him walk away made me ache in

a way I wasn't used to, and I hurried up to my room. I was glad, though. I wanted this time to think. I needed to think clearly so I could decide what to do next.

The same thoughts poured through my head: I had a mate; he hadn't claimed me; Lord Somerville would never allow us to claim each other; nobody knew except me and him; the elder might suspect; I wanted his taste in my mouth again like I wanted air; he hadn't claimed me.

I kept coming back to that. I'd been told so many times, in a hundred different ways, from outright lectures to fairytales, to hints and subtle suggestion, that people would want to claim me if they knew about my magic. They would want to hoard me like they did their gold. But Lew hadn't claimed me. I was partly relieved and partly devastated that he didn't want to.

When I got back to my room, I flopped down onto the bed. That was a mistake. The movement disturbed the sheets and released a faint trace of the two scents that had been caught there: mine and Lews. We smelled so good together. Without even thinking, I threw myself forward and buried my face in the pillows, seeking his scent and inhaling deeply.

The smell of him made my body tingle with energy. It felt like I was just coming alive, and my dick certainly came to life, growing hard and needy just from the faintest trace of him. I debated for a moment whether to lay down under the covers and pull them over my head to capture the aroma and touch myself to the memory of Lew Hoskins' body on top of mine but, in the end, I didn't. I couldn't think clearly with his smell in my room and my dick straining against my trousers and dampening my underwear. I needed to think. I needed a clear head. I needed to get rid of his scent.

I began to strip the bedding, wadded it up into a ball and carried it to the laundry room.

CHAPTER 25: LEW

"Are you going to tell me, then?"

I started guiltily, like a fool. If Nana didn't realise that I was keeping something from her already, she would now.

"Tell you what?" I asked, just to be clear.

"A little birdie told me that our Morgan has magic."

"Yes. Apparently he does."

"You didn't know?" Nana's eyebrow went up in that way it did.

"No, I didn't. I'd have trained him differently if I'd known."

"What kind of magic does he have?"

"Um," I said, because I was a genius.

The other eyebrow rose to join the first one in a look of disbelief. "You don't know, do you? You've been training him for weeks and you didn't know he had magic?"

"No."

"And when you found out today, you didn't think to ask him about it?"

"No." I was sure my face was burning, totally giving away what I *had* done that afternoon.

Sure enough, Nana sat back on the sofa she was on and crossed her legs. Her eyes bore into mine and she spoke softly, which was weird. "Interesting. Maybe you should tell me about *that*, instead."

"What?"

A slow smile spread over her face. I began to sweat. It was really, really hard to keep anything from Nana.

To distract her, I asked, "Who told you he had magic?"

"Laura. And Prince, when he came back after losing Brendan about twenty miles south of here. And Dee. And Dum."

"Dum came to tell you that Morgan knocked him on his arse?"

Nana's mouth twitched into a smile. She looked like she was trying unsuccessfully to restrain it. "Yes, he did. Dee nearly wet herself laughing at him."

I couldn't help but smile at that, either. "It was pretty unexpected."

From across the room where he was sitting

in his armchair and pretending to read instead of ear-wigging our conversation, Gramps gave a little snort.

Nana ignored him. "According to Dum, it felt like lightning had struck him, only it was cold. Some kind of energy, perhaps?"

"Perhaps. All I know is it was blue."

Nana rolled her eyes. "Your keen powers of observation come in handy again, Lew."

"I wasn't the one hit by it."

"No, you weren't. But you might have inadvertently been the cause."

"What do you mean?"

"According to all the witnesses, Morgan was agitated by you. How many times do I have to tell you to sit down instead of looming over me? I'm getting a crick in my neck."

I sat, just like the good grandson I was, and Nana fussed with some imaginary fluff on her skirt until I couldn't bear it any more. "Nana? What did I do wrong?"

"You didn't do anything *wrong*, you just did something. That's different."

"Alright, what did I do?"

"Firstly, you didn't tell me how much of a crush you had on Morgan Somerville."

I bristled. It wasn't a crush, it was love. Pure love. He wasn't just some bloke I fancied because he was fit; he was precious and perfect. I growled automatically, my dragon wanting me to claim him as mine, in any way I could. Neither of us liked reducing the feelings we had for Morgan to 'a crush' and I growled, "He's my mate."

Normally, if I growled at Nana, she would growl right back. She was like that. She was in charge and she needed to keep us all in our place. You basically had to be scary and a bit insane to be the head of a dragon clan, since dragons were difficult to control as a general rule. But, to my surprise, Nana smirked and said, "Yes, isn't he?"

"You knew?" I couldn't believe it. I felt a bit betrayed, actually. "How long have you known?"

The look she gave me was part pity and part disbelief. "I did wonder about it early on. You weren't exactly acting like yourself around him. And then you started waxing lyrical about how bright he shone—"

Gramps didn't even look up from his book when he crowed, "That's when *I* knew."

Nana tutted. "That's not proof, John."

"When people like Lew start getting depressed because virtual strangers lose their *brightness*, it's proof." For the first time, Gramps looked over at me and gave me a reassuring smile. "You see him just the way I see your Nana."

"Nana's bright?" I asked. I might have sounded a bit too incredulous because both of them looked offended. I hastily asked, "Why didn't you tell me?"

"Would you have believed us?"

I thought about that. "Maybe," I admitted.

"Where mates are concerned, I find it best to let them sort themselves out. Neither of them appreciates interference. Not to mention, if things go wrong, the consequences can be... fatal." She was talking about *ruith*, the dragons who lost their mates one way or another, who lost control of their dragons and rampaged until they were stopped. Stopped permanently. Nana leaned forward and her dark eyes locked on mine and I couldn't look away. "But you must sort yourselves out, Lew. Morgan's time here isn't infinite and you need to decide how you want to proceed sooner rather than later."

"Proceed? Surely we'll just—"

Gramps gave an irritable huff. "You're making assumptions, Lew, and that's not the way to do this. You've got to talk to him. If you'd only talked to him in the first place instead—"

"John, I thought we agreed not to interfere."

"No, my darling, *you* agreed not to interfere and *I* said nothing."

She snorted in disapproval but Gramps pointed dramatically at me and said, "That's my grandchild, at one of the most important moments of his life, and you want to leave him to blunder around on his own?"

"Gee, thanks."

"He's oblivious, darling, you can't leave him to fend for himself."

"Hey."

"He's got no experience with these things. Ask him if he had any idea that Brendan was pining away for him. Go on, ask him."

Nana looked at me and raised a questioning eyebrow.

"No, I had no idea, I swear, Nana. I didn't mean to—"

"You see!" cried Gramps. "He's practically helpless."

"Now hold on a min—"

"No, *you* hold on a minute, Lew!" Gramps rarely went into full dramatic mode but he was a sight to behold when he did. He leapt out of his chair and paced the floor. Nana sat back and her eyes followed his movements with amusement and a disturbing kind of heat. "You let Brendan flirt with you and it meant Brendan felt like he was promised something and Morgan used his magic on someone who was a complete stranger to him, after keeping it secret from us for weeks. That wasn't an accident; if he didn't tell you about his magic, it was because he didn't want you to know about it. You're lucky he showed us at all. And now you waltz in here and say you'll probably just do whatever it is you've assumed you'll do, but you haven't asked Morgan what he *wants*. You need to ask him, and you need to tell him what *you* want, otherwise you're going to go round in circles."

I frowned. "I assumed we'd claim each other." All mates claimed each other. I'd never heard of mates not being claimed, once they'd found each other. It was impossible not to, after you'd tasted your mate, smelled their scent, touched their body... I really needed to stop thinking about Morgan's taste and scent and touch or I'd get a hard-on in front of Nana and Gramps and then we'd all need therapy.

"Did you *say* that?"

"No, but it's obvious – we're going to be together. Dragons can't be parted from their mates."

Nana spoke for the first time in ages and her voice was dark. "They can be parted."

"Not- no, they can't," I said, and my dragon twisted inside of me, trying to get away from the nasty thought that we might not be with Morgan forever.

She corrected me gently, but it still sent an actual pain through my body as my heart constricted. "Lew, they can be parted unless they fight to stay together."

I barely heard the command from Gramps, "Go to him, son, and tell him what you *want* and what you'll sacrifice in order to get it."

I was out of the door before he'd even finished. My heart was beating fast and my dragon was confused and anxious, not struggling to get out yet, only flexing its claws and sniffing the air, searching for Morgan. Shit, I'd never understood why dragons *ruith* when they lost their mate, but I suddenly understood with horrific clarity. I didn't think I'd be able to control my dragon if ever I lost Morgan.

When I burst into his room without even knocking, Morgan was in the middle of putting a fresh duvet cover on the duvet. He was standing on the bed, shaking the cover and my brain almost didn't compute what was happening, mostly because I was through the door and on top of Morgan in a second and little details were still catching up with me.

I leapt onto the bed, pushed him back against the wall and kissed him like my life depended on it. He went stiff in my arms for a moment and then his body practically melted against mine and his lips parted for me. I pushed my tongue into his mouth and tasted him again and my dragon was at peace at last.

We kissed for minutes and I wrapped my arms around him, wanting to feel him in my arms. At last, I pulled back enough to look into his eyes and smiled at the blissed-out expression there.

"You have no idea how much I want you, Morgan. Can you hear me?"

He gave a dazed nod but I wasn't convinced he was really listening.

"Morgan?"

"Huh?"

How could anyone help but smile when faced with this man? "I'm going to do everything in my power to be with you. Wherever you want to go, we'll go together. Whatever you want to do, I want to help you do it. I want to be with you forever, Morgan. I assumed you knew that, but Gramps said I was an idiot and needed to tell you."

His eyes lost some of their soft pleasure. "You're not an idiot."

I chuckled and pressed a quick kiss to his lips. "Gramps always says it with love, so I don't mind. He said we needed to talk, and I think he's right."

It wasn't my imagination, Morgan looked a bit wary of that, even though he said, "Ok," in an even tone.

"Morgan? We're mates, there's nothing you can tell me that will change the way I feel about you."

"Oh."

For the first time, it dawned on me that we were standing on his half-made bed. "Are you changing the bed?"

"Yes."

"Why?"

"Um, it had our smell on it."

I blinked at him. "You don't like my smell?"

A blush rose up his cheeks and spread down his neck. I wanted to take his shirt off to see if it spread down his chest, too. "I, um, liked it a bit too much," he said at last.

That made me smirk. I stepped back, jumped off the bed and lifted Morgan down. Before I lost track of things, I went to the door, closed it and locked it. I gave him a questioning look. "Is this ok?"

He nodded and I went back over to him. He hadn't moved. He was just standing where I'd left him, looking small and lost and vulnerable.

"We need to talk about a few things," I said.

"Yes."

"Are you ready?"

For a second, I thought he'd say no. But then he took a deep breath, steeling himself, and then he gave a decisive nod. Fuck, I was so proud of him.

CHAPTER 26: MORGAN

I didn't know what he wanted to talk to me about but I knew it couldn't be good.

I started to explain myself before he could get mad at me.

"I didn't mean to hurt Dum, I really didn't! Is he ok? It- it shouldn't do any lasting harm."

"He's fine. He was back to his normal self before you even made it back to your room." Lew tilted his head to the side and looked down at me. "Yeah, I guess we should talk about your magic, too."

"Too?"

"We'll start with your magic."

That sounded ominous. Did I have to prove myself before he would claim me?

"What do you want to know?"

He lifted my hands and held them between us, studying them with an air of a jeweller valuing two precious gems. I supposed, in a way, my hands – or, rather, my magic – was the valuable part of me.

"I want to know why you didn't tell me you had magic."

That was easy to answer. "Because Lord Somerville told me not to. He said I wasn't to reveal it to you at all. He'll be angry I did."

"Your family don't want us to know?"

"My mother told me I could use it, if- um, if I needed to. If I was in danger." I could feel my face heating and tried to drag some ice into my blood to cool myself down. I really didn't want to tell Lew that I was allowed to burn him if he tried to take me. I didn't want to put him off any more than I already had.

"But your father said you couldn't?"

"That's right. He doesn't like people to know what we can do."

"Why not?"

"Um, lots of reasons."

Lew leaned closer to me and I was almost pressed back against the bed. "Morgan, we need to be honest with each other."

My throat felt uncomfortably dry and I swallowed, trying to get some moisture into it. "Ok. He doesn't want anyone knowing what I can do in case they try to claim me."

I was surprised by the growl that Lew let out. If anyone else had done it, I'd have backed away and prepared to fight, but for some reason, when Lew growled, all I did was stand there and watch his lips pull back over his teeth and feel the vibration of it in the air around us.

"I don't want anybody else to claim you," he said. I was relieved. I didn't want anyone else to claim me, either. Of course, I wasn't sure I'd get a say in it either way, but still. If I could choose, I'd want Lew to be the one who claimed me. The idea of belonging to anybody else made my skin crawl and my dragon fizzed with magic inside, warning me that it wouldn't allow it. That was a new development.

"They won't," I said.

"So your father won't let you reveal your magic in case somebody tries to claim you for it?"

"Yes."

"What would he do if somebody did claim you?"

I eyed Lew warily. "Claim me willingly or un—?"

I didn't even get to finish because the growl was so loud and he snarled, "Willingly."

On reflection, I might have made it sound like I expected Lew to try and claim me unwillingly, which hadn't been what I meant. I'd meant if somebody else had tried to claim me. If Lew tried it, no matter what I'd told myself when I'd been alone in my room, changing my sheets, I knew that the second he kissed me again, I'd willingly bear my neck for him.

It took me a moment to gather my thoughts. I'd forgotten what Lew had asked and struggled to think back. He'd wanted to know what my father would do if somebody claimed me. I had no idea. That was part of the problem. It was the reason that the question kept running round and round my head: What would Lord Somerville do if he found out about me and Lew?

I shook my head like I couldn't even find the words I needed. "I don't know. I'd be no use to him once I'd been claimed, unless it was by someone in the clan."

Lew blinked at me. "Of use to him?"

"Yes."

"What do you mean by that?"

I shrugged. It was obvious.

"No, Morgan, don't shrug me off. Tell me what you mean. How are you of use to him now?"

"Oh, that. Well I'm his son." When that didn't seem to be enough of an explanation for Lew, I carried on. "I'm part of the family and he is the elder. So my magic belongs to him. If ever the family needs it, he can call on me. Just like if your family needed you, your elder would demand *your* talents."

"Demand?"

"Yes. To protect the family." I didn't know what part he was struggling with.

"You're saying that your dad doesn't want you mating anyone outside the family because then he won't be able to use your magic however he likes?"

"You're making it sound bad. It's not like that." But, as I said it, I couldn't work out what it was like, if not exactly like that.

Lew was taking long, steady breaths and his hands went up to my shoulders and gripped them hard. It wasn't like he was trying to hurt me, more like he was trying to steady himself, and I was happy to stand there and support him. "I take it he wouldn't take kindly to you mating somebody outside of his clan, then?"

"Um."

"Me, Morgan. He wouldn't want you mating me."

There was nothing I could do but admit the truth. "No, he wouldn't like that."

"And you?"

I couldn't find an answer. I'd never even considered that I'd get a choice in the matter.

Instead of answering, my mouth opened and a question rushed out. I blurted it out before I could stop myself. "Why didn't you claim me when you had the chance?"

The way he looked at me then was worrying. He drew back and studied me, like he was searching for all the flaws in my face, and I was sure he saw every one that I tried to hide with my mask. I'd never felt so exposed in my life.

"Because it's too important to rush, Morgan. It's not something you can decide in seconds and certainly not in the heat of the moment. We need to talk about it. We need to decide together."

"Together?"

"Yes."

"You mean I'd get a say in it?"

He ground his teeth together so hard I actually heard them crunch. Shit, I hadn't meant to make him angry.

He ground out his answer like teeth being pulled. "Morgan, you get a say in it. Nobody claims you unless you want them to. I'll fucking make sure of it. And that includes me. *Nobody* claims you unless you're willing."

That was a new thought. I wasn't sure whether to believe him at first. Surely he meant well but he couldn't actually keep that promise. How was he going to stop my father letting somebody claim me when I went back home?

I hadn't realised I'd asked that out loud. I had no idea when my mouth had started running away with me, but it was inconvenient.

Lew answered the question I hadn't realised I'd asked.

"You're not going back to that castle unless you'll be safe there."

"Of course I'm safe there."

"Not if your father's going to use you like a bargaining chip, you're not! What did he do? Tell you the savage *curaidh* would ravish you if you let on you had magic? That we'd let one of us claim you to keep you here and use your power like a fucking battery whenever we wanted?"

I'd never heard him sound so angry and his nails had sharpened into claws and were digging in me, but I wasn't afraid of him. For the first time in my life, I realised someone was angry *for* me, not *at* me. Weirdly, even though I was standing there with a furious warrior dragon almost blind with rage, I had never felt so powerful. Lew was angry *for* me. I wanted to laugh.

He carried on. "Is that what he's told you, Morgan?"

"Yes. But it's nothing personal about your family." I wanted him to know that. If it was me, I'd take it personally.

"No?"

"No, of course not. Anyone would try and take our power if they got the chance. That's why we're so careful."

"Careful?"

"Not to give people the chance. Keep them at a distance. Don't get close."

He blinked. "You mean your father kept you locked away like fucking Rapunzel in order to stop anyone getting close to you? Because he thinks they'll claim you if they get the chance?"

"Yes."

"Fuck, I can't believe you let me touch you."

Ok, that had not been what I'd expected. "Um, well, I did. Let you touch me, I mean."

"Do you trust me, Morgan? Not to claim you unless you want me to?"

I swallowed. That was the question, wasn't it? I remembered the dire warnings I'd heard about letting a *curaidh* get too close – about anyone getting too close – and how they'd lure me into a false sense of security, but I honestly couldn't picture Lew doing anything to hurt me. He'd had me pinned beneath him before, totally at his mercy, begging for his touch and almost incoherent with lust, and he still hadn't tried to claim me. A sharp little sword pricked at my heart but I ignored it.

"I trust you."

Lew breathed out like he'd been waiting for the answer. He lowered his head to rest his forehead against my own. I was torn between wanting to soak up the warm comfort he offered and wanting to push my mouth up to his and taste him again.

His breath mingled with mine when he asked, "Can I touch you again?"

"Yes."

He pressed his body forward, captured my mouth with his and I opened to him. His tongue slid against mine and I sucked at it, wanting more of his taste in my mouth. I wrapped my arms around his neck and dragged myself up his body, rubbing against his big chest.

"You can tell me to stop, Morgan. Any time."

I pressed my lips against his more desperately. "Don't stop," I begged. I was well and truly done for if I was reduced to begging, but I had Lew Hoskins in my bedroom and touching me with his big hands and his mouth was on mine and I just wanted to feel more of him against more of me.

I felt his smile under my lips. Having Lew smile as he kissed me might be my new favourite thing.

CHAPTER 27: LEW

I had tried to be a gentleman and not put my hands all over Morgan's perfect body, but he let me and my dragon was pretty angsty after hearing that his father had practically made him wear a chastity belt to keep anyone from claiming him. No, not to keep anyone from claiming him – to keep anyone he didn't want from claiming him. Like it was Barrington Somerville's fucking choice. My dragon had been pretty vocal about how it felt about that, and I'd been right there with it, wanting to rip the throat out of the abusive prick who'd kept Morgan living in fear and ignorance.

It meant that, when I got my hands on Morgan, I sort of lost my mind a bit. I wanted to push inside him and fill him with my seed, and I wanted to suck him off so I could taste him again, and I wanted to wrap him up and protect him, and I wanted to prove to him that not everyone was the monster he'd been told they were, and all of that boiled down to me saying, like a fucking sex addict, "Where's your lube?"

I couldn't for the life of me remember where he'd got it from last time.

He only paused for a second and then went to his drawer and took out the nearly-empty bottle. I growled in satisfaction that he trusted me enough to hand it over without being afraid I'd force a claiming on him.

I turned the bottle on its head and shook it, trying to make the very last of it flow down to the cap so we could use it. "I'll get us some more tomorrow," I said. I was almost out as well, since my lube consumption had increased dramatically the second I'd laid eyes on Morgan. For a moment, I enjoyed the thought of Morgan working himself to the thought of me, and then I wondered what exactly he did to pleasure himself. I was curious to know how far he'd gone. "Do you have a dildo?"

He blushed again and it was a mesmerising sight. He didn't normally blush and it was like I was getting a glimpse beyond the veil.

"I didn't bring it with me. I didn't want anybody to find it."

For my own sanity, I ignored the implication that somebody else would be in his bedroom at all. "But you've used one before?"

"Yes."

If he got any redder, I would die of cuteness overload.

"But not for the last couple of months? Have you used your fingers?"

He answered easily and I began to recognise the pattern: after he closed himself up, I had to work to get a drop of information from him but, once he started, it was like a dam cracking and answers poured out of him shamelessly. His answer was swift and simple. "Yes."

"Fuck!" I gripped my dick through my trousers, afraid I was going to shoot my load at the mere image that put in my mind. "I want to see that some day." Yeah, I was going to have to stop thinking about Morgan working himself open with his slim fingers or I really was going to orgasm before I'd even touched him.

"Get your clothes off."

I have no idea how I managed to pull my joggers and jumper off while I watched Morgan reveal more and more of his delicious skin to me. He'd barely stripped his underwear off before I was on him, sinking to my knees in front of him so I could lick at his abdomen and nibble and suck my way down his sparse happy trail to his dick. I wanted to smell him but I refused to ask him to release his scent again. I really wasn't sure what I'd do if I did smell him again, and I needed to be in control of myself.

Above me, Morgan gasped and whimpered. He was so beautiful when he did that, just let go and threw off the tight mask he wore the rest of the time. One day, he'd be confident enough that he wouldn't need to put the mask back on at all, and then everyone would see what he was really like beneath it. But not quite the way I saw him. I may be trying to be a good person but I wasn't a fucking saint and no way was anybody seeing Morgan in ecstasy except me.

"Fuck, Morgan, you're so beautiful."

With that, I buried my face in his groin and inhaled. My dragon was nudging at me to ask for his scent but I refused. I had to make do with the taste of his pre-come, which I lapped from his slit. It was divine. I could have tasted him all day and still wanted more.

His hands were in my hair, gripping tightly. He wasn't trying to force my head but I got the impression that was more a question of willpower than anything else. It made me want to lick and nibble at his crown until he lost all that tight control and shoved my head down as hard as he could so he could fuck my mouth. But I didn't. That could come later, when he was more confident.

I stood, grabbing the lube and throwing the half-covered duvet off the bed before lying on my back. He stared at me like he couldn't believe the sight of me, and I had to admit that made me feel pretty good.

A smile broke over my face and I said, "You like what you see?"

"You- you look incredible."

"You can touch, if you want."

His eyes darted up to mine and I saw nerves in their depths. Slowly, so he could see what I was doing, I reached down to my dick and gave a few strong tugs. It stood up like a soldier on parade and Morgan's eyes widened as he watched the pre-come glide down my shaft.

He took a tentative step forward and I let him move where he wanted. He straddled my thighs and my hips bucked of their own accord, but he managed to stay on me.

The first touch was a barely-there brush of his fingers and my cock bobbed, seeking out more. I clicked open the cap of the lube and squirted some into my palm.

"You want to take the lead?"

He looked at me, startled, sitting on my thighs with his amazing dick sticking out from his nest of neat curls, and then he carefully shook his head.

It was like a starting pistol went off. I surged up, taking his mouth and owning it. My tongue was in his mouth, seeking out his flavour, and I sucked and nipped at his lips and clutched at him with my free hand. With the lubed hand, I reached for my cock and spread the lube over it, groaning at the feel of it against my heated skin. Once I was ready, I dragged him down onto my body and lined us up so that our dicks notched together and rubbed against each other.

Even though Morgan didn't want to lead this encounter, I didn't want to pin him beneath me, not now I knew he was worried about being claimed against his will. Instead, I pushed my hips up to glide our dicks together and the sensation drove me to the edge quickly.

Morgan was rolling his hips, dragging his cock along my skin and making himself feel good. I loved it. He whimpered and grunted as he got the angle right and my hands slid down to his arse to grip it. I had a bit of an obsession with Morgan's arse. I wanted to eat it and I wanted to fuck it and I wanted to feel it in my palms. It was perfect. The two globes fit perfectly in my hands and I pulled him closer to me, driving him higher as he ground against me.

When he began to lose co-ordination, and I sensed he was close to going over, I slid my hands together and pulled his cheeks open a little. He whimpered again and I barely managed to pant, "It's alright, Morgan, I've got you."

I used my lubed fingers to brush along his crack and run over his tight hole. He thrust harder against me, and the feeling of him gliding against my dick was almost too much. I was so close, I wasn't sure I was going to last any longer. The pressure of his body and the constant movement and the way his stomach slid over the head of my dick was so hot I had to bite down on my need to push him onto his back and bury myself in him. It was everything I wanted and Morgan was giving it to me with utter trust.

The next time he thrust against me, I chased his hole with my index finger and then, when he pulled back to thrust again, he pushed himself back onto the tip.

He stilled, and I worried I'd hurt him. Just as I was about to withdraw my finger and try to soothe him, he surprised me by thrusting his arse back and impaling himself further. My finger slid in, up to the second knuckle, and then I wouldn't let him get any more. He writhed and thrust his hips, and I pushed my finger in and out, timing my thrusts with each of his so he got the pleasure of it as his cock rubbed against mine, and it took almost no time to push him over the edge like that.

He bucked desperately and gave the most erotic moan I'd ever heard as his cock throbbed against mine and I felt his release spill over us both. The warm liquid burned my sensitive head and the feeling of him moving against me and of my finger buried in his clenched channel was more than I could take. I gave a shout and came hard, spilling my load between us and revelling in the slick glide we created as we both thrust through our orgasms and then lay together to let the aftershocks wash over us.

After a few minutes, I slowly slid my finger out of his hole and wrapped my arms around him. His face was pressed against my chest and I could feel his softening cock trapped between our bellies still.

"That was incredible," I said.

"Mmm hmm."

I laughed at his post-orgasm non-verbal responses, and he huffed good-naturedly against my skin as I shook him with my laughter.

CHAPTER 28: LEW

We lay like that for a long time. I thought he was asleep until he said, "You take care of me."

I wasn't sure what to say to that. I didn't know when I'd taken care of him except to make sure he orgasmed when I did, and I thought that was probably the least I could do.

"Do I?"

"Yes. You serve me dinner, did you know that? Do you do it on purpose?"

I shrugged, making him bob where he was still sprawled on top of me. "I want to make sure you eat. And you have to be quick in my family to get what you want, and you're too polite to take it. I don't want you ending up with the dregs."

He pressed his face closer into my chest

and rubbed his cheek against it. "Your hair tickles."

"Sorry?"

He leaned up and looked me in the eye. He looked serious. "Don't be. I like it."

"Glad to hear it." Before I could settle down again and lose the will, I added, "Let me up and I'll clean us off."

He clutched at me tightly for a moment and then let go, rolling off me. I felt the sticky pull where our mess was drying between us, and cringed. I should have cleaned us up minutes ago.

Hurrying into the bathroom, I found a new flannel, made sure the water was warm and soaked it. Morgan watched me as I came back in and I felt the need to say or do something, but I didn't know what. I felt like he was waiting for something.

As gently as I could, I cleaned his stomach and groin and his soft dick. He let me move him how I wanted, which I found simultaneously sweet and erotic. I felt he would let me do anything to his body, if he trusted me enough.

When I finished, I went back to the bathroom and rinsed the flannel and began to clean my own mess up, scrubbing at my skin quickly so I could get back to Morgan. As soon as I finished, I flung the flannel away and went back into the bedroom, picked the duvet up from the floor, pulled the cover over it properly and drew it up over Morgan's exposed body. I didn't like to cover him up, since I kind of liked the view, but I didn't want him to get chilly, either.

I slipped into the bed beside him and pulled him back on top of me so his head rested on my chest. It felt so right to have him there. His hand settled on over my heart and he began to stroke his fingers up and down my skin tentatively, like he was waiting for me to tell him to stop. I pressed a kiss to the top of his head and he let his breath out.

We lay like that for a long time and I was almost lulled to sleep by Morgan's gentle fingers, but then he spoke, asking his question so quietly I almost didn't hear it.

"Lew, are you disappointed it's me who's your mate?"

I lifted my head to look him in the eye, half convinced I'd not heard him right. He was facing away from me and I had to tilt his chin up so I could see his face. "Why would I be disappointed? You're perfect, Morgan, don't you know that?"

"Oh." The sound was small and his voice was tight, and I felt more than saw the threat of tears behind his eyes. Dragging him up my body, I twisted so he was lying flat on his back and I was leaning over him, supporting my weight on my arms and looking down into his face.

"What made you ask that?"

He swallowed and said, "It doesn't matter."

It bloody did matter, if Morgan thought for a second that I wasn't fucking ecstatic to have him as my mate. *My* mate. I wanted to mark him so everyone would know it, and I wanted his mark on me, so I could have a constant reminder of it when he wasn't right there beside me.

"Tell me." I sounded a bit gruff and scolded myself. I didn't want him to think I was angry with him.

"It's just- not even my own family likes me that much," he said, and gave a little shrug like it didn't really bother him either way. But he'd let me back in again and I saw the truth of it in his eyes. He really believed that, and it hurt him.

Pressing a kiss to his lips, I closed my eyes and wished untold torment upon the people who had failed to show Morgan that he was loved.

"I'm so pleased you're my mate, Morgan. There's nobody in the world I could want as much as I want you. I like you more than anybody I've ever met. Every part of you, inside and out. My whole family likes you."

It was the truth, with just two exceptions, and I didn't mention them. Brendan *had* liked Morgan, right up until the point he realised Morgan was the man I wanted and not him, and Dane didn't like anybody, really, so Morgan probably shouldn't take that personally.

I gave a little smile, trying to coax some happiness back out of him. "Trust me, my family isn't subtle. If they didn't like you, you'd know it." When he didn't look like he believed me, I carried on to prove my point. "Nadia wants to adopt you," I said and my smile grew when I saw the laughter flash in his eyes. "Hannah and Ed spent a whole day telling everyone they were going to be *uasal* instead of *curaidh*, just like their Uncle Morgan, until Jill had to break it to them that it didn't work that way. Brenda thinks the sun shines out of your arse because you were kind about her cooking and she's been looking up recipes to try out for you, which she never did for the rest of us. Dimpy felt safe enough to try and spar with you, even though he's not fought anyone in forever and you didn't knock him on his arse like I know you could have. Gramps thinks you're great and has secretly started to knit you a scarf for Christmas. It's tradition. All the family has one."

The amusement shone out of Morgan's face as he said, "It's not so secret now."

"Ah shit, you're right. Well, when he gives it to you, just act surprised. It probably won't be hard because he's not that good at knitting. He makes scarfs because he can only knit in straight lines." I cringed. "Well, they're nearly straight. It might not be instantly recognisable as a scarf, to be honest. You'd think that after a few hundred years, he'd have managed to get the hang of it."

"I'll tell him I love it, no matter what."

I couldn't help but kiss him for that. That, right there, was why my whole family was as in love with Morgan as I was.

"Your Nana scares me a bit," he whispered. I laughed at that and he chided me. "She watches me really closely. I just know she knows something I don't."

"Nana always knows everything, so don't think you're the only one who feels like that. It's unnerving at first but you get used to it." While I'd been away, I'd forgotten what it was like to have Nana's sharp eyes on me, and it had taken nearly four years to get used to the feeling again. "It's her job. She's head of the family."

"She doesn't act like Lord Somerville."

I was pretty glad about that, but didn't think it wise to say so. "No, she doesn't. But she loves us and she'll protect us with everything she has."

"Really?"

"Yes, Morgan – you're my mate and that makes you family. We're going to keep you safe from everything, I promise."

Morgan reached up to brush his fingers over my lips and I couldn't help but smile at the tingling feeling they left behind. There was something important I had to say, though. "Morgan, no matter what, I'm glad you're my mate.

I can't imagine anyone more perfect than you. You're everything I ever wanted in a mate."

Tears slipped out of the corners of his eyes and trailed into the hair at his temples.

"Ok."

That 'ok' was all I needed to know that he believed me.

CHAPTER 29:
MORGAN

I spent the whole night with Lew. We talked on and off into the evening, and I learned, little by little, what life had been like for him growing up, and in the Fife Army and coming back to a house ruled by his elder. What amazed me most of all was that Lew seemed oblivious to his own importance. He didn't see that he was one of the greatest warriors the clan had, or that the elder confided in him and entrusted him with training her warriors, or that nearly everyone in the castle wanted a piece of his time, or that it wasn't just Brendan who thought he was a complete treat they wanted to devour (I was guilty of that one myself), or that he seemed to feel responsible for the others even when there was no way he could change them.

As we talked, two warring emotions clashed inside me. Pride wanted to rule me and make me crow that this was my mate and he was utterly, utterly perfect and everyone agreed with me, but insecurity bubbled up from the pit of my stomach and made me sure that there had been some terrible mistake if Lew Hoskins was the mate of someone like me.

I wasn't aware of drifting off to sleep but I woke up pressed against Lew's body and his arms held me tightly to him. I rubbed against him wherever I could touch and we kissed and talked and slept.

In the morning, we kissed ourselves into wakefulness and I worked my way down his body, revelling in the ability to touch him and feel his shape beneath my lips and the only thing I wanted that I couldn't have was the taste of him from his skin. When he concealed his scent, his body became tasteless and scentless. The sounds he made were sexy and his voice was rough from sleep and talking half the night.

"Morgan," he said, and I loved to hear my name on his lips. "Fuck, that feels so good."

He pushed his hips up to meet my questing mouth and I made my first attempt at giving a blow job. I had a general idea of what to do, and I tried to remember what it had felt like to have Lew's mouth on me the day before. The memory made my whole body tight with need and the feel of Lew beneath me and his groans and then, finally, the salty taste of his pre-come made me so aroused I couldn't concentrate. I sucked as well as I could but Lew was thick and heavy and I couldn't fit him all in my mouth without choking.

When I gagged, I pulled back, embarrassed, but he stroked a hand down my cheek and said, "Just suck the head. It feels so good, Morgan," and I did what he asked. I couldn't get enough of his taste in me and his groans vibrated through my whole body and his hand worked the rest of his dick until it was pulsing.

My first taste of his semen was a shock. I'd tasted mine once and vowed not to do it again, but the pleasure that exploded in me when I tasted Lew meant I chased his flavour and sucked hard, wanting to draw more out, and I licked and mouthed at his whole dick, trying to get any drops I might have missed.

At last, he pulled me off him and his expression was what I might term awestruck. He dragged me up the bed like a rag doll and lay me down, and then he sucked my soul out of my dick. At least, that's what it felt like.

Afterwards, he kissed me gently and I could taste myself on his tongue but it was mingled with his flavour and I didn't mind it so much.

Lew smiled down into my face and I thought how wonderful it would be to wake up like that every day, or even some variation of it. Just waking up in the same bed with Lew would be enough, actually.

"Are you coherent yet?"

"Mmmh. Yes," I said. I sounded a bit slurred but pretended not to notice. I don't know why my mouth didn't function properly after orgasm, it wasn't like it had ever happened when I'd got myself off. Then again, I'd never come as hard as I did when it was Lew bringing me to completion, so maybe my body needed more recovery time.

He chuckled, obviously *not* pretending not to notice. I would have pouted if I thought I had enough control over my facial expression. I didn't.

Lew sat up and swung his legs over the side of the bed. "Come on, let's get up now or I'm going to get hard again and then I'll never let you out of bed."

I followed him up and into the shower. He pushed me in first but didn't join me and he even left the tiny bathroom so I couldn't even watch his incredible body as I washed mine. When I went back into the bedroom to dress, Lew slipped past me and I heard the shower start again. I got dressed slowly, not quite sure what to do with myself.

I have to admit, I had got lucky with Lew; he came out of the bathroom still drying his hair and his towel was so low on his hips that I could see the top of his public hair. Every time he moved, his muscles flexed and my focus on his body was absolute. Under my gaze, his dick hardened until it tented his towel and then he flung the towel he'd been using to dry his hair at me. I only just caught it before it slapped me in the face.

"Stop looking at me or I'll ravish you."

I gave him a quizzical look. Did he think that was a threat?

We barely made it out of my room before noon but, when we did, we were both freshly-showered – again – and dressed and not sporting erections, so I counted that as a win. I had never been that obsessed with sex before I met Lew and, even then, even when I'd been touching myself every day and usually more than once a day, I'd never felt desire quite like it. Looking back at my existence before I met Lew, it seemed pretty sexless and stale. But then, I'd never been allowed lovers and I'd always known that my father would choose somebody to claim me, which, weirdly, didn't seem to be that sexual. I think I'd blocked that whole area from my life as a precaution against future pain or regret or disgust.

When Nadia spotted us from the other side of the entrance hall, I actually felt Lew cringe back and I was sure I began to blush again.

I'd never blushed before, I had no idea why I'd lost control over my face right then. She knew. I only had to look at her to see that.

She walked right up to us and neither of us could do anything but stand there was wait for whatever happened.

She jabbed Lew in the chest with one slim finger, which was much less than I'd seen her do before. Nadia seemed to take the dragons' advanced healing ability as licence to do more damage. At least, she did with Lew. With me, she hardly touched me and, when she did, she was always gentle. I'd actually started to like her touch, if I'm honest.

"I'll get to you in a minute. You can be thinking about what kind of explanation you're going to give me."

Lew stuttered, "Um, you see—" but she cut him off.

"I said in a minute."

He closed his mouth and I wanted to snigger. It suddenly occurred to me how funny it was that Nadia – who was titchy compared to Lew – could make this big, tough *curaidh* quake and stammer. As I looked at her, she met my eyes and I realised that I could see the same amusement in her eyes that she must see in mine. When I had first met her, I'd been a little afraid of her. I'd assumed she hated her family and that was why she shouted at them. Then I'd started to like her and I'd thought that she was just easily angered. But at that moment, I finally understood, and it was very simple: Nadia found it hilarious to mess with them.

I almost spluttered out a laugh. It was through sheer force of will that I restrained it, but I was sure my lips twitched.

"You," she said, directing her extremely false ire onto me, "owe me a demonstration."

"Of what?"

"Of the blue lightning that everyone is saying you can shoot from your hands. You know, the magic you *never ever mentioned to me*, even though we are best, best friends?"

"Oh, that," I said. I still wasn't sure how I felt about that. I had been told not to show anyone at the Hoskins' castle. I'd already let *that* cat out of the bag, though, so I didn't see the harm in showing them again. A handful of them had seen it already, and they all knew about it.

"Yes, that, Morgan. I can't *believe* you didn't tell me. How am I supposed to look people in the eye if they think I'm behind in my gossip? *Dimpy* knew about it before I did and he still has a blackberry phone and hasn't even heard about Prince's accident yet. If I'm behind him, I'm *decades* out of touch."

Lew asked, "What about Prince?"

She waved a hand dismissively. "Oh that, never you mind. We're talking about Morgan here."

I was almost positive that she'd made up Prince's accident just to mess with Lew. I wasn't sure about Dimpy's mobile, though. I hadn't concentrated on him as much as I should have the day before, since some people had had their hands all over Lew and it had made me insane in a way I hadn't known I could get, but Dimpy did strike me as the sort of man who still wrote things out by hand, probably with a fountain pen. I was amazed that he even *had* a phone.

She grabbed my hand and I happily followed along behind her. "Come on, we're going outside so you can show me your mojo."

"Oh, I'm not supposed to—"

"No, Nadia."

Nadia stopped. She turned. She did it slowly, so Lew had a lot of time to realise his mistake. The more I saw of her, the more I was convinced she was the best actress I'd ever seen. I nearly believed she was mad at him, but she was still holding my hand and her touch was soft and her thumb brushed my palm briefly. People couldn't be angry and touch somebody so sweetly at the same time.

"Excuse me?"

"He- Morgan hasn't agreed to it. And we don't know anything about his magic." Lew looked down at me from where he stood close, like he was going to protect me from his tiny cousin. "We don't know how much energy it takes, or how long it takes him to recover, or whether it hurts. You can't just demand a demonstration."

"It doesn't hurt. It makes me tired, though. I try not to do it unless I have to because it leaves me pretty weak for a while afterwards."

Nadia's thumb stroked my palm again and she said, "Will you tell me about it?"

"Yes. And I don't mind showing you a bit. I can just use less of it, that way it won't make me so tired."

"Great!"

She began to drag me forwards again but I resisted.

"Can we stay inside? I know people saw it yesterday, and everyone knows about it now, but I'd rather not show them again, not unless I have to. Lord Somerville said I wasn't to show you at all."

Beside me, Lew growled quietly and I saw the excited amusement fade from Nadia's eyes.

"Sure, we can stay indoors. You can show me another time, if you want. I can ask Lew to explain himself instead, since we'll have time."

"No, no, I don't mind." I didn't want to throw Lew under that bus. He looked like he was still trying to work out what he was going to have to explain to her and, again, I was sure she was making up her outrage just to see what he'd come up with. My respect for Nadia went up. She was good.

"Right, where shall we go that's got room for people to go flying around when they're hit by lightning?"

When Lew answered, "The armoury," I actually gasped.

"You're going to take me in there?"

He frowned. "We don't have to go there if you don't want to. Do you not like weapons?"

"No, it's not that. It's just that, I've never been- never mind."

I felt both of them move closer to me, Nadia still holding my hand gently and Lew pressing his hand into the small of my back. It was comforting.

"What is it, Morgan?" he whispered.

"I've never been allowed in the armoury before. At home, I mean."

"Why not?"

"That's only for the warriors and elders."

Lew was growling again and Nadia practically snarled, "Well not here, it isn't. It's for all the family. Come on."

She tugged me along behind her and I stumbled along. I was going to the armoury. I was family.

CHAPTER 30:
MORGAN

Watching Lew as he showed me the armoury was quite something. I was a little overwhelmed, to be honest. I couldn't believe that he and Nadia were showing me a part of their clan's defences that I had never even seen in my own family home; I was amazed by some of the weapons and armour that were stored there; I was completely besotted by Lew's casual way of lifting swords down from the wall and balancing them in his palm like he held them every day. I might have asked him about every sword there, just to see him swing them with his big arms, if it wasn't for Nadia saying, "Come on, I want to see what Morgan can do. Put the pointy-pointy things down, Lew."

He did, and I followed the two of them

through the secure doors and into a large open area. It looked something like a school gym, if it had been crossed with a high-security prison. It was a large room – big enough for a couple of dragons to tumble around in it in dragon form – and there were mats and bars and benches against the walls.

"This is where we practice with the more powerful weapons. The ones we don't want to take outside."

Reading between those lines, they were the weapons that they didn't want anybody else to get a look at. The ones they wanted to keep secret so none of the other clans would think to try and steal them, or prepare adequate defences to protect themselves against if they decided to start a war.

It occurred to me then that perhaps I shouldn't be showing Nadia everything I could do. If they knew, they might find the right armour to use so my magic wouldn't have any effect.

Lew slipped his arms around my waist from behind and pulled me back against his chest. "Are you sure you want to show us your magic again?"

"Yes."

That was true. I kind of wanted to show both of them, actually. I wanted to watch Nadia's face when she saw it for the first time and soak up the excitement I could feel emanating from her. And I wanted to show off a bit for Lew, if I'm honest. There wasn't much I could do to impress my mate, except exist, recite my family history, and demonstrate my magic, and I'd nailed the first one already, didn't think he'd be interested in the second one, and so demonstrating my magic was the only thing I could do that might make me look a bit cooler than I was.

Nadia asked, "What exactly is it? Laura said it looked like lightning."

"Kind of. It's energy."

"Does it hurt?"

I gave her a wry look. "Me or whoever I hit?"

"Both."

"It doesn't hurt me, it just takes a lot of energy to use. As for the people I hit... I'm told it does hurt a bit. And it's cold."

Both Nadia and Lew spoke at the same time. "Cold?"

"Yeah, cold. Like ice."

Nadia tilted her head to one side. "Huh. A dragon with ice magic. Who'd have thought it?"

I shrugged. It was what it was.

"Lew, go and stand over there." She pointed a few metres away, further into the room. He gave me one last squeeze and then went to stand where he'd been told. "Now," she said, looking at me, "Show me what you can do."

"You both need to stand back a bit in case I hit you."

She rolled her eyes. "You're *supposed* to hit Lew. Why do you think I put him over there?"

"Hey," he cried, and I had to swallow my laughter again. Poor Lew sounded actually offended that she'd sacrifice him.

"I'm not hitting Lew."

She rolled her eyes. "It won't do him any lasting damage, you said so yourself."

"No."

"*Fine*, I'll get one of the dummies."

While I tried not to snigger and Lew muttered about his *least favourite cousins*, Nadia went over to a large trunk and dragged out a life-sized doll. It looked something like a scarecrow, with a huge padded chest and its head stuck on at a slight angle.

"Help me prop it up."

Lew and Nadia set it up between them and then stood back, and I moved slowly forward until I was close enough that I was sure I'd be able to hit it. Missing the target altogether wouldn't make me look particularly cool in front of Lew.

Taking a deep breath, I reached inside for my magic. I'm not sure how it was supposed to go, but my instructor at home had always said I was too slow. He said I should be able to whip my magic out at any moment, and I'd never been able to think of that without picturing myself whipping my dick out.

Needless to say, that wasn't how I called upon my magic. For me, it was a bargain. My dragon had the magic and, when I wanted it, I asked my dragon for it. It might have been slow, but it was the only way I knew how to access that particular power.

Because I'd known I'd need it, since that was what we were here for and all, my dragon had already been stirring inside me, drawing my magic up so I could tap into it. I could feel it just below the surface of my skin, prickling like ice. I was always amazed that I didn't get frost forming on my skin when I used my magic, but I never did. I guess that was just fanciful.

"Ready?" I asked.

"When you are."

I raised my hands so my palms were pointing at the target. One of the disadvantages – or advantages, depending on how you looked at it – was that I basically looked like I was surrendering when I was preparing my magic. I had my hands up, palms out, exactly like I was trying to ward off blows. My instructor had told me that I needed to change my stance and my father, when he'd watched me once, had told me never to perform magic in that style again because it made me look weak, like a coward, but my dragon wouldn't release the magic to me unless I did it that way.

When the magic emerged, it was blinding, blue light that fizzed from my hands and arced towards the dummy target, striking it and blowing it into three pieces. It let it burn for a couple of seconds and then stopped and turned to see Nadia's face.

It was better than I'd expected. She looked perfectly torn between shock and amazement. "That- that's astounding, Morgan." I was incredibly flattered.

"It's beautiful," said Lew. I glanced at him and saw his eyes lingering on me like a caress, and my whole body heated with the praise.

"How do you feel?"

"Pardon?"

Nadia repeated herself. "How do you feel, Morgan?"

"Oh, I don't know."

"Well think about it."

I did. I felt tired. Not sleepy but as though I'd just gone on one of Lew's infamous 'we'll just go for a gentle jog for twenty miles or so' runs. At the same time, I felt good, though. For the first time, I wondered whether using magic gave off the same endorphins that exercise did.

"I feel ok. I'm tired, like I've done a workout, but I feel good."

Lew coughed, and I realised he might be thinking that we had done some pretty intense work-outs that morning. Nadia watched me closely and it was almost like when the elder looked at me, only less intimidating. I didn't expect her to casually order her warriors to behead me or something, which I kind of did expect from the elder. There was a particularly gruesome fairytale that the *uasal* told about the little prince who wandered into *curaidh* territory. There was a lot of beheading in it. And a store of treasure, a pot of boiling oil and a *uasal* king with the power to turn dragons to ice. One of our nannies had been particularly fond of that one and we'd heard it every day before bedtime, which had been just the right timing to give me nightmares, thank you very much.

Nadia clicked her fingers. "Lew, a chair, if you please."

He brought over a chair and then wasn't sure whether Nadia wanted it for herself or for me, so he dithered in the middle until Nadia cried, "Urgh, men," and took the chair from him, set it down beside me and then practically forced me to sit in it.

"I'm fine, really."

"You're tired," they both said at the same time.

Lew crouched down beside me and put his hand on my knee. Where he touched, my leg warmed up and I realised that I was cold from the icy magic. His hand felt nice.

Nadia's dark eyes scanned us and I felt entirely seen in that instant. She definitely knew. Then she gave a wicked grin and asked, "Do you want to see Lew play with some of the weapons?"

Did she really need to ask? My tongue was practically hanging out at the thought.

I tried to play it cool, though. Somehow, I don't think either of them was fooled. "I suppose. If he's happy to."

Nadia cackled and said to Lew, "Get the Beheader, it's awesome."

"What?"

My voice might have come out a bit loud and high-pitched but any weapon called The Beheader was not what I wanted to see. Not at all.

Lew's hand squeezed my knee and he spoke in a low voice. "I'll show you whatever you want, Morgan. What would you like to see?"

"I don't know."

"Do you want to come and look at the weapons and I'll show you how to use the ones you like?"

"Yes."

Very much yes.

Nadia whined, "But the Beheader is awesome, Lew. It's massive and I never get to play with it because I'm not strong enough."

"Is it magic?"

Lew shook his head. "No, it's just massive."

"It's big enough to behead a dragon – in dragon form." I was a bit disturbed by how

Nadia's eyes glowed at the thought. Maybe that fairytale had been based on fact, after all.

"You realise it's never actually been used in battle, right, Nadia? I mean, it's not the most practical weapon."

Nadia pouted. "But I like it."

"Then *you* can drag it behind you into battle and try not to chop your own arm off with it. Stupid thing, it's far more effort than it's worth."

Nadia huffed and I felt a bit better.

As we walked through the rows of pikes and spears and shields and swords and daggers, Nadia said, "Just point at anything you want to see Lew use. You earned it by being spectacular. Like, seriously, I'm still kind of blind here from the magic." A soft smile touched her lips and she sighed wistfully. "I wish I could have seen you hit Dum with it. I bet it was glorious."

I didn't feel it was politic to respond to that, since it had, in fact, been great. But he was their cousin, so I didn't really think it wise to say so.

Lew, however, did answer. "Yes, it really was that good." He gave me a little smile that promised big things. "Morgan is officially a badass."

The feeling of pride that reared up inside me was a new one. I felt like a king, smug as anything that Lew Hoskins thought I was cool. And then I noticed the empty space on the wall and asked, "What should be there?"

CHAPTER 31: LEW

My first thought was that it had to be Dee and Dum. They'd been known to 'borrow' weapons before, and then they always returned them, spotlessly clean and undamaged. It was creepy, mostly because there had to be a reason they were so clean. Nobody had to clean an axe unless they'd used it to chop something and got it dirty. Simple, innocent training wouldn't get it dirty and they certainly wouldn't bother cleaning them unless they had to. I couldn't help but shudder every time they presented me with some weapon or armour they'd borrowed, shiny and polished, wearing identical smiles that promised they'd definitely tell me exactly what they'd done if I made the mistake of asking. So far, I'd never made that mistake, and I was glad of it.

"Hmm, that space should be a dagger."

Nadia shrugged. "Maybe somebody borrowed it."

I cringed, and she eyed me keenly. "You want to tell me exactly why that's a problem, Lew?"

"Uh, it's just it's a *biorach* dagger." Which meant it was sharp and strong enough to pierce a dragon's hide, which, needless to say, most metal couldn't. At least not without a lot of hacking, and some precision stabbing. Basically, to kill a dragon in dragon form with an ordinary sword, the dragon had to stand still and let you do it. Plain old metal didn't cut it with dragons. No pun intended.

"Ah." She had summed the situation up.

Thinking about what we'd need to do next, I realised that somebody would have to go and tell Nana, and that it was likely to have to be me. I eyed Morgan, contemplating just for a second whether it would be better to send him, since Gramps liked him so much and that was likely to make Nana a bit more reasonable. But then I realised there was no way I'd send my sweet little mate into the lion's den, so to speak – dragon's lair? – and, since I was Gramps' favourite anyway, it was probably best I told them. I'd just make sure Gramps was there when I broke it to Nana.

Then, in a flash of inspiration, I realised that Nadia hadn't said it did have to be me.

"Bagsy not telling Nana," I said. I might have shouted it, actually. Morgan jumped.

Nadia sighed in a very put-upon way, and said, "Very well. I'll do this for you, Lew, but you owe me big time."

She booped Morgan on the nose as she left and it was only when she was already out the door that I realised and said, pointlessly, "But you're *not* doing me a favour, you're just- oh, never mind."

Instead, I turned to Morgan and asked, "What kind of weapon do you want to see me use?"

Morgan looked at me like I'd grown an extra head. "We're just going to carry on?"

"Why shouldn't we?"

"Because... you've been robbed."

"We haven't been robbed."

The look he gave me was pure disbelief. "If something valuable is missing, that means you've been robbed, Lew."

I used my most soothing voice to reassure him. "Morgan, we haven't been robbed. Nobody can get into the house—"

"Someone might have got in."

I realised then that he was probably thinking of the maybe-break-in at his own family castle.

"Nobody can get into here, Morgan. And, if they did, they would have taken something else rather than one little dagger. It's not the most dangerous weapon or the most valuable."

"Oh. But somebody took it, though…"

"Yeah, it must be someone who can come in here, which means it has to be family. They probably just borrowed it."

"Why would they need to borrow it?" Morgan asked, and then instantly cried, "Sorry! I didn't mean to ask that, it's none of my business."

"You can ask," I said. "Somebody probably wanted to… do something with it."

"O… k. That's not worrying at all."

I cringed again. "It was probably Dee and Dum. They like to play with things like that."

Morgan glanced around him, like he expected the two lunatics to have snuck up close behind him. "Now I really am worried."

"They won't hurt anyone here." I said it confidently, hoping I was right.

"Did—?" Morgan began, and then stopped.

"What?"

"Did Dee mean it when she called you 'baby brother'?"

"You caught that, huh? I was kind of hoping you were too distracted to notice."

"Oh?"

"Yeah." I dropped my head into my hands and my voice came out muffled by my fingers. "I didn't want you to know I was related to the insane one."

I felt Morgan's gentle fingers on my wrist and he tugged my hands away from my face. Despite the anxiety I'd seen etched into his face earlier, there was a little thread of amusement, too.

"I hate to be the one to tell you this, Lew, but your whole family is insane."

I groaned. "I know."

Morgan was standing right in front of me and he put his hand on my chest, and I couldn't deny that it felt right to have it there.

"Don't worry about it, though. I love them all anyway. And I love you."

For some reason, he seemed *surprised* that I pushed him up against the wall and pinned him there with my body, bringing my mouth down to his and kissing him, tasting him, like I'd been starved of him for weeks. But what did he expect after telling me that he loved me? He *loved* me. I'd never in a million years have thought Morgan would be the first of us to say it. At that point, I wasn't even sure he was interested in sticking around.

I kissed him and moaned into his mouth, loving the feel of it, of him pressed against me, and lost all sense of time.

Behind me, I heard a cough, and spun around, crouching into a defensive stance and already growling. It was Dimpy, standing in the doorway and fidgeting nervously, like he was deciding whether to run or not.

At the sight of him, I calmed. "Sorry, you just surprised me."

He gave me a tentative smile and asked, "Can I come in?"

I was glad he hadn't come in before, since I might have attacked out of sheer instinct if I'd felt threatened, especially when my vulnerable little mate was beside me. As I thought that, I realised two things: firstly, that was probably exactly why Dimpy hadn't come any closer, and, secondly, he now knew about me and Morgan, whatever it was we even were.

"Sure, come in. We were just..."

Thankfully, Dimpy cut me off. "Nana sent me down to check the rest of the armoury. She says something is missing."

"That's right."

It was only when Morgan shifted that I noticed I was pressed up against him, holding him against the wall and instinctively shielding him from view. I eased away and watched Dimpy walk around the other side, leaving the showcases and cabinets between us. He was studying the array of weapons and armour on the opposite wall with intense interest.

"Did you notice that anything else had been touched?"

"No." I went over to the far end of the

room and rounded the corner, wanting to look Dimpy in the eyes. It seemed strange that he was there. "Why are you really here, Dimpy?" Ok, so I wasn't great at subtle. Sometimes, I just had to ask outright.

He squeaked, and I felt bad for startling him. "To check the rest of the armoury, like I said. I didn't mean to... intrude."

His eyes darted down, almost too quickly to notice, but I did notice and then I realised what was making him blush and stammer. I was really fucking hard from where I'd been rubbing against Morgan and my dick was jutting out the front of my jogging bottoms. It looked pretty fucking obnoxious, even to me.

"Ah, shit. Sorry, Dimps."

"No problem," he said, studying that wall really closely.

That still didn't answer my question. "Wait, Nana sent you to check everything? But one of the family must have taken the dagger."

"Oh, um, well, you see, normally it's only... certain people who take weapons. And they always tell Nana what they've taken. No-body takes without permission."

"So you're saying it might not be Dee and Dum?"

"I'm saying I'm here to check whether any-thing else has been taken as well."

He was good at not answering that particular question.

"Ok, we'll get out of your hair."

I'd like to say that he didn't look relieved, but I'd be lying. I turned to go and Morgan walked ahead of me to the door. Before I'd gone more than three steps, though, Dimpy coughed and said, "Um, Lew? Can I have a- a word, maybe?"

Morgan glanced back over his shoulder to check with me and then left.

"Yes?"

"It's none of my business, and I didn't mean to eavesdrop, it's just you were- and I was right outside- and it's not like I could have avoided-"

Dimpy was worse than I was at articulating things when he was nervous. Which was ironic, because he had more letters after his name than in it, with all the qualifications he had.

"It's ok, whatever it is."

"Right, well, I couldn't help but notice you didn't say it back. That was all."

And with that, he basically fled to the other side of the room.

CHAPTER 32: MORGAN

Ok, so maybe Lew hadn't told me he loved me back but then I had sprung that on him suddenly, and I'd done it without meaning to, as well. It's just that I'd been looking into his eyes and he looked so adorable and handsome that it had just sort of slipped out. And it was true.

But he had taken me to the family armoury and shown me the secrets inside. That had to mean he loved me, right?

I would have been content to leave it as it was. I would have spent the next few months exactly as we were, being trained by Lew and kissing him and making love at night (and, ok, sometimes during the day, as well). But Fate had other ideas. And, by Fate, I mean my father.

Lord Somerville was something of a force of nature. Since I could remember, I'd seen him coming and simply got out of the way, which is exactly what I would do if I saw a tornedo or a tsunami or an earthquake heading my way. Who wouldn't?

That meant that, when I got a call from Alfie, I was a little jumpy about it. I always was. There was just some instinct in me that expected it to be bad news. I have no idea whether that makes me a terrible person or not.

I answered the call just as I reached the top of the first flight of stairs leading to my room.

"Morgan? Are you ok? Are you safe?"

Panic shot through me. "What happened, Alfie?"

"I can't- are you ok, Morgan?"

I took a deep breath and tried to talk calmly. When Alfie got like that, he needed calmness and reassurance. I knew from experience that, if I got agitated and started demanding answers, he'd get even worse and neither of us would make any sense. So I stated by answering his questions.

"Yes, Alfie, I'm ok. I'm perfectly safe. Are you ok?"

"I- it's not that I'm *not* ok, it's just that—"
"What do you mean you're not ok?"

I admit, I might have screeched that a little loud. Alfie grumbled on the other end of the phone, "Mind my ears, Morgan. I told you, I'm ok."

"No, you said you're not *not* ok, which means..." I thought about it. "...that you are ok. Fine. Whatever. The point is, you phrased it badly."

Behind me, Lew barrelled around the corner, already shouting, "What happened?" His eyes were wide and he was scanning the corridor, looking for threats.

"Nothing happened, sorry. My brother decided to *lie* to me."

On the other end of the phone, I heard Alfie huff, "I didn't lie. I can't help it if my words aren't coming out right. It's probably a concussion. Wait, do you need to have hit your head to get a concussion?"

Lew and I both answered at the same time, pretty much giving away the fact that everyone was listening in to all aspects of this conversation. "Yes."

"Oh, well it can't be that, then," mused Alfie. "I didn't get shot in the head."

"What do you mean you were shot?"

I was back to screeching again. Lew winced and then walked right up to me and put one arm comfortingly around my shoulders. I was glad. I felt so helpless, being so far away from Alfie.

"It was only in the arm."

I needed those deep breaths again if I wanted clear, straight answers. "Alfie, tell me: were you shot?"

"Yes."

I resisted more screeching, but only just. My jaw was gritted tightly together when I asked, "Where were you shot?"

"Over by the boundary, where our den is."

Even as most of my brain was taken up with the fact that my baby brother was shot, a little part of it was spared to drop its head into its palms and sigh that now Lew thought Alfie and I had a den, like children playing in the woods.

"I meant where on your body."

"I told you, my right arm."

"Can I take it from the fact that you're chatting to me that you are not in immediate danger?"

"Yes."

"Where are you?"

"In my bedroom."

"Have you told someone?"

"Yes. I told Lord Somerville and then Mother, and she sent me to get my arm looked at. Glenwise had to cut the wound open again to get the bullet out because it had got lodged."

I ground my teeth. That meant he'd been standing there waiting for someone to help him for probably over an hour, if he'd begun to heal over the bullet-wound.

"And are you going to recover fully?"

"Glenwise says I'll be fine by tomorrow. It hurts a bit and he wasn't very sympathetic. He kept telling me not to be a baby but he was there with this scalpel and you *know* I don't like blood."

I turned into Lew, pressing my forehead against his chest. I wanted nothing more than to go to my sweet brother and give him the hug that nobody else would think to give him. It occurred to me then that having Glenwise slice his arm open and root around for a bullet might be the first human contact Alfie had had since I'd gone.

"I'm coming to see you."

"Um, that's what I wanted to talk to you- well, I suppose it doesn't matter, if you're already coming. But I didn't want you to come home just because of me. I suppose it's not because of me, though, is it?"

"I am coming home because of you, Alfie, I'm coming to see you." I looked up at Lew and asked, "Can I go now? I can be there by tonight."

Lew was frowning. For a second, I thought he was frowning at me and I'd done something wrong, but then he held my hand – with the phone in it – and asked, "Alfie, what did you ring to talk to Morgan about?"

"Which one is that, Morgan? Is it the hot instru- never mind! I didn't say anything. I was just asking which *curaidh* he was, I wasn't guessing."

Alfie was the worst liar I'd ever met. He was also a big-mouth because Lew's lips quirked up and he said, "It's Lew here. I'm Morgan's instructor. Tell me, Alfie, does that make me the hot instructor or is there—?"

I pushed at Lew, mortified that he'd find out I'd been talking to Alfie about him. Alfie – bless him – didn't want to land me in it but he knew he was a terrible liar and so he went for something that wasn't a lie. It also didn't do anything to stop it being entirely obvious that Lew *was* the hot instructor.

"Um, I don't know any of you so I can't say which of you is the hot one. Not that Morgan's said any of you are hot, you're not. You're probably not. Not that you're not pretty, I'm sure you're very attractive. Just nobody's mentioned it either way."

"Yeah, thanks Alfie, I'll take it from here."

"Sorry, Morgan. *Is* he the hot one?"

I glared at a sniggering Lew and answered tightly, "Yes, he is."

"Is he going to escort you home?"

"Um…"

"Yes, I am."

I looked up at him. "Are you sure?"

He shrugged. "Sure, why not? We can get there by tonight, see Alfie, spend tomorrow with him and then be back here by nightfall."

That sounded like a brilliant plan.

Alfie, though, said, "You're not going back. To the *curaidh*'s, I mean."

I wanted to sigh because talking to Alfie was often quite hard work, but a niggle of worry began to gnaw at my stomach and I had to ask, really calmly, "What do you mean I'm not coming back?"

"Oh, yes, that's why I rang you." Brilliant, I thought. Now he tells me why he rang me. Not to tell me he was shot or anything.

"Yes?"

"Lord Somerville's a bit… annoyed."

Which meant he was furious.

"He, um, was talking about protecting the borders and there was a bit of a fuss about whether or not whoever-it-was that shot me was inside the territory or not. I'm not allowed to leave the house now, in case they can get in, but they think the gunman – or gunwoman, I suppose, since I didn't see them, and there's no reason why it shouldn't be a woman – in fact, we don't even know if it's a dragon but there's no smell so Seren reckons it would probably be a dragon—"

"Alfie? The point?"

"Oh yes! I'm not allowed near the borders because they reckon whoever-it-was stayed on the outside and shot in."

"So you're safe now?"

"I suppose. It's just we had that- um, that incident, you know, the other week, and, um, there might be a connection. Or not. Anyway, Mother said she didn't like you being away from home at a time like this, and Lord Somerville said you needed to stay where you were and learn to earn your keep, and *she* said you'd be more useful at home, and *he* said you'd be more useful when he's got you mated—"

Lew's snarl cut him off. "Nobody claims you without your permission."

"Um, Morgan? Are you ok? If you're hurting my brother, I'm going to come over there and... do something really terrible. And don't be put off because I don't know what that is yet. It'll be worse than you think, because I'll have time to plan it. Morgan?"

"I'm ok, Alfie. Lew wouldn't hurt me. None of the Hoskins' would."

"What did he mean about being claimed?"

I didn't think that was a conversation that we could really have over the phone, with me standing in the corridor in the Hoskins' castle. "I'll talk to you about it when I see you."

"If you say so. I just wanted to warn you that you might be summoned home. Depends if Mother wins or not."

"Ok."

I said goodbye to Alfie, he promised to rest, and to let me know how he was later that night and again in the morning, when he should be fully healed. As I hung up, Lew took my hand and led me along the corridor towards his bedroom.

"My room is nearest," he said. "And I want to talk to you."

We got to his door, he pushed it open and, as I moved past him, he breathed in my ear, "And I've currently got more lube than you."

It meant I stepped into his room with equal parts trepidation and excitement. I was so screwed.

CHAPTER 33: MORGAN

The first thing I noticed about the room was that it didn't have Lew's scent in it. I'd known that already, since I'd been in it before, and since dragons kept their scent shielded, but it did mean I wanted to pout because I couldn't smell my mate.

And it was still so weird to think of Lew as my mate. Incredible, yes, but weird.

Behind me, Lew shut the door and locked it. Even a week ago, I'd have panicked at that sound, but now I didn't get so much as a murmur of unease. There was no way Lew would hurt me.

He stood by the door and tilted his head, studying me.

I shifted from foot to foot, uncomfortable. "What?"

"I've never heard you sound like that before."

"Like what?"

"Unguarded, I guess. Passionate. Except, you know, when we're having sex. But that's a different kind of passion."

He was looking at me strangely, as though he was trying to work me out. I wasn't sure whether it would be good for me if he did. I wasn't sure whether he liked seeing the passion or whether he was turned off by it.

"Did it bother you?"

"No, Morgan, it didn't. Not at all. I just- I'm not explaining this very well." He ran a hand through his short hair and then sighed. "You really care about Alfie, don't you?"

I blinked at him. That was a stupid question. Of course I cared about Alfie. "He's my brother," I said, since apparently it needed explaining.

Lew smirked a little and I absently thought that it looked good on him, that kind of quiet confidence.

"Yes, but you don't sound like that when you talk to your mother, and you don't sound anything like it when you talk about your father. I've only ever heard you sound quite like that when you talk about Alfie."

"Alfie's special," I said.

Lew's smile became broader and he

moved nearer to me so we were standing chest to chest, and he raised his hands to settle on my hips.

"Yes, he is. I like him, and not just because he called me hot."

"He didn't call you hot, *I* called you hot."

For some reason, I didn't want Lew thinking anyone else got to have an opinion about his looks at all. He shouldn't care about what anyone else thought, he should only care whether *I* found him attractive.

That smile stretched his lips as wide as they'd go. He looked like he'd been given the best toy on Christmas day.

"Yes, you did, didn't you? And don't think I don't appreciate it."

"Don't start using double negatives, you'll get as confusing as Alfie."

He sniggered and said, "Is he always like that?"

"Like what?"

"Calm down, I didn't mean anything bad. I told you, I like him. He must be something else for you to love him as much as you do."

"He is. He's..." I struggled to find the right word. Everything I could think of made him sound too weird. I didn't want to say 'special', even though that's exactly what he was, and I didn't want to say 'unique' either because that made it sound like his beautiful personality was too different, so I settled on, "Perfect."

It felt right.

Lew lowered his mouth to mine so that our lips were barely touching, and then he said, "*You*'re perfect, Morgan. Did I tell you that already?"

I shook my head.

"Well you are."

As he spoke, our lips brushed together and I felt the teasing tingles along the sensitive skin and barely resisted pushing forward for more.

He carried on, and I was entranced. "I love you, Morgan. I know it seems quick, but it isn't, not really, not for us. I would have said it back to you earlier but you blindsided me. I wasn't expecting it."

I pulled back, worried that I'd gone too far. "You don't have to say it back."

"I mean it. I love you, Morgan. I love you." He punctuated each sentence with a tiny kiss, and my whole body buzzed with happiness.

We were lying on the bed, kissing in a slow, leisurely way, exploring each other's mouths with our tongues and each other's bodies with our hands, when my phone rang again. At any other time, I might have ignored it, but Alfie had told me that Lord Somerville might be summoning me back home, so I scrambled off Lew, my hard dick deflating at the mere possibility that I was about to talk to my father.

It took me a moment to find my phone, since it had fallen out of my pocket where Lew's big hands had been all over my arse, and so, when I answered, I barely caught a glimpse of the name on the screen and my father began the conversation by snapping, "Finally. What took you so long to answer?"

"Um..." I definitely wasn't going to tell him what had actually taken me so long. I didn't think there were many things that would make my father lose his cool but me casually telling him that my phone had fallen out of my pocket because I'd been humping my *curaidh* instructor would definitely be one of them. I didn't fancy hearing that meltdown.

"You're coming home." Lord Somerville didn't believe in breaking bad news softly. He said it how it was. "I have informed the elder, and everything is arranged. You will receive an escort to the castle tomorrow morning."

"Tomorrow?" I couldn't keep the devastation out of my voice, which was an amateur error.

"Yes. I wanted you to come back tonight but the elder insisted it was impossible. Couldn't arrange it in time. Not enough discipline."

I said nothing, not sure what I could say to tell him he was wrong that wouldn't make my father angry. Beside me, I felt the growl coming from Lew. I didn't think my father heard it – it was more a disturbance in the air, rather than a noise.

Lord Somerville continued. "Be ready to leave. You'll come in the car, so pack your belongings. You won't be returning."

That broke my silence.

"But- but Father, why? I mean, I'm here to learn—"

"I have changed my plans for you, son. Don't be difficult."

"I didn't mean—"

"And don't interrupt. You'd better not have learned any *curaidh* manners, I won't have them in my castle."

"No, Father."

"Report to me when you arrive."

I knew the tone of his voice, and that was the end of the conversation. Before he could hang up, I blurted, "Wait, Father, tell me: why am I being summoned back?"

"Because I wish it."

"Can't you tell me?"

"Watch your tongue, son. I'll have to re-teach you your manners, I see."

I said nothing, knowing it would be worse if I did.

"You'll come home because you'll be more use to me here. Certainly more use than you are now."

He disconnected the call and I sat there

stunned. Even for Lord Somerville, that had been abrupt.

Behind me, Lew was still growling softly, a constant vibration in the air.

"Did you- did you hear that?" I asked, closing my eyes and hoping – even though I knew it was useless – that Lew hadn't heard my father speak to me like that. I felt ashamed that my mate had heard me being reprimanded.

The words came out on a growl, almost indistinguishable. "I heard."

"I guess I'm going, then."

The words broke something in me. Saying them aloud was much worse than hearing them. I could almost have pretended it was a dream until then.

Lew was beside me in an instant, his voice in my ear and his arm around me.

"No, you're not."

"I have to go. Lord Somerville summoned me."

"But… I don't want you to."

He looked frustrated, like he couldn't think of a better way of explaining himself than that, but, strangely, it was the perfect thing for him to say. I clung to him.

Eventually, I managed to get my mind in order enough to ask, "Will you come with me?"

"Yes, of course."

I clung to that, too. The idea that I would

have Lew with me for just a little longer.

We stood in the middle of his room, pressed tightly together, my phone on the floor where I'd dropped it. I didn't remember doing that.

At last, Lew spoke. "Do you want to go, Morgan?"

"It doesn't matter what I want."

"Of course it matters."

"No, it doesn't." I was very certain of that. I had a lot of evidence for that. "Lord Somerville has summoned me. I'll go. There's nothing else to it."

Lew pulled back from me, forcing my head up to look me in the eyes. "That's not all there is to it. I'm asking you, Morgan, do you *want* to go?"

Slowly, I shook my head. I didn't know what Lew could possibly do to persuade Lord Somerville to let me stay, but if there was any chance he could, I'd take it. I wanted to stay. I wanted to be wherever Lew was.

CHAPTER 34: LEW

"Y ou're not going back there if you don't want to."

Morgan shook his head. "I have to go, I've been summoned."

That he thought he could be summoned like a dog made my dragon prickle and its spiked tail lash. We weren't going to allow it.

However, I was aware that I might be a bit much for Morgan if I began to hand over control to my dragon – it wasn't something I normally did, and for good reason – and so I changed the subject. Slightly.

"What do you think he wants you back for?"

"Um, I don't know."

Something in the way he said it made me

sure that Morgan knew *exactly* what he was being summoned for.

I raised my eyebrows at him. He squirmed, which was the cutest thing I've ever seen, but I made sure to keep my face hard rather than melt into a puddle of goo. I wanted an answer.

"I really don't know," he cried at last. It came out on a puff of air like he'd been holding his breath. "You heard him; he didn't say! He just wants me to go back and be useful."

If I hadn't learned to read Morgan so well, I might have been satisfied with that. But I *had* learned to read him, and there was something he was keeping back.

"Morgan?"

"I- I think he's going to mate me off." His voice was small and it nearly broke me.

My first instinct was to deny it. I didn't want that to happen and, while I was denying it, my dragon was roaring in my head loud enough to drown out my words.

"What makes you think that?"

"He said I had to be useful. I've never been useful to him before because I can't control my magic well enough. The only thing I can think of that would help him is to make an alliance with somebody. You know, somebody powerful. Be their mate."

The dragon's roar burst out of me and I felt my skin shimmer with the moment just before my shift. Fuck, I needed to calm down. I was getting nearly as bad as Dane; if I didn't get a grip, I'd break my newly-replaced windows trying to push my dragon form out of my room.

I closed my eyes and breathed deeply, talking to my dragon in my head. *He's ok, he's standing right here in front of you, he's safe. Calm down, or you're going to scare him. Let him talk, you arsehole. Listen to him, then we can work out how to stop this.*

When I opened my eyes, with my dragon barely concealed behind them, I expected Morgan to be looking at me with horror, but he wasn't. He was staring with a look of wonder on his face.

"I'm sorry about that, I'll do better," I promised.

He reached out a hand to touch my cheek. "You're so beautiful when you shift. Was that because you don't want me to mate somebody else?"

I swallowed. "Yes."

He was *my* mate. I was his. How could I ever belong to anyone but him? If he mated someone else, I wouldn't be able to survive.

Shit. I realised, with sudden certainty, that, if I lost Morgan – however I lost him – my dragon would *ruith*. It would just rampage until somebody stopped it.

Outsiders – shifters and witches and sprites and fairies and humans who knew about dragons – all thought that a dragon's *ruith* was in anger. It wasn't. It was always in despair. They thought it was to destroy things, to break whole buildings down and spew fire, but it wasn't. It was to goad somebody into killing them. It was a complete loss of control.

In my family, nobody would kill someone if they got a bit out of control, if they were violent or angry, we'd just capture them, bind them, wait for them to calm down, and then help them solve whatever problem had caused them to get angry. That had happened just the year before, when Uncle Milton had shifted and destroyed a section of the south wall in anger. Sure, he'd been angry, but he hadn't been beyond help. Right at that moment, he was probably playing with his kids. That had been a moment of emotion for him, and he'd overcome it. A *ruith* was an eternity. There was no coming back from it. Outsiders killed a dragon who was rampaging out of fear and desperation, and dragons would kill them out of mercy. It didn't matter whether we even knew them or not, we'd do it. I'd done it, just the once.

Forty years into my career as a soldier, my unit had been sent out to stop a dragon's *ruith*. Twenty of the finest soldiers I'd ever met, four of us dragons, and we barely managed to kill it. I still remembered the way it looked, the way it fought with no regard to its safety. It was unnatural. And, in the end, I still believe it *let* us kill it. I saw its eyes. Sometimes, in the night, I remembered those eyes. I'd never been able to fathom the depth of emotion I'd seen, never understood why it had destroyed so much, and allowed itself to be destroyed in turn. At that moment, with Morgan in front of me and the feeling of being right on the edge of losing him, I finally understood. And it scared me.

"I told you, you're not being claimed by anybody you don't want."

"I don't think my father will listen to reason."

"I'm not asking your father, I'm telling you – you're not being claimed unless you want to be."

He tilted his head, studying me. I never felt more seen than when Morgan's silver-blue eyes fixed on me and scoured my face.

"Will you stop it?"

"Yes." I felt that was a promise I was making, and I was just fine with that.

"You know if you do that, you'll anger Lord Somerville?"

"So? You're not his property, he can't just use you how he wants."

"You'll break your alliance with the Somervilles, if you anger him."

I thought about that. For all of two seconds. It really didn't matter. Nothing mattered except Morgan.

"Somerville can fuck off." I was so witty when I was riled, I know.

"You can't make decisions like that. That's your elder's place."

"Nana won't mind. Not if keeping you here is keeping you safe. She'll tell Lord Somerville to fuck off herself."

I kind of wanted to see her do just that, actually.

For a horrible moment, I saw Morgan's eyes become watery and a single tear slipped over his lashes and ran down his cheek.

"You mean- I can stay here with you?"

I was on him in an instant, wrapping him in my arms and crushing him against me. I had to remind myself not to hold him to me too tightly, but I wanted all of him pressed against all of me.

"Of course you can stay, Morgan. You're family. You're my mate. I *want* you here, with me."

"Oh."

It seemed I had to keep reminding him of that.

His face was pressed against my chest, between my pecs, and his voice was slightly muffled, but he asked, "Can I still go and see Alfie?"

I pulled back just slightly, just enough so that I could peer down and see his face. "Yes.

We'll go to the Somerville castle tomorrow and you can see Alfie. We'll tell your father that you're my mate and that you're coming back home with me."

I meant every word, which is why I was a bit surprised to hear Morgan laugh. It was just a burst of laughter, barely a couple of seconds long, and it had a slightly hysterical edge to it.

"You can't do that."

"Yes, we can."

"He won't let me leave again."

"You mean he'll keep you there and force you to be claimed by someone else?"

I saw the fear flit over his features. "Yes."

"I'm not going to let that happen, Morgan."

"How are you going to stop him? All he has to do is have you thrown out and then he can do what he wants with me."

I did not like the fact that Morgan seemed to accept this was normal behaviour. But he was right. Unless I was beside him, there was nothing I could do to protect him. And if I left him there, unclaimed, anybody who was bigger and stronger than him would be able to force a claiming on him.

Then I had the best idea I'd ever had.

"What if I'd already claimed you?"

CHAPTER 35: MORGAN

My heart beat furiously in my chest at the possibility that Lew Hoskins would claim me.

"You would do that?"

"Seriously, Morgan? Don't you know that I want to?"

That sounded like a trick question. "Uh... do you?"

"Yes, I want to claim you. I want to be yours – I want you to be mine. I know I said we couldn't rush this decision, because it's a lifelong commitment and it's not like we can undo it, but I *want* to be mated to you for the rest of my life. I love you, Morgan."

I thought about it.

That probably wasn't the most romantic thing to do, under the circumstances, but I needed to get things clear in my head.

If Lew claimed me, nobody else would be able to do it. I'd belong to Lew already. The deed would be done, and there would be no undoing it.

If I mated somebody without his approval, though – and a *curaidh* no less – my father would be angry. Not just annoyed, but absolutely furious. I asked, needing to check, "And you're sure I could stay here with you?"

"Yes. We'll stay wherever you want to."

Ok, so if my father disowned me, I'd have somewhere to live. That was ok. And he wouldn't be able to hurt me because I'd be living in a *curaidh*'s castle with a whole host of warrior dragons to protect me, assuming they decided I was worth the trouble. I couldn't exactly see why they would, though.

"Won't your family be angry? To lose an alliance with the Somervilles?"

Lew shrugged. Shrugged! Like an alliance with my family was something he could take or leave.

"Right," I said, thrown off balance a bit. "You need to ask your elder's permission, though."

At that, Lew grinned. My heart beat an extra beat at the sight of it.

"I think we already have Nana's blessing."

"Um, are you sure? You don't sound sure."

He did sound sure, actually, but he'd said he *thought* we had her permission, and that wasn't quite the same as *knowing* we had it.

Lew growled, "I'm not asking anybody's permission to claim my mate. Except yours. Yours is the only opinion that matters."

I don't know why, but I felt my dragon swell inside me, puffing up with pride. I'd never felt that before. Normally my dragon stayed small inside me, unnoticed and unremarkable. Clearly, it liked us being important to Lew. If he didn't watch out, my dragon was going to get a big head.

Still, I tried to be logical. "But it affects her whole clan. Won't she be angry—?"

"Nana will support us, not matter what. She wants us both to be happy and she's not stupid enough to stand between fated mates."

He dropped a tiny kiss to my lips, making them tingle.

"Besides, even if she is angry, she'll get over it. And I'll feel much better walking into your father's castle tomorrow knowing he can't force a claiming on you."

I didn't think we'd really covered his elder's potential anger properly, especially since he'd just admitted there was the possibility that she really might get angry about us.

"Will she be angry because it's me or angry because it'll cause problems?"

"She won't be angry with us, Morgan, she'll be angry with your father. Besides, Gramps is cheering us on. He's a romantic at heart. And I'm his favourite grandchild. Trust me, Nana won't get a say in the matter."

I almost believed that. If the woman could mate a human, she was probably absolutely besotted. Maybe having her mate on our side was enough.

"Do you think we should ask, though?"

"I told you, I'm not asking permission. It's our business, not anybody else's."

The more I thought about it, the more that made sense. If Lew claimed me behind his elder's back, it would mean she had plausible deniability. Not that I really thought that would stop Lord Somerville holding her responsible.

As I considered, Lew kept his arms looped around my waist and looked down at me, waiting patiently. I flushed as I realised I'd been thinking about it too long.

"I'm sorry, I didn't mean to take ages. I- I was just thinking. Not that I need to think about whether I want you to claim me, but—"

I was silenced by a kiss.

"It's alright, Morgan, I don't mind. I'm not rushing you. I want you to be sure about this and, if you're not sure by the time we leave tomorrow, that's fine. I'll only claim you when you're ready. Not before. I'd rather wait forever than claim you and have you regret it."

He actually shuddered when he said that, like he thought I'd regret letting him claim me, like it actually pained him to imagine me resenting the power he'd have over me.

I realised then that I found it ridiculous to be standing there waiting when what I wanted – what I'd wanted for weeks – was to have Lew Hoskins claim me as his own. I wanted to belong to him. It would cement our bond, yes, but I was his anyway. It was ridiculous to wait.

I leaned forwards and went up on my tiptoes. "I want you to claim me, Lew. I'm yours already."

I might have expected to see relief in his eyes, or even satisfaction. I didn't expect to hear a sob escape his lips and to see tears brimming in his eyes.

"I'm sorry," I cried. "Was that wrong?"

"No, no! It was perfect. I feel like such a tit, crying when I've just got everything I wanted, but... I just feel so happy."

I was stunned. I couldn't help it. I started to laugh. I was so filled with joy that I couldn't stop myself. I couldn't remember the last time I'd laughed like that – it had probably been when I'd been with Alfie, who always seemed to make me laugh.

As I laughed, I pulled myself up Lew's body, wrapping my arms around his neck and kissing him. I tasted the salt on his lips, mixed with his own unique flavour, and I dived into his mouth to taste more.

"Fuck, Morgan, I- you're everything."

I didn't know what he meant, but I'd go with it. If Lew Hoskins thought I was everything, then I'd be happy with that.

We kissed for a long time, in no rush to do more, and Lew held me close to his body so I could feel the ridges of his muscles and the hard press of his erection in my thigh. As he kissed me and ran his hand over my body and rubbed against me, Lew gradually worked me up into a state of arousal that had me panting and begging. Apparently, I wasn't proud.

"Please, Lew, please."

"I've got you, Morgan. I'm going to make you feel good."

I was already feeling pretty good. I was feeling amazingly good, actually. I could hardly imagine feeling better but, if Lew wanted to try, I was just fine with that, too.

He manoeuvred us both over to his bed and pressed me back against it. I fell onto the covers with a grunt and he stood back to look at me. If the look on his face was anything to go by, he had a thing for flushed and writhing blondes.

He stripped and I was disappointed it was over so quickly. That is right up until the point he stood naked before me and then I thought he was probably a genius for getting undressed as quickly as possible.

As he stood there, I stared, taking in his broad chest and long legs that were thick with muscle. His cock was hard and pointing directly at me, like a challenge.

Lew smirked and stroked a hand along his length, making it bob. "I guess I have to strip you, huh?"

Oh yeah. I'd forgotten about my own clothes.

As I reached for the hem of my shirt, Lew's hands batted them away and he pushed me back down against the bed, crawling over me and straddling my legs.

He unbuttoned my shirt very deliberately and I couldn't help but buck up every now and again. My dick was desperate for any kind of pressure and my pants weren't cutting it.

At last, my shirt slid open and I sat up so Lew could slip it off my shoulders. He was panting, as turned on as I was, and I felt a rush of power. Getting my trousers and pants off was much quicker. I practically kicked them off and Lew let me, tugging them over my feet and throwing them onto the floor.

When he kissed me again, my body lit up as though it was bathed in firelight. I could feel his warm skin against mine, the little hairs tickling against my chest and my legs, and his gloriously erect penis rubbing against mine. I was already so hard I was actually worried I wouldn't make it.

He broke the kiss and panted against my mouth, "Fuck, you turn me on so much."

I was beyond words but the way I gripped his body, trying to press it harder against mine, must have let him know that I felt the same way.

"I'm going to prep you. Let me know if you want me to stop – I don't want to hurt you."

I nodded, and Lew leaned over to the bedside table to pick up a bottle. I could feel myself blush when I saw it, since it was what anyone else would think was a normal amount of lube for someone to have. I swear Lew knew what I was thinking because he chuckled and kissed my heated cheeks.

I heard the cap snick open, and saw Lew shift so he was braced above me on one arm, and then I felt a warm wet grip on my dick. It wasn't what I was expecting, and I yelped, bucking my hips to thrust my dick further into that grip.

He let me rut into his hand for a while and then he slid his hand away and I gave a tiny whine. I really was shameless in bed. Or maybe it was only in bed with Lew.

Shifting again, he pushed my legs up, bringing my knees towards my chest. As I felt the first slick glide of his fingers down my taint and around my hole, I tensed up.

He murmured sweetly, "It's alright, Morgan. Let me in."

One finger circled my entrance and probed it, barely dipping inside. It was the strangest sensation, to have warm fingers there that weren't my own. And then he breached me, pushing his finger inside. I felt full already, and my body tensed. It took me a moment to realise that Lew wasn't moving, that his finger was still inside me, and he was pressing gentle kisses to my lips and jaw and ear.

When I'd adjusted to the feeling of him inside me, I gave a small grunt and pushed down on him, forcing his finger all the way in. His cock, which was pressed against the side of my arse, throbbed at the movement and I longed to feel it inside me.

He eased his finger in and out, slicking me up and spreading the lube. It felt incredible and he drove me steadily higher, towards my climax.

That steady climb was halted by the second finger he added. I'd used my own fingers before, but they weren't as big as Lew's and just two of his stretched me wide already. My erection flagged and he moved slowly, easing me gently open.

I wanted more, I knew that, I wanted the feeling of being full, of being joined to Lew completely, of his skin and his taste and his smell.

Unable to tell him what I wanted without

words, I forced my tongue to co-operate. I was nearly coherent when I said, "Your scent. Smell you."

I knew what I meant. I was so grateful that, apparently, Lew did as well.

Gradually, I was bathed in Lew's scent. It was deep and earthy, with a hint of wood and smoke. My cock throbbed as I took my first deep lungful of it and my whole body drew tighter with need. I felt like his scent infused every cell of my body, filling me with pleasure.

I began leaking pre-come faster and whimpered and twisted my body, trying to get more of Lew inside more of me.

"Your scent, Morgan. Release your scent."

I had to bargain with my dragon for that, just like I had to bargain for magic. My dragon controlled both, and it guarded both jealously. I was almost incoherent and wasn't sure I'd be able to concentrate enough, but my dragon was vibrating with the feeling of Lew on top of us and inside us, and it willingly surrendered.

CHAPTER 36: LEW

F uck, Morgan's scent nearly pushed me over the edge. I had to rear up onto my knees, with my fingers still inside him, and grab the base of my dick with my free hand. At least my nose wasn't pressed against Morgan's neck any more, or I really would have come just from his smell. There was nothing like it. I felt the pre-come leak from my slit and run over my fingers, even with my fist clenched tightly.

I tried to breathe deeply to get myself under control but, each time I took a breath, Morgan's scent filled me. It felt like being immersed in water, only I could breathe and the water was making my whole body prime with pleasure. Alright, so I wasn't the best at metaphors when I was this turned on. I was desperate for Morgan, any way I could have him, but my body knew – and my dragon knew – that we had to claim him. It was an instinct I hadn't been aware I had; I'd never felt the desire to sink my teeth into somebody's neck before, to bite through their skin and mark them as my own. But, fuck, I felt that with Morgan.

My desire made my control start to slip. I felt my eyes shift and I fought my dragon back, gripping the base of my dick hard and sliding my fingers in and out of Morgan's arse. I wanted to drive him as high as I was. If I wasn't so desperate to claim him, I'd make him come just from my fingers, suck his cock into my mouth and swallow his seed, but I needed to be inside him.

I pulled my fingers out slowly and wiped the remaining lube on my dick.

"Are you ready for me, Morgan?"

He gave a whine and nodded his head quickly, desperately. I felt the grin break over my face at the sight of him writhing beneath me. Fuck, he was the ultimate sexual fantasy.

I moved to line my dick up with Morgan's hole. The first touch of his skin against my sensitive head was almost too much and I was glad I still had my fist clenched around the base or I'd have gone off just from that.

My dragon wanted to push inside him, bury my dick in Morgan's arse and sink my teeth into his neck. I knew I'd come straight away, if I did. But I couldn't do that, not yet. There was no way I'd risk hurting Morgan.

I moved slowly, feeling my whole body shake with repressed need, and pushed my length inside Morgan's tight hole inch by inch.

"Breathe, Morgan," I whispered, and he took a deep breath.

When I was fully seated, I held myself above him and looked down into his eyes. They were wet and shiny and filled with emotion.

"I love you, Morgan."

"Love you."

Leaning forward to kiss him gently, I lowered myself down on top of him, pressing his legs down against his chest and settling my body over his. When I was ready, when I was kissing Morgan deeply and he was moaning constantly, and I could feel the wetness of his dick as it leaked pre-come, I began to move.

It was at once exquisite and painful to move inside him. The pleasure was so intense it was almost too much, and I wanted to go slow, to make sure Morgan felt the pleasure he should. As I rocked in and out of him, kissing his lips, dipping my tongue into his mouth, and murmuring how much I loved him, I gradually shifted my position so my dick stroked inside at a different angle. I knew I'd hit the spot I wanted when Morgan's whole body bucked up and he let out a keening shout that nearly deafened me. I pushed my lips to his and tried to drink that sound, wanting it inside me.

Having found his prostate, I kept that angle and moved slowly in and out, brushing against it again and again. Morgan began to sob, "Please, Lew, Lew," and I felt my dick throb inside him with the sound of my name on his lips.

I was moving as slowly as I could, but my body was demanding more and my balls were drawing tight. I wanted Morgan to come. I wanted to feel him fall apart beneath me.

Reaching between us, I found his dick and started to stroke. He began to orgasm at the first touch of my hand and I felt the way his cock throbbed in my palm, I smelled his release, and I came deep inside him from the pulsing tightness of his muscles around my cock.

My orgasm blinded me for a moment and I went light-headed, floating on euphoria, shouting Morgan's name. I hadn't even noticed my dragon push to the surface but I dropped my head instinctively to where Morgan had tilted his to the side, and used my sharp teeth to bite down.

I groaned as another wave of pleasure washed over me and my spent dick pulsed inside Morgan.

I was nearly as incoherent as he was, but I had to tell him, so I grunted, "Claim me."

His face was pressed to the side of mine, I tilted my head, exposing my neck, and I felt Morgan's lips graze the skin, kissing me. I wanted him to do it, I wanted that pain and that pleasure, if it meant I could wear his mark on my neck.

He sank his teeth in suddenly and I grunted, almost too exhausted to come. My lips pulled back in a smile at the feeling of the last of his come spurting between us.

I was practically boneless and lay heavily on top of him for a moment before trying to heave myself up. I wanted to take the weight off him, but he murmured, "Uh uh," and the arms that were wrapped around me clung tighter.

That was alright with me. I'd lay right where I was forever, if I could.

At last, I eased back, though, and let my softening dick slip out of him. I didn't have the energy to stand up just yet but I did manage to roll myself to the side so I wasn't squashing him any more. I also wasn't ready to let him out of my arms, so I dragged him with me as I rolled until he was sprawled on top of me, his sticky come and sweat between us and our mingled scents thick around us.

"Fuck, that was incredible, mate."

"Mmm hmm."

I chuckled, amused that someone as articulate as Morgan became so incoherent after sex, and my dragon rumbled with satisfaction that we'd been the ones to make him lose his words.

I stroked a hand down his back, revelling in my freedom to touch him. "I love you, Morgan. I'm so glad you claimed me as your mate."

"Didn't think... want me to claim... you too."

I could feel the way he was fighting to get the words out, which was adorable. "Of course I did. I'm so proud to belong to you. And to have you as my own. Nothing can part us now."

"Mmm good."

"Let me get up and I'll clean you up."

"Mmm minute more."

Laughing, I relented. "Alright, just one minute more."

CHAPTER 37:
MORGAN

I could totally get used to sharing showers with Lew. He held me up the entire time, which was handy, since my legs were decidedly unstable, for some reason. I actually considered that an advantage, since it meant I could stay pressed against Lew's hard muscles and warm skin, which was exactly where I wanted to be.

"Can you talk properly yet?"

"Don't know what you mean," I said, putting my nose in the air.

"Sure you don't."

Damn, he was smug. And it was really hot.

As we stood there, letting the suds rinse down our bodies, Lew said, "Conceal your scent again. I don't want anyone else scenting my mate."

I gave a little shiver as he called me his mate. It was official: I was his mate. We'd claimed each other. I still couldn't believe he'd let *me* claim *him*, too. I'd assumed I'd wear his mark and he would just... say he was mine. I couldn't deny, though, that I got a thrill from seeing the already-healed bite mark on his neck.

My fingers reached out automatically to touch it, but then stopped. I looked at Lew, waiting to see if he'd let me.

"You can touch. You can touch me anywhere, anytime, alright, Morgan?"

"Yes."

The skin under my fingers was smooth and warm, and I could feel the difference in the surface texture as I traced my fingers over the round scars that made up my bite mark.

I looked up at him, keeping my hand on his neck. "Are you going to conceal your scent, too?"

I know I didn't need to worry that his family would harm him if they scented him, but still. It was weird for a dragon to just walk around and let people smell him.

Lew frowned. "I *am* concealing my scent."

"Oh." Maybe it was just because there was so much of his scent in the air, but I could still smell him.

"Are *you* going to conceal *your* scent?" he asked.

I checked with my dragon. It had drawn our scent back in, making sure we were untraceable. I was sure of it. At least, my dragon was sure of it, and it was one of the things it was pretty anal about. "I have," I said.

"I can still smell you."

"It must be my scent in the air. It hasn't dispersed yet."

He leaned in to me, putting his nose to my neck right where his mating mark was, and I felt his tongue flick out to run along my skin, making me shiver, and then I heard him take a deep breath.

"No, it's not just left over. I can smell you still; you're still giving off your scent."

My heartrate sped up. That would be bad. If I couldn't conceal my scent, I couldn't hide. And it would mean my dragon was mistaken, which it never had been before. Inside, I felt my dragon huff in disapproval; it was sure my scent was concealed. But Lew said it wasn't.

"I can't be." My voice sounded panicked, even to my own ears.

"It's alright, Morgan, don't worry. We'll deal with it. You're probably just unsettled still. You're not used to revealing your scent at all, maybe it'll just take a little while for you to pull it all back in."

"Yes, that must be it," I said, but my heart still beat fast and my dragon assured me my scent was hidden.

As we continued to shower, though, my unease grew. "No," I said. "I can still smell you. That means it's just our scent still in the air. We probably gave off more scent than we realised and it's taking ages to clear." It wasn't helping that Lew's scent was making my body respond, since it was the sexiest smell I'd ever encountered. If I could distil an orgasm into a smell, that's what Lew would smell like.

He frowned. "I'm sure I can smell you." Again, he leaned down and pressed his nose into my neck and drew in a long breath. "I *can* smell you. You're giving off your scent still." He leaned back to look me in the eyes. "How strong is my smell? Is it fading already?"

Breathing in, I shook my head. "It's still strong. No, wait, it's not as strong as it was when we were, um, you know." I can't believe that I couldn't say *fucked* and I can't believe I blushed, as well.

"So it's just taking its time dispersing?"

"No." I was sure it was stronger than that. "I can still smell it, it's just it's not... as strong. I can't explain properly."

He tried to keep his face calm but I saw the tightening of his jaw. Lew was worried. That, unsurprisingly, did not help.

"Are we broken?" I asked.

"No, we're not broken. Nothing about you

is broken, Morgan. We're just..." I watched him struggle for an explanation. "Adjusting."

Right. Adjusting. That explained it.

We finished our shower in silence, Lew got us out, dried us, and helped me to get dressed before yanking on his own clothes.

"I think we should go and see Nana. And don't look so worried, she won't bite. I told you, we'll be fine."

That was all very well but the two of us had just destroyed whatever tenuous alliance she'd had with Lord Somerville and there was no way she'd be pleased about that. I really, really hoped her human mate was there so he could calm her down, just like Lew said.

As we left his room, Lew closed the door, leaving the window open so the last of our scent could diffuse into the atmosphere, but we both knew that was useless. He was still giving off a faint smell of earth and smoke and something else that made it uniquely *Lew*'s scent. I kept checking in with my dragon, who was still insisting that it had withdrawn our scent, but Lew kept casting worried glances at me so I was fairly convinced that he could still smell me. It meant I was incredibly nervous to step into the corridor of the Hoskins' castle where just anybody could come up to me and scent me. I didn't like to leave a trail behind me that they could track.

"Come on, it's not far."

Lew took my hand and we hurried along the thankfully deserted corridors until we reached her door. Lew knocked, and I glanced around us to make sure nobody else was around.

"Come in."

Lew had to tug me inside the room, which was surprisingly dainty and pleasant. The elder sat on a pretty floral sofa in front of a low coffee table, and her black eyes swept both of us, taking in our tense faces and the mating marks freshly made on our necks.

Even though I was afraid, and even though I swear I was blushing – again! Even though it wasn't like me at *all* – I still felt a strange satisfaction from wearing that mark. I was Lew's. He'd claimed me. She couldn't undo that. Nobody could undo it. I was his forever.

The elder stayed silent and motioned with one hand for us to go in further and take a seat. It was only when he moved that I even noticed her mate stand up from his chair by the window. He grinned wide at us, his eyes tacked to our mating marks, and he rushed forward and wrapped Lew in a hug, slapping him on the back and saying, "I see you finally got your head out of your arse."

When he pulled back, Lew said, "Um, yeah?"

I wanted to snigger at that, but I didn't.

Then the human turned to me and I was engulfed in the same hug. I froze, not sure what to do. I'd never been hugged by a stranger before. I patted him carefully on the back, making sure I was gentle – I didn't want to break the Hoskins' elder's mate, since I could only imagine how badly that would go for me.

"Congratulations, son," he said into my ear.

"Mmm," I said, trying to sound like I wasn't about to burst into tears. Apparently, I was not successful.

John pulled back and took my face in his hands. They were surprisingly warm. I have no idea why I'd expected a human to have cold hands.

"Welcome to the family, Morgan."

That was it. I burst into tears.

CHAPTER 38: LEW

I t irked me to see anyone's hands on my mate as he cried, but since it was Gamps, and since Morgan clung to him like a child, I let it go.

As Gramps soothed Morgan and patted him gently on the back and cooed, "It's alright, let it all out. It's been a long time coming and you're safe now," I met Nana's eyes. I knew, somehow, that she knew what I was thinking. I gave her a rueful smile.

"Come and sit down, Lew."

I was surprised that she didn't snap at me not to loom over her, which she usually did. But, as I moved forward and studied her, I saw that she looked grave.

"Nana, we—"

I started to explain, not sure what I was

going to say, since I wasn't going to apologise for claiming my mate, especially since it meant he'd be safe going back to his family.

"What's wrong?"

Shit, Nana always could read me too easily.

"Um, Morgan can't conceal his scent, um, at the moment," I said. He'd told me he could smell me, too, but I was sure I'd concealed it like normal. I realised that Nana had probably scented him as he'd walked in. I didn't like that.

"Yes, he can. His scent is concealed."

"Um," I began, not sure how to contradict her.

"Sit *down*, Lew."

Yep, there it was.

"And Morgan *has* concealed his scent. I can't smell him at all. I'd have told you if I could." Nana wrinkled her nose, as if the thought of scenting my mate was unpleasant. "And stop frowning at me."

"Sorry, Nana," I said, and eased onto the sofa opposite hers. I didn't like having my back to Morgan, though, and I twisted round to see him.

He peeked out from his hug with Gramps. "I- I *have* concealed my scent?"

He looked tentatively hopeful.

"Of course you have."

Gramps gave Morgan's shoulders a squeeze

and began to lead him over to the sofas. "Yes, you have, son. But you're a mated man now – you two will be able to scent each other regardless."

"What?"

"That's right. Nobody else will be able to smell you, but you'll be able to smell each other."

Gramps spoke with the air of a man who'd never quite understood why dragons were so twitchy about letting people scent them.

"How do you know?" I asked. After all, he was human. His nose wasn't as sensitive as ours.

He huffed, flapping his hands and wafting Morgan towards me. I reached out and snagged Morgan's hand, pulling him into my side and wrapping my arm around his shoulder. As he sat, I got a whiff of his scent. It was faint, but it was there. It was also delicious and I wanted to bury my face in his neck and inhale. That could be awkward, if I could always smell Morgan, since that pretty much meant I'd always be turned on.

"I," said Gramps, with an air of offended dignity, "can smell your Nana's scent, even when she conceals it. Even with my paltry human senses," he added, glaring at me.

I rolled my eyes. He was such a drama queen. I loved him.

Morgan exhaled, and I saw the relief on his face, even as he tried to keep his mask in place. I pressed a kiss to his temple, wanting to share his relief with him, wanting to comfort him.

"More important than that," said Gramps, sitting on the sofa next to Nana, "is your Mating Party."

"Our what?" I asked, just as Morgan tilted his head in confusion.

"Your Mating Party! Congratulations on becoming mated. You know, the whole family will want to celebrate this." His eyes sparkled, just as they always did at the thought of getting his whole family together. "It's going to be huge."

It was sweet of him, to want to throw us a party, to celebrate the most important thing that had ever happened to us. And, I suppose, he wanted to make a bigger fuss because it was me, his favourite grandchild, and Morgan, whom he was already coming to see as one of his own.

Nana, though, put a stop to that.

"No."

He turned to her with a gasp. "No? What do you mean *no*?"

"They're not having a mating party, John."

"But- they've just claimed each other. They're mates. We need to celebrate."

"No."

Gramps, in full flow now, put his hand over his heart and said, "But Edith, I've been planning this for *weeks*."

"Gramps! What do you mean you've been planning this?" I was pretty outraged myself, actually. "Why didn't you tell me?"

"Because your Nana has a non-interference policy when it comes to mates." He gave a dismissive huff and Nana let him. She'd never let me do anything so disrespectful, I knew that. "Pft. If you hadn't got a move on, I was going to have to come up with something to throw you two together. Lock you in the cellar, perhaps? You're not afraid of the dark, are you, Morgan?"

"Um, no." Morgan sounded baffled, which was about normal for one of Gramps' rants.

"Good. Wouldn't want to traumatise you."

"John, you don't need to lock them anywhere. They're already mated."

"Yes, yes. But just in case, I like to have a plan handy. If I could get Dane and his—"

I didn't want to hear about Dane. And I didn't want Morgan to hear how his monstrous cousin had broken poor Dane's heart.

"Gramps!"

"Don't give me that look, Lew. You should have claimed him the second you saw how bright he shone."

Fuck, I was sure I was blushing. I glared at Gramps for bringing up Morgan's *brightness* and he sniggered, totally unrepentant. Morgan glanced at me from the corner of his eye and I got the feeling he was going to be asking about that.

I made a mental note not to tell Gramps any more secrets.

"We'll have it tonight," he said.

"Have what?" I'd got lost somewhere in the middle of that conversation.

"Your party!"

Nana spoke again. Her tone was firm. "No."

Gramps deflated. Even he didn't push her too far.

Nana looked at Morgan and I tightened my arm around his shoulders.

"Morgan, I take it you got a message from your father?"

"Yes, Lady Hoskins."

Nana twitched. She hated being called that, probably because it was a *uasal* title and she didn't want to be associated with it. She softened her features, though, and said in quite a pleasant voice, "You'd best call me Nana, now you're family."

Morgan swallowed and I knew he was swallowing down his emotions again. On the basis that he called his own mum 'Mother' and his dad 'Lord Somerville', I didn't think he'd got a lot of affection over the years. Well, he was going to get all the love he could handle with us.

"I received a call from him earlier. He wants you to go back to his castle."

Morgan nodded.

"Since that is our agreement, I will go through with it. You will return to your father's house tomorrow." I saw the glimmer of something in her eyes, then, and thought for a second it was her dragon, but I dismissed the idea. It couldn't be. I'd never seen Nana's dragon before. "He will no doubt see your mating mark. I suspect he won't like it."

Morgan shook his head.

"In which case, you are free to choose whether you stay with him or return with us."

I wanted to shout *he's staying with me* at the top of my lungs, but I held my tongue. It was Morgan's time to choose.

"I'd like to return here, with Lew."

He got one of Nana's rare smiles for that. "Of course," she said, and carried on like she'd expected nothing less. "We'll leave early tomorrow morning and conduct our business at the Somerville castle as quickly as possible. I want to get this over with."

I could see she was tense. She expected trouble. *I* expected trouble. No way would Lord Somerville let Morgan go without a fight. Who would?

She looked round at Gramps, who was slumped back like a wilted flower. I swear I saw her lips twitch at the sight of him sulking.

"And then you can have your party tomorrow evening, to welcome Morgan properly."

Gramps face lit up and, when I snuck a look at Morgan, his face was impassive but I could still see the mixture of relief and excitement in the depths of his silver-blue eyes. Nana had nailed it. I knew Morgan was worried that he'd be kept at the Somerville castle, and in one fell swoop she had reassured him that he'd definitely be coming home with us, and had given Gramps a project to work on all day that would keep him busy so he didn't have time to worry.

Damn, she was good.

"Lew, send Laura to me, will you? Then you're free for the rest of the afternoon. Both of you."

I gave her a grateful smile and pulled Morgan to his feet, trying not to consider the possibility that Nana knew I was about to go and find Laura and then spend the rest of the day exploring Morgan's lean body with my tongue. Which I definitely was.

CHAPTER 39:
MORGAN

"Do you think I'll be able to see Alfie?"

"Yes."

"Do you think he'll let us leave again?"

Lew's voice was steady and patient as he replied, "Yes."

"You won't let them take me away?"

"No."

I'd been asking the same questions, on and off, all morning. Lew, to his credit, was still answering them. If it had been me, I'd have stopped bothering, probably, but Lew had the patience of a saint and he answered like I hadn't asked it before, and he didn't get annoyed that I didn't quite trust his family to protect me.

It wasn't like I didn't trust them, more like

I knew what my father was capable of and wasn't sure they were worried enough. They all looked too calm. Anyone about to anger Lord Somerville – and in his own territory, no less – should look much, much more worried.

"He's going to be angry," I said. Again. I'd definitely said it before.

"I know," said Lew. He squeezed my hand where he'd been holding it for half an hour already as we drove south towards the Somerville castle. "But we'll face him together, Morgan, as mates."

I nodded and held his hand tightly and tried not to ask any more stupid questions.

As we drew nearer, two of the cars in front of us peeled off the convoy. And, yes, we had a convoy. The *curaidhs* were out in force, which I liked a lot. Not that it would do much good if they were on the outside of the border and we were on the inside. Still, it was nice to know they were near.

"They'll stay close," Lew said to me. He reached over with his free hand and pulled at the collar of my shirt, dragging it down my neck so he could see his mating mark. I'd chosen the shirt with the highest collar, and I'd worn my blazer as well. I was hot and uncomfortable. I had no idea how I'd ever spent all day in an outfit like this, but I had, for years.

"Nearly there," said the driver. I had been

introduced, but I couldn't for the life of me re-member her name. My blood had been pounding in my ears as I'd climbed into the car and any-one I'd met early that morning was just a faceless blur.

Partly, it had been anticipation of return-ing to my father, and partly it was the sight of Brendan, who'd returned home the evening be-fore, contrite and apologetic. He'd apparently begged Nana to let him help protect the two of us, and she'd relented. When he'd hugged Lew and slapped him on the back, flashing a wide grin and saying, "Sorry, I just got a bit crazy there for a while," I knew I should have felt relieved. But I didn't. Lew had forgiven him too easily and nobody else seemed bothered that he'd taken a chunk out of Lew's shoulder just a couple of days before.

I was bothered. I'd talked to Brendan quite a lot and I'd seen how much he fancied Lew. That, I could understand. Turning on Lew, I couldn't. And to see him standing there grinning and act-ing like just another bro grated on me, somehow. I didn't believe it. He couldn't have fallen out of love that quickly. At least he had been in the car behind us all the way here, not sat next to us.

My whole body tensed as we drove through the gates leading to the castle. I felt a flash of something, some residual magic, and it sizzled against my skin, almost like it knew I had no business there any more; I wasn't a Somerville any longer.

We drove slowly up the long drive, winding this way and that, barely catching a glimpse of the castle. When we finally saw it in its full glory, I couldn't help but see it with a stranger's eyes. It was light grey, clean and neat. There had been extensive refurbishments made so that it looked sleek and modern. I hadn't given it much thought before, but I found that I preferred the Hoskins' homely old castle, strange as that may seem.

As we came to a stop, I dropped Lew's hand. The longer I could keep Lord Somerville from knowing that I'd mated him, the better. I had an awful feeling that we weren't all going to make it out of the territory that day, and I prayed it wasn't a premonition.

Two footmen in smart blue uniforms came down the steps to open the car doors and I slid out of my seat and began to walk into the castle, trying to hear Lew behind me. I didn't dare to turn around to check, since I was sure Lord Somerville was having us watched and I'd been trained, long ago, to always look straight ahead as though there was nobody else around me, especially if it was only servants and *curaidh*.

When I heard Lew's footsteps on the polished tiles of the entrance hall, though, my heart settled and I followed the footmen and Lady

Hoskins – Nana – into the drawing room.

I heard him greet Nana, and then I saw him again for the first time in months.

The sight of my father sent a spike of fear trough me and I tried to school my face. It was harder than I remembered. I was trying to put on a mask, but I'd not used it in so long that I wasn't fast enough. At least he couldn't smell my fear. That would probably have done us all in.

Lew, though, must have noticed my change in scent because he moved closer to me, standing right beside me so that our arms brushed. I was torn between shuffling away and just flinging myself into his embrace and clinging on like a baby monkey.

The choice was made for me. Lord Somerville's voice was cool and crisp.

"You are dismissed. I will send for you when I wish to speak to you." Beside me, I could smell the anger that rolled off Lew.

"Yes, Father."

Lew turned to come with me, but Lord Somerville's voice cut into us. "I will speak with your instructors."

I knew exactly what he meant. He wanted to know what I'd learned, what I'd revealed, what progress I'd made.

I gave a bow of my head and turned to leave. Lew shifted into my path, blocking my way. He didn't want me out of his sight. I could understand that. I didn't want to leave his sight.

"Someone will escort you," he said. He needed to stay and talk to my father, since he was the one who had been training me.

Brendan stepped forward. "I'll do it, Lew."

Lew gave a curt nod and I found myself walking out of the room with Brendan behind me. The skin at the back of my neck prickled and I wanted to cover it. I didn't like exposing my neck to him, not after the way he'd bitten Lew.

"Let's take your things up to your room," he said. There was something in his voice that I'd never noticed there before.

I didn't want to remind him that I hadn't really bought anything with me, since I fully intended to leave again that day. Maybe he'd missed that part of the plan, since he'd only just got back.

Instead, I said, with as much dignity as I could, "The servants will see to it."

"Why don't you show me your room?"

It wasn't that I didn't want Brendan in my room – anyone could go in there from now on, for all I cared – but my dragon began to shimmer inside me. It had never really had much of a say before, always staying low and quiet, releasing my magic when I asked it, but always reluctantly. Now it seemed suddenly to have an opinion. The trouble was, I didn't know what. Did my dragon sense something? Was Lew alright?

Just as I was turning back towards the drawing room, hoping to stand outside and listen at the keyhole – yes, I wasn't subtle – my cousin Seren came down the stairs. From the way he looked around, I suspected he wasn't meant to show his face until the Hoskinses had left.

"Morgan! Good to see you."

That was news to me. Seren had never been bothered about me one way or another before.

"Um, yeah, good to see you, too. Brendan, this is Seren, my cousin. Seren, this is Brendan, one of Lady Hoskins' clan."

I did not want to try and remember exactly what his relationship was to her, and I didn't want to remind him of how closely he either was or wasn't related to Lew.

Seren gave a brief nod in his direction and then asked me, "Why don't we have a chat?"

"A chat?"

"Yes, catch up on each other's news."

I was pretty sure he wouldn't have any news. He wasn't allowed out of the house, even before there were any trespassers. But that reminded me, and I wanted to know about that, so I said, "Sure. Shall we go to Alfie's room? I want to see him."

"Alfie's been taken out for the day."

I stopped walking. "What?" That had never happened before. Like, ever. Alfie had never left the castle grounds, just like I'd never left them until the day I'd gone to the Hoskins' castle.

Seren shrugged. "A treat, I suppose."

"O…k." I liked the sound of that less and less.

Brendan said, "Maybe we should go somewhere private."

Seren latched onto that idea. "Yes, let's. We'll go to my room." He cast a regal look at Brendan that made my neck heat with embarrassment. If anyone else had been the subject of that look, I'd have hated it. It was utterly disdainful. "You may leave us."

Brendan grinned. "No can do. I'm sticking with Morgan."

Seren wanted to talk to me more than he wanted to put Brendan in his place, and so he agreed, leading us both up to his room. I got the impression that he was glad to get out of the open, too, which only confirmed that he wasn't meant to be seen.

When we got into Seren's room, I looked around. It looked just like my room had – high-ceilinged and wide enough for a couple of dragons in dragon form to move around, as long as they didn't try anything particularly acrobatic. And it had white walls, oak furniture, white bedding. All very clean and minimalist.

In fact, if it wasn't for the fact that his

bed was pushed up against the far wall instead of standing in the middle of the room like mine, and that I *knew* we'd walked through his door, it could actually be my room. It was weird, to stand there and be almost sure it was mine. I hadn't realised before that my room had been so un-touched, so bland.

Seren walked into the middle of the room and I went over to the window, looking out. It overlooked a section of the garden just round the corner from the front door. I leaned to the side but I couldn't see any of the Hoskins' cars.

Even in my own family's castle, I felt isolated and unnerved being out of sight of everybody.

"How are you, Morgan?"

"Um, yeah, I'm well," I said, spinning round so that the side of my neck with my mating mark was towards the window instead of towards Seren. Not that he could see it underneath my collar or he'd have said something by then. Still, I didn't want to chance it.

"How did you find living with the *curaidh*?"

"It was, um, good. It was good. I enjoyed it."

Seren nodded. Something was wrong. Nobody in my father's clan would think it was normal to enjoy living in a *curaidh*'s castle.

He asked, "And the *curaidh*? How were

they?"

"Ok."

"Are they all well?"

"Um, yes? As far as I know?"

"You were trained by their warriors, weren't you?"

"Ye-es."

I glanced at Brendan, who was standing by the door and watching us openly.

"Did you find Lewis a good instructor?"

"Yes."

"And, oh, what is his name? The other warrior, the big one? Dane, is it? Was he an adequate instructor?"

"I wasn't taught by him."

"Why not?" Seren snapped. "Was he not there?"

"No, he was there. He just... didn't teach me. I get the feeling he doesn't like *uasal* much."

My cousin was not too difficult to read, once you noticed his eyes basically gave away his emotions. For years, Seren had walked the castle with an air of despondency. It was allowed to talk to him, I suppose, but it had never been encouraged. The rumours around him were many and varied, and Alfie and I had tried to stay away from anyone who might draw Lord Somerville's focus onto us. Seren definitely had Lord Somerville's attention, though we were not sure why.

He took a step towards me, seemingly

without realising.

"Dane likes *uasal*. We- he worked for Lord Somerville."

I didn't know what to say to that. "Well he didn't like me."

"You didn't see him at all?"

"Not much."

"Did he come here with you today?"

"No."

Something inside Seren deflated. He looked more tired. Not just drooping shoulders and long face, but I swear his skin changed colour, becoming duller. The dark circles under his eyes – the ones that almost no dragon had, since we healed so quickly and rejuvenated – became more pronounced.

As I stood there, looking at him and actually *seeing* him for the first time, I realised that Seren looked sick. He looked human.

"Seren, are you ok?"

"Yes." He drew himself up tall, trying to look regal – I recognised the stance, I'd used it enough myself – and flicked a hand dismissively. "It's none of my concern what the *curaidh* do. If you don't mind, I'm going to rest now."

He looked like he needed it.

"I'll go in a second. Just one question: what happened to Alfie?"

"I don't know. He was shot."

"Yes, but how?"

"I don't know, Morgan. Why would I know?"

"Alfie says you think it was a dragon. Did you see anyone?"

"No, I didn't. I was inside the house."

He sounded weary, like he'd been asked these questions already. I knew, as well, that he never left the house. But I wanted to know what had happened to my baby brother.

"Why was Alfie out by himself in the first place?"

Seren glared at me. "I wasn't aware he was a prisoner."

That had a slight ring of bitterness to it and I felt bad. It wasn't Seren's fault that Alfie was shot, and I didn't want to rub it in that he was basically a prisoner himself.

"Are you- do you know when he'll be back?"

"After the *curaidh* leave."

"That'll be too late."

"Why? When they go, Alfie will come back and you can spend as much time with him as you want."

I couldn't tell him that I was leaving. Unfortunately, I'd forgotten that Brendan was there, standing against the door, listening to every word.

His mouth pulled up in a sneer as he said, "He thinks you're staying, Morgan. How sweet.

He's wrong, though, isn't he?"

Brendan began to pace towards me, and I tracked his movement across the large room. My dragon fizzed with magic inside me, and I didn't know why. It had never reacted like that to anyone. What did it want me to do?

"Brendan, what are you—?"

"And you, Morgan, you think you're coming back home with us. Well, you're wrong, too."

"What do you mean?"

"You're not coming home with us."

He looked serious. His eyes were dark and glowering. They were hard and unforgiving.

"Brendan—"

"You should have just left him alone, Morgan."

"Who?" I had a pretty good idea who he was talking about already, but for some reason I thought it would buy me time to ask, and he was stalking nearer and nearer and I was pressed right back against the window sill.

"Lew. We were getting on fine until you came along."

"Brendan, you have to understand—"

"If you go away, Lew and I can go back to the way we were."

"You can do that anyway. You can be friends."

He screamed the next words, right in my face. Because, yes, he had got that close to me and

I hadn't known what to do to stop him.

"We're more than friends!"

I tried to be gentle. "No, you're not. You were good friends."

"He would have loved me, if you hadn't turned up, always flirting with him and fluttering your blue fucking eyes at him."

I had never fluttered my eyes at *anyone*.

"I don't—"

"You're not coming home with us, Morgan. Do you understand?"

I couldn't take my eyes off him to look at Seren. If I told Brendan I was definitely going home with Lew, Seren would hear. On the other hand, Nana was about to tell Lord Somerville just that, so what did I have to lose?

"I'm going home with Lew. He's mine."

My dragon filled me, pressing against my skin. It felt *right* to say it, to claim Lew as my own, and my dragon approved. Perhaps that was what it had been waiting for.

As I marvelled at how powerful I felt, with my dragon filling me, I failed to notice the knife that Brendan pulled from behind him.

I noticed when he stabbed me, though. Boy, did I notice that.

CHAPTER 40:
MORGAN

I looked down, amazed to see the flash of the knife between us and see the spurt of blood that washed over my shirt from the wound. It was in my side, scraping just below my ribs, and the knife had sliced through a good inch or so of my flesh.

The pain burst inside me, and I grabbed my side, pressing both my hands to it. For a second, I wasn't sure if he'd killed me. The whole world tilted and there was a tangle of limbs and two screams. I wasn't sure if one of them was mine.

It took a second for me to get my bearings. I was on the floor, by the window, and Seren was beside me, sprawled on the floor with Brendan where he'd launched himself at Brendan to save me. It was lucky he'd seen Brendan unsheathe that knife, even if I hadn't. He had been just in time. He was smaller than Brendan, though – we both were – and he had only knocked him over, hadn't actually harmed him.

Brendan struggled with Seren as I tried to drag myself up, clutching my side where my wound was pouring blood. Seren thrashed but he was weak. Or maybe Brendan was just much stronger than I'd given him credit for, because he smacked Seren across the face and my cousin crashed backwards, hitting his head on the floor with a *thunk*.

That knife flashed again and I saw it raised above Seren's neck, so I flung myself forward, knocking Brendan over so he sprawled on the floor again. The agony in my side told me that had been a mistake, but Seren wriggled out from underneath Brendan's legs, struggling and unco-ordinated and desperate. We'd just bought our-selves seconds.

"Are you ok?"

Seren had his hand pressed to his left thigh, and there was a red stain under his palm that was growing even as I watched it. He'd been cut. At least it hadn't been his neck. His voice was high and afraid. "I can't help you, Morgan."

"What do you mean?" I was dragging him away, across the room, and he was leaning heav-ily on me. Brendan struggled to his feet and faced us. The knife was back in his hand.

"I can't- just run, Morgan. Get out. Get downstairs."

"I don't—"

"Get downstairs! They'll protect you." Seren tried to shove me, but he toppled and I grabbed him under his arms and held him up.

Brendan snarled and I saw his teeth lengthen. He was starting to shift.

Seren's voice was urgent as he said, "Run."

I was going nowhere. No way was I leaving him alone with Brendan. I gripped Seren with one arm around his waist and lifted the other hand, palm outwards. Brendan didn't even pause and his skin began to flicker with scales.

I reached inside, to my dragon, and asked it for magic. It granted me my wish. Not only that, but it gave me magic faster than it ever had before.

Blue light shot from my hand, straight at Brendan. It threw him backwards and he hit the window with a crack.

Lowering my hand, I waited. There was a second or so of silence and then Brendan groaned. He lifted his head and growled.

"Brendan, stop this, it's not you. You'll be killed, Brendan. Lord Somerville will kill you if you do this."

A horrible sneer pulled at his lips. "You don't know, do you?"

"Know what?" That answer gave away

that, no, I didn't know whatever it was.

"You're disowned."

Seren's body went limp beside me and I clung to him, having to use both hands to grab him and keep him from crashing to the floor. It twisted my body and split my wound open further, making me cry out.

I glanced at Brendan and panted, "You're lying."

"Really? You think all of the Somerville security is suddenly just deaf and blind? Or do you think you're not under their protection any more?"

What he said made horrible, terrible, deadly sense. There was no way he'd be able to bring that knife into Lord Somerville's castle otherwise. He wouldn't have been allowed upstairs. He'd have three dragons on him already, if they were watching the Hoskinses like they were supposed to be. I felt cold. Disowned. There must be others outside, right then, watching this and doing nothing.

Seren pushed weakly at me. "Get out, quickly."

I held him tighter. Brendan had decided to remain in human form. He gripped the handle of the knife hard, so hard I could see the whites of his knuckles, and he walked across the room towards us. I dragged Seren back with me almost to the bed.

I raised my hand again, and Seren sagged lower as I released him. But I needed that free hand.

My dragon released my magic to me again, faster this time, almost instantly. I watched in surprise as it arched out of my palm and across the room. The problem was, Brendan was prepared for it that time and he rolled to the side.

I flung another burst of magic, and he dodged again. I did not have the practice I needed to hit a moving target. Normally, my dragon was too slow to release my magic, and there was no way I could respond to a threat so quickly. Now, even with the quick responses, my aim was off. I was also getting tired from the draining energy.

Brendan was barely two metres away, rippling with scales that would protect his skin from the blast, and I raised my hand to throw every last particle of magic I had.

That was when there was a crash behind him. I flung my free arm over my face as glass sprayed everywhere. There was a shattering sound and a deep crack and then a thud, and I looked up to see a large dragon bursting into the room through the window. The whole window, including the frame, disintegrated and the dragon landed on its feet in the middle of the glass and bits of rubble from the wall.

It was huge. It was bigger than Lew by nearly two metres, and its giant head was dark grey and filled with teeth as long as my whole hand.

Brendan spun to face it, and raised his hand. The dragon's head snaked forward, and they both moved at the same time. Brendan stabbed the knife down into the dragon's neck and the dragon closed its jaws around Brendan's torso.

I heard the crunch of his bones. It made my whole body revolt and I vomited up my breakfast, right there beside them.

The dragon let Brendan's body slip out of its jaws and he rolled onto the floor, dead. Then it turned its black eyes on us. I raised my hand, palm out, and prepared myself, much good it would do me, to fling magic at that monster.

Seren's voice was weak and confused. "Dane?"

The scales began to shimmer and the bulk of the dragon began to dwindle and then Dane was standing in front of us, completely naked. He had blood pouring out of a wound on his neck and it ran down his shoulder and chest.

"You're hurt!"

He reached up to touch the wound and shrugged. "It's already healing."

"What are you doing here?" Seren asked.

Dane's voice was as deep and curt as ever. "Sent as security."

"Oh, right."

While they talked, my eyes were rivetted on Brendan's body. "Is he... dead?"

"Yes."

"Are you sure?"

Dane nudged Brendan's arm with his foot. It flopped around, but otherwise Brendan didn't stir. "Yes," he said.

I threw up again, letting go of Seren, who crumpled down. Luckily, we were right by the bed and he collapsed to the floor and managed to prop himself back against it.

Dane was glaring at him. "Why isn't that wound healing?"

Seren looked down at his leg. His face was greyish in colour, in a sickly way, and his breathing was laboured.

"I think he broke my rib."

Dane stepped forward, his angry glare making me shiver. "Why aren't you healing?"

Seren's voice was weak but his words were clipped. "It's none of your business."

Dane straightened up from where he'd been in the act of crouching down in front of Seren. His face was livid.

And that's when Lew burst through the door.

I knew it was Lew even before I saw him. Somehow, I knew it was him, and then a second later, his smell hit me. It was filled with panic and anger but it was still distinctly him.

He was on top of Dane, tacking him to the floor, before I'd even opened my mouth.

CHAPTER 41: LEW

He'd been toying with us.

The bastard dickhead cock-faced Lord Somerville had been playing with us by bringing us here, and I was not happy. Beside me, Nana was still and silent, which was a danger sign.

And we knew he'd been playing with us because he'd just got bored with it and told us.

"You have broken our agreement."

It occurred to me that, actually, we'd upheld our side of the bargain pretty well, since Morgan had been sent to train with us and I'd trained him. In fact, I'd done quite a good job, in the end.

Lord Somerville carried on. He looked right at me as he said, "You have defiled my son and tainted him." Looked like he knew about all the sex, then. He shifted his focus to Nana. "You will leave my territory immediately, or I will consider it an act of war."

She stood. She was calm, which freaked me out a bit.

"I, and all of my clan, will leave your territory." She kept her eyes on Lord Somerville, even when she addressed me. That was wise. "Lew, go and get Morgan."

For the first time, I saw some emotion flicker over the man's face. It was anger.

"You will have no further interaction with my son."

"On the contrary, Lord Somerville; I shall. He's one of mine, now."

Barrington Somerville bolted out of his chair, standing rigid with fury. "He is mine."

I couldn't restrain myself any longer. My anger and possessiveness rolled out of me as I growled, "He's *mine*." I'd never sounded like that before. I'd never heard so much of my dragon in my voice – normally, if my dragon took over too much of me, I became unable to speak at all, and in our dragon forms, we couldn't form human words. I would have scared myself, if it weren't for the thrumming fear already coursing through me. Where the fuck was Morgan?

I didn't care that I was in another clan's castle, I didn't care that Lord Somerville was said to have magic that could blast a human in two, I didn't care that I was leaving Nana to face him alone – she could more than take care of herself, and there were more of us just outside the door – I just ran to find Morgan.

As I followed the faint trail of his scent upstairs, I was so incredibly grateful that I'd claimed him, and that I could scent him even when nobody else could. I'd never have found him, otherwise. But, tracking his scent, I burst into a large bedroom to see Morgan covered in blood and smelling of puke, with a slim man collapsed beside him and looking like he was about to pass out, Brendan lying still on the floor in a growing puddle of blood, and Dane, naked, furious, standing over them. I didn't think. I didn't question. I just launched myself at the only person in that room that seemed to be an immediate danger to Morgan.

It was just unfortunate that Dane was probably one of only three of our clan who could kick my arse.

I took two heavy blows to my stomach and one to my face. It connected with my cheek and nearly broke my skull. I didn't manage to actually hit Dane, since I could either punch him or roll him away from Morgan and I chose to do the latter.

"Lew! Leave him alone. Seren? Lew!"

Morgan was shouting but he wasn't making any sense. Another voice said, softly, "Dane?" and then Dane let go of me. It was sudden and I made a grab for him, since he was moving back towards Morgan.

"Lew, he saved us." That was Morgan's voice. I dropped my hold of Dane and rushed over, grabbing Morgan and pulling him back towards the door, away from Dane and away from whoever-it-was beside him. The slim little *uasal* looked in a bad way. Maybe he had internal injuries.

"Are you hurt, Morgan?"

"Just a cut. It was Brendan."

"Shit! And Dane?"

Morgan gulped, and he sounded queasy when he said, "He bit Brendan in two. Brendan had a knife."

I cast my eyes over Dane again. The wound on his neck was still bleeding, which, for a dragon, wasn't great. It was only a little trickle of blood, though, so I didn't think he was in immediate danger.

"Dane, how bad are you hurt?"

He turned his head but didn't move his eyes to me, just kept looking at the man who had collapsed by the bed. "I'll be fine." He couldn't take his eyes off that man. If I had to guess, I'd say that was Seren, then.

"Is he healing?"

Seren was slumped down and Morgan

stepped towards him, but someone came in the door behind us and I grabbed him, shoving him behind me.

"Lew?" It was Laura, and she took the room in at a glance. "We're going. Nana says we can do it the old-fashioned way."

"Right."

I went to Brendan's body – he was already cooling and most definitely dead – and flipped him over. The knife slipped from his fist and I picked it up.

"Shit, this is the *biorach* dagger that was taken from the armoury. Dane, are you going to be able to fly with that wound?"

"I said it's already healing."

So he said, but Seren was nearly unconscious and I didn't want Dane bleeding out and going the same way while we flew home.

"Can you—"

Laura interrupted me. "Dane, Nana says you're to come home. It's an order."

He dragged his eyes off Seren to look at her. She stepped back, hands up in surrender. "I'm just passing it on. She's commanded it."

Quickly, I flipped Brendan again, searching for the dagger's sheath. When I found it, I snagged it and slipped the dagger inside.

I looked at Morgan, putting my hand on his pale cheek. I hated to see the blood that soaked his shirt and stank of iron and pain and fear. But at least Morgan's scent had changed now. There was relief in it. And I would soak that up and fly him home.

"Take this. It's sharp enough to cut a dragon's scales. Anyone you don't like comes near you, cut them. Anyone, Morgan. No exceptions."

"Ok."

I began my shift, felt my teeth lengthen and my claws come out, and said to Morgan. "Get ready to hold on."

I shifted, tearing my clothes off me and leaving them where they fell. I pushed my body low to the ground, snaked my head round and tried to curl my neck around Morgan as he tucked the dagger into his belt and climbed onto my back. He didn't hesitate, and that gave me a surge of power.

When I felt him settle on me, his legs either side of my neck, just where my shoulders widened out, I moved across the room. He felt stable on my back, a natural part of me, and I eased over the partly-broken sill of the window, trying to ensure I didn't bump Morgan against any shards of glass or sharp edges.

As soon as Morgan was out the window, I pushed off from the wall and took to the air. Letting my wings out, I circled round to the front of the house where our cars were lined up, waiting to drive away. Everyone was inside them, except

Daniel, who was already in the air, beating his wings to keep himself steady and airborne, like treading water. He was the only dragon I'd ever met who could stay practically still in the flight.

Behind me, I heard Laura take to the air and then, nearly a minute later, Dane gave a low growl and swooped around the corner.

Nana was standing outside the last car. As we flew over them, she saw Morgan on my back and saw all three of her grandchildren were out, and she got in the car, slamming the door. The car set off immediately.

I turned my head to glance behind me and saw a row of *uasal* on the front steps, three in dragon form and three in human form. I got a bad feeling about it. No way would Lord Somerville just let Morgan fly out of his territory. Nobody would let Morgan go, I was sure of it.

CHAPTER 42: MORGAN

I could feel the magic of the boundary push against me. We were flying right over the cars we'd arrived in, and they were heading up the drive at a surprising speed – fast enough to keep up with a dragon in flight, anyway.

As we drew nearer, I felt that magic push harder. It wasn't going to let us out. The gates ahead of us were closed and normally they'd have opened by now to let the cars pass. We drew nearer and nearer and they still didn't open.

Lew gave a shriek and one of the dragons ahead of us – I'd lost track in the confusion, it was either Laura or someone named Daniel – dived towards the heavy gates, twisting round as they dropped so they hit them with their back claws. They gave off a loud creak – iron bending against its will – but they stayed firm.

The dragon retreated, obviously intending to get another run-up, but I knew that it wasn't going to work. Those gates were magic. My father's magic. Brute force wouldn't open them.

I reached inside for my dragon, prepared to bargain. I didn't have to. My dragon didn't just grudgingly release a trickle of magic to me like it normally did, it pushed up a fountain of it. I was overwhelmed by it, filled too quickly with the kind of power I'd never had before, and it crackled around me.

For a second, I felt a jolt of panic that it would harm Lew where it crackled over the top of his scales, but he just kept flying. He didn't even notice.

My dragon sizzled inside me, fizzing with energy. Pushing my legs against Lew's neck to make sure I had a tight grip, I held up both hands, palms outwards. I drew the magic to me, feeling it surge around me and nearly blind me as it crackled around my head. Then I flung it at the gates.

I was hoping to make a crack in them. I was hoping that, if I could create a little tear in the magic, some brute force might work to prise them open. I did not expect what happened.

The gates blasted apart with a screech of iron and continued to spark with blue magic even after I'd stopped throwing it. The two gates were bent and crumpled to the side of the road and the Hoskins' cars drove straight through the gap, while the four dragons swooped through them and we were out of Somerville territory.

We flew further, and I kept my eye open, scanning the surrounding fields and woodland and skies for signs that we were being followed or watched. I saw nothing.

Eventually, the last car in the convoy tooted its horn twice and all the cars slowed to a stop, while Lew took us down and landed lightly on his feet. He twisted his head round to look at me and I flung myself forward, onto his neck, wrapping my arms around him.

"Are you ok?"

He couldn't answer in dragon form, but there was no pain or fear in his scent.

Behind me, Laura said, "Get in Nana's car. Dane, she said you were to go with Daniel in the first one."

Slithering down Lew's huge, scaled body, I couldn't help but notice his powerful shoulders and legs. I'd never really seen much beauty in our dragon forms, but Lew's body was incredible. I'd never felt so powerful as I had when I was on top of him then. Standing under his neck, with his huge chest looming over me and his incredible long, muscled neck, I felt absolutely safe for the first time in forever.

Laura said, "Get on with it, Lew. Nana's waiting."

He began to shift back into his human form and I realised he was about to be naked. I felt a dash of panic, then, that I was about to get a hard-on from the sight of him, right before having to go and sit next to his Nana.

"What is it?" he asked as soon as his jaw could form words again. "What frightened you?"

I shook my head. No way was I about to tell him that.

"Morgan, tell me," he insisted and glanced around us, trying to see what had given my scent a burst of panic.

"Nothing."

"Tell me." His voice was commanding and his hand wrapped around the back of my neck, comforting.

"You're naked," I said. Stupid, I know.

He let out a surprised bark of laughter and then scooped me up, carrying me to his Nana's car and sliding me into the seat through the open door. He slid in after me and closed the door and I found myself sitting between Lew and the elder. There was probably nobody in the world better protected than me at that moment.

The car was large, with tinted windows, so at least no random human would see inside and wonder why a load of naked people were driving around. Nana flicked a blanket at Lew and he wrapped it around himself and then put his arm around me, pulling me close.

"Well that went well," he said.

Nana sighed. "It could have gone worse."

I was amazed that she was being so understanding. I'd just broken her alliance with my father. She should look a lot more worried than she did.

Lew also didn't seem worried. He leaned back in the seat and put his head back on the headrest. It looked like he might go to sleep. Then he yanked his head up and looked at me.

"Are you healing?"

I pulled my shirt up to look at the wound. It was already scabbing over, although it was hard to tell from all the drying blood around it. I wrinkled my nose. It was pretty gruesome. And, I realised, I would probably smell of sick. Great.

"Yep," I said.

"Nana, he was wounded by a *biorach* dagger. Can you have someone ready to look at him when we get home?"

"Yes. Who had the dagger?"

"Brendan. It was the one missing from our armoury."

She nodded. "He must have come back and taken it."

"But... why?"

Lew sounded absolutely baffled. I wasn't sure whether to tell him that it was because of him. I thought about it for about five seconds and then decided that my generous-souled Lew never needed to know that. He would only feel guilty.

Nana said, "We'll never know."

That's right, I thought. *It's a mystery.* And then her eyes flicked to me and I was absolutely certain that she *did* know. And she knew I knew, too. Huh.

"Nana, Dane was hurt as well."

"He'll be looked at, too."

I remembered the sight of Seren collapsing on the floor, deathly-pale and bleeding. I'd thought he was going to die. God, I hoped he'd be ok. He didn't deserve to die. He didn't deserve any pain.

Lew asked, "When did Dane even get back? I haven't seen him since he took off."

Nana didn't answer, and so I told Lew, "He said Nana sent him as security."

Lew grunted. "I'd never question your wisdom, Nana, but that was fucking stupid."

Her voice was hard when she replied, "If I wasn't worried that you'd get blood on my seats, I'd let you feel my claws for that."

"You mean you don't want to embarrass me by kicking my arse in front of my mate," said Lew, and pulled my further into his side. He was warm and I felt the last of the tension leave my body as I pressed against him. I felt so safe, it was wonderful. And, if I could protect him from his

Nana's wrath, that was good too.

Nana sniffed. "Something like that. Your reprieve won't last forever, though."

Lew chuckled. "Got it. Why'd you send him, though?"

There was a pause while Nana decided what to say. I was used to those pauses with Lord Somerville. The difference was, Nana actually answered.

"I didn't. I haven't seen him since he left. We both know he went to the Somervilles, and he stayed there."

I sat up, pushing out of Lew's hold. "Wait a minute, Dane's been at the castle all this time?"

"Yes."

"Why?"

Lew fidgeted. He was a terrible liar. "I don't know."

I turned in my seat to face Nana. She raised one eyebrow at me. "Perhaps we can wait for explanations until we are home."

It was phrased like a suggestion, but I got the feeling it wasn't, really.

I nodded and Lew pulled me back against him, draping the blanket over my shoulders and resting his cheek against my head. "I'm so glad we got you back, Morgan."

"Me too."

"And you were fucking awesome with that magic. I've never seen anything like it. Nadia's going to be so pissed off that she missed it. I didn't realise your magic was that strong."

"It isn't. Not normally," I said.

Nana's voice cut across us, reminding me we weren't alone, even cocooned in our blanket. "Yes, we'll talk about that, too, when we get home."

I suddenly realised how Lew felt when Nadia prodded him in the chest and told him she'd get to him later.

CHAPTER 43: LEW

Morgan was going to recover fully. The wound was healing nicely and Nana said it would heal just like any other wound, even though it had been made with a bio-rach blade – they cut through scales, but they weren't magic and there would be no lasting side-effects.

Still, I wanted to wrap my mate up and take him to my room, lay him down and snuggle him, telling him everything would be alright, that he was amazing, that he was safe. The problem was, Nana wanted a word.

When we walked in to Nana's sitting room, I was a bit surprised to see Dane there. More worrying was that Gramps was nowhere to be seen. I shouldn't have been surprised, since he'd been running around making 'preparations' when we got home and had banned me from going near the dining room, but it made me uneasy that we didn't have his calming presence. On the other hand, if he was going to arrange the little surprise I'd asked him about, then he needed to get cracking, so it was probably for the best.

I was well prepared to defend my mate from both Nana and Dane, and to tell them he didn't need to answer any questions.

I was not prepared for him to start asking them.

He looked straight at Dane, who was sitting on one of Nana's little sofas like a bear on a toadstool, filling two people's seats, his knees almost up to his ears. Sometimes I thought Nana kept those low sofas just to make the bigger dragons uncomfortable when they visited her.

"Did you shoot Alfie?"

I made a noise in the back of my throat and practically threw myself in front of Morgan, expecting Dane to get up and strangle him or something. He didn't. Which meant I'd barrelled into my mate for absolutely no reason. And I looked like a fucking tit.

Dane shot me a quizzical look and then gave his attention to Morgan again. "No."

"Did you see who did?"

"No."

"Nana said you were there."

"I was over the other side of the estate when it happened."

Morgan narrowed his eyes. "Convenient."

He had gained a fuck load of confidence if he was prepared to piss Dane off, that was for sure. I kind of liked it. The new confident Morgan was making my heart sing and my dick hard.

Dane shrugged. "I was watching someone else. Didn't know the kid was going to get shot, did I?"

"Were you watching Seren?"

I held my breath. I would have bet all my savings that Dane would say no, but he shrugged again. "Yes."

Morgan's eyes narrowed again. "How?"

"What do you mean 'how'? I kept my fucking eyes on him, that's how."

"But Seren never leaves the house. You can't see the house from the boundary, even with dragon eyesight, even from the air, even with high-powered binoculars. We know. We designed it that way."

Dane gave his classic shrug. "I got in."

"How?"

"Your security isn't as tight as you think it is."

"No, that's not possible."

Dane started to get irritated. I was surprised it had taken that long – he'd had to be civil for a whole minute there. "Just be glad I did get in. If I hadn't been watching, you'd be dead."

"Yes, I meant to ask you about that, too. Did the Somerville dragons really just watch Brendan attack me?"

"They were sent into the house. There wasn't anyone guarding you."

"Was Brendan lying about me being disowned?"

Nana interrupted. "I'm afraid you have been disowned, Morgan. I'm sorry."

Morgan looked Nana in the eyes. "Disowned by Lord Somerville or by you?"

"Him."

He squared his shoulders, standing proud. He looked so tiny and breakable but he was strong as fuck.

"Then I'm not disowned, am I? I've got my clan."

My heart filled to bursting then and I grabbed Morgan to me and hugged him. He patted me on the back, soothing me, and if I had been able to appreciate the irony I would have, that he was comforting me after everything he'd been through.

"You're one of us now, Morgan. No going back."

"I don't want to go back," he said. "But I don't want Alfie to be in any danger. If people can get in, it means he might get hurt again."

Dane spoke. "They're tightening up security. I nearly didn't get in this time."

"This time?" asked Morgan.

At the same time, I said, "You still got in, though."

"I'm good," was Dane's answer. I thought it was probably true, but I also thought he had more incentive than most. He wanted to see his little *uasal* lover from afar. I almost asked if Seren was alright, but I didn't want to remind Dane that he'd been hurt in case Dane flipped again.

Morgan's eyebrows drew in slightly. It was the closest I'd ever seen him come to frowning. "But if people can get in – even if they're exceptionally good – it still might leave Alfie vulnerable. He got shot!"

Dane coughed. I glared at him. There was something he wasn't telling us. "Out with it."

He ignored me.

"Or I'll get Nana to ask you."

Nana, of course, was standing right there next to us, looking on with sharp black eyes and a grave face. She'd been through a lot today, too.

Dane's mouth drew into a line but he answered. "It was Brendan who shot Alfie. He wanted to get Morgan to go home."

"But- that's horrible!" Morgan cried.

I put my arm around him. There wasn't much else I could do right then to comfort him.

Nana asked, "Are you sure?"

"Yes, Nana. He thought Morgan would go home alone, or maybe with only one or two escorts."

My heart beat fast at the thought that we had nearly done exactly that. "What was he going to do?"

"My guess? Exactly what he did. Try to kill Morgan. If it had just been one escort, he might have been able to wrangle it so he escorted Morgan, but I doubt it. He might've been able to take one person out, with the element of surprise. Or he might've tricked them into thinking he'd been sent as a replacement. Whatever he planned, he wanted Morgan dead."

My heart was still beating fast and Morgan laid his head on my shoulder, sensing my distress.

Dane continued. "You threw a spanner in his plans when you came out in force. He still got Morgan alone, though. Good job I was watching. Nobody else was."

We both knew that it hadn't been Morgan that Dane was watching but, since I was so fucking grateful that he'd saved my mate's life, I didn't call him on it.

"Dane, I—"

I didn't know what to say to express my gratitude.

Morgan gave him the sweetest smile – a little tilt of his lips – and said, "Thank you, Dane. I'm sorry you got hurt."

"Glad to help. 'Course, I didn't know you could blow secure iron gates up with your magic at the time, so maybe I shouldn't have bothered."

"I can't do that. I mean I *did* do that but I can't now. I tried a while ago, to call my magic up. I can still use it but it's not the same."

Nana gestured at the sofa opposite Dane. "Sit down, Lew, you're looming."

I sat down and dragged Morgan down beside me. I wanted him in my lap but didn't want to do that if it would make him uncomfortable.

Nana said, "You've been trained to repress your dragon, Morgan. You don't talk to it much, do you?"

He shook his head.

"*Uasal* are like that, sometimes. Trained into domestic obedience. You'll find your dragon coming out more and more soon, now you're allowed to talk to it, and now you've found Lew. It won't be pushed down, not now you've tasted your mate."

There was something in the way she said that last part that was weird, some sort of emphasis I didn't quite catch. But she moved on, and I dismissed it. We'd tasted each other. We'd claimed each other. Morgan's dragon could come out whenever it wanted to.

"The magic you performed on the gates was remarkable. You have that power inside you. Perhaps, in years to come, you'll be able to draw on it alone. But for now, you'll only be able to access it to that degree when you're riding Lew."

I frowned. "Why? What do I have to do with it?"

Nana sighed, like I was a kid asking questions I should know the answer to already.

"Because, Lew, you're his mate. And you're a *curaidh*. There's a reason that the most feared warriors in history have been *curaidh* and *uasal* pairings. When the *uasal* finds their mate in a *curaidh* and rides them, both their powers grow. Strength and flight, with cunning and magic. It's a deadly combination."

"I thought that was legend."

She really did roll her eyes then. Yep, I was the slow kid at the back of the class.

"I'm going to send you to Dimpy for lessons if you carry on."

I decided to sit quietly. I liked Dimpy and it wasn't that I didn't want to spend time with him but sitting indoors and reading books wasn't my idea of fun and I didn't want to see Nana follow through on that threat.

"So... why did Lord Somerville summon me back if he wanted to disown me?"

I could see Morgan was puzzling through everything, going back over things one at a time. He liked to think things through. That was probably for the best, since I usually didn't do that. He'd be good for me. I smiled automatically at the thought that we'd have years and years for his good habits to wear off on me.

"He had not disowned you at the time. He wanted you home. It was only when he realised that you were mated to Lew that he disowned you."

Yeah, that little episode was burned into my memory. The way Barrington Somerville's disgusting fucking face had gone livid at the thought of Morgan not belonging to him any more. Fucking prick.

Nana smiled faintly at the memory. "We had a few words after you left, Lew. I informed him of the change in Morgan's circumstances. I think he took it remarkably well."

That probably meant he hadn't taken it well at all and Nana had enjoyed seeing the dickhead rant and rave.

Morgan's face had gone pale. "Did he say anything?"

Nana tapped her finger against her chin. "Nothing of note, no."

"Did he maybe say anything about killing me?"

"Not that I recall."

Unsurprisingly, that little bombshell bothered me. "Morgan, why would he talk about killing you?"

His eyes were huge when he looked at me, and I saw the certainty in them when he said, "He won't take that well. It's an insult to have one of your clan taken from you. It shows weakness."

Nana sounded positively breezy when she said, "That sort of thing is nonsense. If he'd been reasonable, he wouldn't have disowned you. We could have united the two clans with a mating and he could have had a whole other clan's worth of power at his fingertips. It's his fault he lost you."

"He won't like it," Morgan repeated. "He won't want to be seen as weak."

Nana smiled comfortingly at Morgan.

"Don't worry about that, Morgan. You're safe here. You're a Hoskins now, and we protect our own. Why don't you go and get ready for the party? John's going to be itching to get going as soon as he's finished fussing – he has no patience."

Firstly, I thought it was rich of Nana to say Gramps had no patience.

Secondly, she was clearly deflecting.

"Nana? Did Lord Somerville say anything about hurting Morgan?"

"Do you really want to know?"

"Yes."

"Fine. He said he'd kill him before he let a load of *curaidh* have him as their bitch."

Morgan whimpered. I wasn't sure whether it was the death threat that scared him or the insult.

I was growling as I asked, "Do you think

he'll try anything now we got Morgan out of there?"

"No." This time Nana smiled broadly, showing her human teeth. "I don't think he will. But it doesn't matter either way. Morgan's one of us. I protect my family." Her eyes began to glow with fire and I caught the glimmer of her dragon lurking behind them. "I told Somerville to come and get Morgan, if he dared."

Three growls rumbled out low and threatening, my own joining with Nana's and Dane's and reverberating round the room. We wrapped our growls around Morgan, telling him we'd keep him safe. He was one of us now, and we'd protect him.

CHAPTER 44: MORGAN

The Hoskins' medic had looked at my wound and pronounced me fit. It had already scabbed over and all I had to do was wash the rest of the blood off me and brush my teeth to feel nearly back to normal. The wound ached, but considering how the day had gone, a bit of discomfort was neither here nor there.

"Are you sure you're up for this?"

"Of course," I said.

Lew walked over to me and pressed his whole front against me so we were chest to chest.

"If you don't feel up to it, I can tell them we're not coming."

I reached up to kiss him on the lips, revelling in my freedom to kiss my mate and loving the taste of him as he dipped his tongue into my mouth. He hands went to my hips and one of them wrapped firmly around me and the other stroked gently against the skin just behind my cut. He was so wonderfully attentive, it made tears push against my eyes.

I pulled back from our kiss, blinking hard to try and banish those tears.

"Did I hurt you?"

"No. Not at all."

He smiled, and my heart beat an extra little beat at the sight of it.

"Do you want to go downstairs?"

I couldn't help my excitement. I knew Gramps was throwing a party to celebrate our mating, and I was sure it was more to give him the satisfaction of having all his family together, but a selfish little part of me shone with pride that the party was for *us*. We were special, even if it was just for one night.

I tried not to let my childish glee show through too much. Lew was taking it all in his stride and it occurred to me that maybe I was blowing it all out of proportion. Still, no way did I want to miss my own party.

"Yes, please. I want to go."

"Did the Somervilles ever have parties?" Lew asked. I'd noticed that he never referred to them as my family any more, and he never referred to their castle as my home. They were the people I'd been born to, and their castle had been a place I'd lived, but I was a Hoskins now and this was my home.

"Yes," I said, my excitement waning a little. I looked down at my clothes. I was wearing a pair of dark blue jeans and a shirt with no tie. "Do I need to change?"

Lew cocked his head. "Why would you need to change?"

"Because... is it a dinner party?"

"God no. Is that the kind of party the Somervilles have?"

"Yes."

"Sounds boring."

"They are," I agreed. "And I was only ever allowed to go to one, anyway, when Seren did something that angered Lord Somerville and wasn't allowed to go; I had to replace him at the last moment."

Lew dragged me to him again and peppered my face with kisses. "Well this party is not going to be anything like that, I promise. Are you ready?"

"Yes."

We walked out of Lew's room together and he slid his arm around my waist, pressing me against his side.

Since we'd got home, Lew had practically decided to wear me as an accessory at all times. His hands were constantly on me, and I couldn't have been happier. I'd trail around behind Lew for the rest of my life and be perfectly content, but it was even better when he touched me, holding me at his side. It was a constant reminder that I was his; he touched me because I was his mate, and it soothed me to feel that connection to him.

We got as far as the ground floor when two whispering voices caught my attention.

"Here they come!"

"We need to tell Gramps."

"No, wait, we've got our surprise."

There followed some high-pitched giggling and some scuffling, and then, as we rounded the corner at the bottom of the stairs, we were met by two little children, a girl and a boy. They'd both put on their best clothes and they both had glitter all over their faces.

They rushed at Lew and he let go of me to catch them and scoop them up.

"Wow, don't the two of you look beautiful?"

Both children beamed and the little boy said, "Hannah did my make-up. Do you like it, Uncle Lew?"

"I do. It suits you."

The kid's eyes shone at the compliment and I wanted to burst with love for Lew. He turned to me.

"This is Hannah and this is Ed. They're my favourites, but don't tell anyone that. I don't want people to be jealous."

The two of them giggled and I smiled at them.

"We've got a present for you, Uncle Lew. We're supposed to tell Gramps when you're coming down but we needed to give your ours first."

He set them both down and crouched in front of them.

"What is it?"

Ed pulled a little package out of his pocket, wrapped in shiny pink paper and topped with a disproportionately large bow.

"Wow," said Lew. "Who wrapped this? It's the best wrapping I've ever seen."

Hannah drew herself up with pride and declared, "*I* did. But Ed chose the paper."

I decided I kind of liked Hannah. And Ed.

I watched Lew unwrap his present and was amazed when a string of bright orange plastic beads fell out into his palm.

"Oh, wow," he said, and I got the distinct impression that he was as surprised as I was and was stalling for time.

The children didn't notice. They gabbled proudly.

"We made it for you."

"Because you liked ours."

"And we didn't want you to be left out."

"And you said you wanted one."

"Do you like it?"

"Are you going to wear it?"

They both held up their wrists, where they each had a bracelet of the same orange beads, and Lew gave them an enormous smile and said – so convincingly I actually believed it – "I love it! Of course I'm going to wear it, now I get to have a matching bracelet, just like yours."

He pulled the garish jewellery onto his wrist and I noticed that the beads were strung on elastic and stretched a bit over his muscled wrists. Hannah and Ed looked thrilled.

"We knew you'd like it!"

"Don't tell anybody we gave it to you, though, or they'll all want one."

Lew shook his head solemnly. "I won't, this is just for me, right?"

"That's right." They nodded, and then turned to me. "We wanted to get you something, too, Uncle Morgan, but we didn't know if you liked orange."

"*Do* you like orange?"

I had the feeling that, if I said yes to that, I'd end up with an awful bracelet as well. But they were looking at me with adorable little eyes and identical expressions of absolute faith that orange was the best colour, and I said, "I love orange."

They scampered off, shouting, "Wait there a minute, we need to tell Gramps we saw you!"

Lew stood and took my hand, bringing it

up to his lips.

"You might regret saying that."

I was definitely going to get a bracelet before the week was out, I knew it.

And I was secretly thrilled.

CHAPTER 45: LEW

Gramps had out-done himself. We walked into the west room as the sun set outside, casting the whole place in a rosy pink glow of colour and making Morgan light up like an angel. His cheeks were flushed with pleasure and, as he stood there in amazement, taking in the sight of the whole family gathered, I realised that he'd never had an actual party before.

His eyes were everywhere, taking in the people in party hats and wearing fun clothes, and the balloons that were clustered around the walls and the streamers that were strung between them and the giant banner that I was fairly certain the children had had a hand in making, which said: *Welcome Home Morgan*.

I felt his hand tighten around mine, where

I was holding it. He didn't say anything and, as I studied his face, I saw he was working hard to keep his mask in place, but it was slipping and there were tears in his eyes again. I saw his Adam's apple bob as he swallowed.

Nana was standing at the front of the crowd, as I expected – she was the head of the household, after all. I expected her to say something, though, make some kind of speech, and she even opened her mouth to do it, but Gramps was standing beside her and he raised his glass and cried, "To Morgan, and his mate Lew," and everyone cheered.

Morgan buried his face in my chest and I held him there, looking at Gramps over the top of his head. I saw everyone cheering and shouting, "To Morgan!" and "Congratulations!" And I saw Nana turn her head to Gramps and raise one eyebrow.

He grinned sheepishly and raised his glass again, and I saw his lips move rather than heard his words, but I was sure he said, "To you, my darling."

He seriously had Nana wrapped around his little finger, because she chinked her glass with his and they drank together.

By the time Morgan had composed himself, Gramps had flapped his hands at everyone to tell them to disperse and Nana had glared the few stragglers away. They were all over the other side of the room, and their gentle chatter filled the air.

"Sorry, I didn't mean to embarrass you" Morgan mumbled.

"Don't be sorry. You didn't embarrass me. Nobody minds."

"I didn't mean to cry again." He looked up at me and his face was just so beautiful. "I never normally cry. I don't know what's wrong with me."

"You've never let it out, that's all. There's nothing wrong with you now, it's normal to feel things."

I led him further into the room, and we gradually met the rest of the family and I let them ogle my mating mark, which I'd deliberately kept visible for that exact reason. Firstly, I knew they'd all want to see it. Secondly, I was proud as fuck that Morgan had claimed me and I wanted to point at his mark and let everyone know about it.

Morgan stayed by my side and seemed happy to absorb the cheery atmosphere, rather than talk. That was alright, I knew he'd need time to be fully comfortable being in the middle of my mad family.

There were only two times when I felt him tense.

The first was when Dane came over and Morgan's scent changed ever so slightly. It wasn't fear, I didn't think, but it smelled a bit like nausea, and I remembered the smell of vomit that had been beside Brendan's body. While I wanted to be the one to protect Morgan, I didn't mind that it had been Dane who saved him that day. I wanted Morgan safe. And I didn't want him to feel sick every time he looked at me, picturing me dealing the killing blow to Brendan. I was hoping that the feeling would fade in time, but, still, I was glad it had been Dane to kill Brendan and not me.

Dane congratulated us both, shook Morgan's hand, and nearly broke my ribs in a hug. I wished I could make him as happy as I was, but there was nothing I could do. He stayed for a minute and then left. Even in that minute, I'd seen him shift from foot to foot and flex his muscles. He wanted to be doing something, not standing around talking. Nana saw him leave, and she let him go, so I assume he wasn't going to do anything dangerous.

The second time Morgan tensed was when I felt the prickles of unease up my spine and spun around to see Dee and Dum standing right behind us. I backed away automatically, pulling Morgan behind me.

"Dee, Dum, good to see you."

They smiled identical evil smiles.

"Wouldn't miss it for the world."

"We wanted to congratulate you in person."

Dee held out a neat little box with a bow

on it. It looked like a jewellery box.

"We got you a present."

I eyed the box but didn't take it. Experience had told me to be wary around those two.

She held it out to Morgan, who reached out to take it. I snatched it quickly, not wanting his hand to get blown up or something if it turned out to be a joke.

"Don't worry, little brother," said Dee.

"It's not a bomb this time," said Dum.

Morgan squeaked, "This time?"

They both shrugged, mirror images of indifference.

Morgan stepped tentatively closer to them. "Um, about the other day," he began. "I'm sorry I hurt you."

I frowned. I didn't want him apologising for using his magic. If it was what he had to defend himself, he needed to use it. "Don't apologise to him. He deserved it."

Dum pulled an expression of innocence onto his face that didn't fit well at all. "I have no idea what you're talking about. Nothing happened."

Dee bared her teeth in a wolfish smile. "He means about knocking you on your arse, Dum. You remember, when he beat you in a fight? When you were taken out by a tiny little *uasal*?"

Dum glared at her, which was fine by me. The less attention they gave me and Morgan, the better.

"Oh yes," he said dryly. "That." Turning back to Morgan, he said, "It was a pleasure."

I seriously didn't know if he meant meeting him or fighting him or being nearly blasted to death by him. With Dum, it could go either way.

Dee was staring at my hand, which still held the little box. "Aren't you going to open it?"

"Sure, sure I am. It's not anything dangerous is it?"

They both shook their heads. The glee on their faces made me wonder.

"Right, ok," I said, trying to build myself up to opening the thing. I kind of twisted round a bit so my back was to Morgan. I was hoping if it *was* something dangerous, I would absorb most of the blast.

I lifted the lid and slammed it down again.

"What the fuck is that?" I demanded.

"It's our mating present to you," said Dum.

"To welcome Morgan to the family," said Dee.

"It's a finger," I said.

Those grins split their faces again. "Not just any finger. Brendan's finger."

I held the box up and glanced at Morgan to make sure he was ok. He didn't look like he was about to bolt, so that was good.

"Why would we want Brendan's finger?"

"Because," said Dee, like it was obvious,

"It's his trigger finger."

"The finger he used to shoot Morgan's brother."

I met Morgan's eyes and he looked as queasily baffled as I was. "Right, well, thanks for that. It's very... nice."

"No problem."

"Glad to do it."

"It's symbolic."

"That's right."

I told myself not to ask, but I didn't listen to myself.

"Symbolic of what?"

"Of what we'll do to anyone who hurts our family."

My dragon rumbled inside me, but it wasn't a warning. I might almost have said it was agreeing. That was bad, if my dragon thought Dee and Dum were right. Nobody should think those two were right about anything. I should probably have a word with my dragon about that at some point.

Morgan surprised me then. He held out his hand to shake Dum's hand, and then Dee's. "Thank you. It's a wonderful thought."

I nodded, not sure what else to do, and then thought to ask, "How did you even get it?"

My enquiry was met by two blank stares, which I correctly assumed meant I didn't want to know.

Smiling at my half-sister and my cousin... relative... whatever, I dragged Morgan away and tried to put the box somewhere that wasn't on me and also wasn't within easy reach of any children. I shoved it on the top shelf of the sturdy old bookcase and tried to ignore it for the rest of the evening.

Needless to say, Gramps' present was much nicer. And it made Morgan light up like the sun, rather than turn green.

Gramps presented Morgan with a box. The fact that the box had air-holes in should have given it away, but Morgan still seemed stunned when he opened the lid and inside was a tiny white kitten with one black sock on her front left paw and on the tip of her right ear.

He lifted her out of the box and cuddled her to his chest.

"She's beautiful," he said, and the tiny cat licked his hand. He stroked his fingers down her back and along her tail. It was short and stumpy, with a bald patch at the end where the fur wouldn't grow back.

"She was in a bit of a bad way when they found her but the shelter says she's perfectly healthy now."

"She's lovely. Does she have a name?"

"No. They said you could name her."

Hannah and Ed were instantly by Morgan's side. "We already named her."

Gramps pretended to look sternly at them. He wasn't fooling anyone.

"I said Morgan could name her."

"But we had to take care of her *all* afternoon!"

"And we looked after her really well."

"We couldn't just call her 'cat' could we?"

They had a point.

Morgan asked, "What did you name her?"

The two kids chorused at the same time, "Frosty."

"Why Frosty?" I asked, peering down at the bundle of fur currently rubbing her cheek against Morgan's chest. She didn't look frosty.

"Because she's white, obviously."

Obviously.

"You know, like a snowman."

They both began to sing, "Frosty the snowman..."

Morgan nodded. "That's perfect."

He was already one of the family if he couldn't say no to those kids.

"Shall we... take her for you, Uncle Morgan?"

"To look after her for you."

"It's past her bedtime," said Hannah, and that clinched it.

"Yes, thank you." He handed over the kitten with a last longing look at the fluffball and Hannah and Ed scurried away to play with her.

"You don't have to let them do that," I said into his ear.

He looked up at me and smiled. Properly smiled. "I don't mind."

In that moment, I could see the happiness shine out of him. Fuck, he really was bright.

CHAPTER 46:
MORGAN

Nadia prodded me in the chest but it was a gentle prod, not like the jabs she gave Lew.

"You know, I'll have your babies, if you want me to."

What?

"Um...." I said, not sure how to respond to that. "I'm mated to Lew."

She rolled her eyes. "Yeah, I caught that, genius. That's why I'm offering. I'll carry your children, if you want me to."

"Like... surrogate?"

"Yeah, but on the condition that it's your sperm. I don't know why, but it's creepy as hell to think of carrying Lew's baby inside me." She shuddered. "Some things are just wrong."

"Um," I said again, but this time it was because I was overwhelmed. "You'd do that?"

Nadia gave me a soft smile and stroked a finger down my cheek before booping me on the nose. "I'm sure. I never offer to do anything unless I'm sure. And Lew's going to be one of those fussy-fussy dads and I could use a bit of pampering."

Lew appeared out of nowhere and pressed himself against my back, wrapping his arms around my waist and leaning his head on my shoulder.

"I don't fuss," he said. Even as he said it, I felt his fingers gently trace around the healing cut in my side, checking it. I barely managed not to laugh at him. I did sink back into his embrace, though, going pliant under his hands.

Nadia snorted. "Pft, you're going to be the worst."

He got indignant about that. "Hey, I'm not. I'll have you know I was a soldier in the Fife Army. I'm tough. And... unfussy."

"Of course you are," Nadia said, eyeing the bright orange beads around his wrist.

Lew huffed and I felt a laugh burst out of me. I was filled with so much joy that it had nowhere else to go and I laughed long and hard at the two of them.

"Fuck, Morgan," Lew breathed into my ear. "Your laugh sounds so amazing."

I flushed. "Really?"

In answer, he rolled his hips forward and I felt the bulge of his erection pressing against my butt.

Nadia said, "You're *both* the worst. Now get out of here and I'll cover for you."

"Won't Gramps be upset if we leave?"

She gave me a smirk and I felt the smile in Lew's lips as he pressed them along my neck, basically ensuring I'd do whatever he wanted anyway.

"Gramps is a romantic, so no, he won't mind."

Lew rolled his hips again and I pushed my butt back against his groin before I even realised I was doing it.

"Come on," said Lew, and grabbed my hand. We were out of there in seconds and, halfway up the stairs to Lew's room, he dragged me against him and began owning my mouth with his kisses. It made walking difficult, but I really didn't care.

Suddenly, he picked me up and I wrapped my legs around his waist. He carried me up the rest of the stairs and I rubbed against every part of him I could reach. His hands were holding my arse, gripping it tightly and massaging it. I pushed back against him, wanting more. I wanted him inside me.

"Please, Lew," I begged against his lips.

We crashed through his bedroom door and he stumbled around closing it behind us and getting us over to the bed. When he dropped me down to the floor, he held me up by one hand around my bicep and ripped at my shirt with his other hand. I helped him and soon I was completely naked.

He stepped back, and I stood there before him, feeling exposed.

"Fuck, you're so hot."

I was glad Lew thought so. I, however, had nothing on him. I watched him strip, and stroked myself slowly to the sight.

"I want to watch you stretch yourself, Morgan. Is that ok?"

Nodding, I climbed onto the bed and lay on my back. Lew passed me the lube and I wasted no time in getting some on my fingers, lifting my legs so my knees were bent and my feet were flat against the bed. I was too turned on to waste much time. I wasn't there to tease myself, I was there to stretch my hole so that I could get Lew inside me.

My first finger pushed in quickly and I barely felt any pain. I pumped it in and out a few times, enjoying the sensation, spreading the lube around and loosening my channel. Adding a second finger was only a little harder but adding a third made me wince.

Lew's hand clamped down on my wrist.

"Stop. You're hurting yourself."

"I want you inside me."

"Oh, baby, I'll get inside you. Just take it slow. I want you to enjoy this as much as I am."

For the first time, I realised that Lew's expression was one of absolute hunger. His eyes were glittering with lust and his pupils were blown. He watched my fingers like he was enchanted and I felt another surge of power that I could do that to him. He wanted me that much.

When I began to push my fingers in again, I took my time. With two fingers inside me, I pushed them in and out, gently scissoring them so the third finger wouldn't sting so much. Lew's hands roamed over my thighs and my hips, sending delicious tingles all over my skin and driving me higher already.

"Touch your prostate," Lew commanded, and I slid my fingers in further and crooked them forward, searching for my gland. I hit it and my hips bucked and my cock leaked pre-come as the pleasure shot through me.

"God, Morgan, you're beautiful. I want to watch you come apart."

"Please," I begged, and he leaned down to lick a stripe up my cock.

By the time I added a third finger again, I was right on the edge of coming. I was moaning almost constantly and my dick bobbed desperately. Nothing I'd ever done when I had touched myself before had come close to feeling this good.

Lew slid inside me slowly. He touched me gently and stroked his hands over my skin and kissed my lips and jaw and neck. It was incredibly sweet and amazingly erotic.

At last, when we were joined, I looked into his eyes again and saw in them all the love I could ever want.

"Love you," I choked out.

"I love you too, Morgan. So much."

He moved, and it sent ripples of pleasure through my channel. The way he pressed inside me grazed my prostate with each slow thrust but never pressed it hard enough for me to come. His scent was filled with musky sweat and arousal and I was filled with him, in every sense, and breathed him in.

He began to drive into me harder, and I felt him nearing his orgasm. I was so close to mine I hurt, my cock throbbed without any touch and my whole body was absolutely wracked with the incredible sensations of Lew Hoskins making love to me.

Panting, Lew kissed me briefly and then leaned back, kneeling over me and driving into me at an angle that pushed his hard dick right against my prostate again and again. My balls were tight and my spine was tingling and I came hard, spurting come over my own stomach and chest just as Lew gave a roar above me and filled me with his hot seed.

When he was spent, he collapsed on me and I clung to him.

He spoke into the soft skin of my neck, right where his mating mark was. "I never thought I could be this happy, my sweet mate. Do you think we'll always be this happy?"

"Mmmm."

He chuckled and licked my mating mark.

"I knew you'd agree."

LEAVE A REVIEW

I hope you enjoyed Family of Fire!

If you did enjoy reading this story, please leave a review.

Reviews help new readers to find the authors and stories they'll love, so let them know what you think.

I appreciate each and every review you leave me!

Hope x

OTHER BOOKS
IN THIS SERIES

I loved writing Lew and Morgan's story.

My new DRAGON'S MATE series is every-thing I love about fantasy, shifters, fated mates and happily ever afters.

The next book in the series is Dane's story.

Find out why the man he fell for – Morgan's cousin Seren – broke up with him so suddenly. If you suspect selfish Lord Somerville might have something to do with it, you're right.

When Seren finds himself in serious trouble, there's nobody he can turn to. Except Dane. But while Dane can't understand Seren or forgive him, there's no chance for the two of them to be together. And staying apart might just be more dangerous than either of them realised.

Read DRAGON'S MATE 2 to find out if Dane will ever forgive Seren, and what he'll do to keep Seren safe.

Sign up to my newsletter to be the first to know when the next in this series is available.

OTHER BOOKS BY HOPE

THE ASSISTANT CRISIS

(Magician's Luck 1)

Al is the most respected magician in Britain. But he's clueless when it comes to love.

So when he finds himself with an assistant, and that assistant is gorgeous, clever, strangely sweet and *bossy*, he's at a complete loss.

As more assistants try and replace Sean, Al needs to show Sean that *he*'s the only assistant he wants.

And if Sean decides to show Al that they can be more than that, then who is he to complain?

The first in the MAGICIAN'S LUCK series. M/M Romances with a sprinkling of magic. Clueless magicians, surly assistants, steamy interludes and a happy ever after.

THE FAMILY MISFORTUNE

(Magician's Luck 2)

Al has found himself the perfect man! His assistant, Sean, is a talented magician, absolutely gorgeous, sweet and just bossy enough.

Now all Al has to do is introduce Sean to his family. But will his family have something to say about their relationship? If Al's suspicions are correct, they probably will.

Al needs to convince his mother that Sean is there to stay. And, more importantly, he'll have to convince Sean as well.

A NEW NORMAL CHRISTMAS

(standalone)

My first Christmas story, written especially for December 2020. It proves that love can be found, even in the hardest of times and a little Christmas magic can go a long way.

WISH FROM THE HEART

(Bric-a-brac Love 1)

A standalone romance in my new series. A

prickly genie, an adorkable master, three wishes and true love.

After being turned into a genie by a vengeful ex, Jordan likes to think he's pretty cynical. But the surprisingly sweet man who buys his bottle in a bric-a-brac shop – and Jordan with it – keeps surprising him at every turn. He's not playing by the rules at all, and Jordan is in danger of giving him much more than the three wishes he's entitled to. He could end up giving Pat his heart.

STAY IN TOUCH

Sign up to Hope's newsletter and see what's new on her website www.hopebennettauthor.com.

Find her on Goodreads.

Follow her on Amazon.

Say hello on Twitter @HopeBennettAut1.

ABOUT HOPE

Hope is a M/M Romance and Fantasy author. She is an absolute believer in true love, head over heels for a happy ending and always on board for a sprinkling of magic in her stories!

If she's not curled up with a good book, she's out hiking. At least, she tells people it's hiking but really it's just walking with sensible shoes on. She loves to reach the countryside when she can.

Hope embraces the British stereotype by being addicted to tea, glorious tea. She drinks it from mugs and doesn't understand why anyone would try to talk to her before she's had her first one of the day. Let's just say that mornings aren't her time to shine.

Where she really shines is in her writing. Sign up to Hope's newsletter to get updates on her latest releases.

Printed in Great Britain
by Amazon